To JUNE

Best Wishes

[signature]

DEAD WRONG

A Dan Shields Mystery
The detective who breaks all the rules

MARK L. DRESSLER

© 2021 Mark L. Dressler – all rights reserved.
Published by Satincrest Press, USA
ISBN: 978-0999062333

Editor: Heather Doughty – HBD Edits
Proofreader: Joshua Suhl
Formatting: Liz Delton
Cover Design: Jeanine Henning – JH Illustrations
Author Photo: Jessica Smolinski

CHAPTER 1

Homicide was his business, and no two killings were the same. Each new crime scene added a chapter to Dan Shields' never-ending murder book. The veteran detective had seen a slew of victims killed by bullets, knives, and other dastardly weapons that left spatters of blood resembling Jackson Pollock paintings.

▲

Dan's phone rang, and he glanced at the digital clock on the nightstand next to his bed. The blue numerals read 3:13 a.m. Yawning as he rolled over to answer the annoying ring, he read the caller ID and knew it wasn't good news. "Can't you lose my number?" he asked Captain Harold Syms.

"A student and a security guard at Hartford City College are dead."

Running his hand across his face, Dan pushed the covers off himself and sat up. "What do you mean dead? Shot, stabbed?"

"Dead. Go find out."

"Thanks. I'm gonna want overtime."

"Right. Call your partner."

He flicked on a lamp and reluctantly headed to the bathroom. "What happened?" his wife, Phyllis asked.

"An incident at Hartford City College. Nice way to start a week. Go back to sleep. I have to call Scotty."

"I'll make you coffee," she said as she reached for her fluffy, pink bathrobe and slid her feet into matching slippers.

The rudely awakened detective took a quick shower, skipped the shave, and dressed. He walked downstairs into the smell of freshly brewed coffee and grabbed the thermos off the kitchen counter. After kissing his wife, Dan retrieved his locked-up weapon from the front hall closet compartment.

"It's raining," she said from behind.

He donned his old tan raincoat, put on a hat, and dragged his tired body to his garaged vehicle.

Driving in darkness from Suffield to the college with little traffic ahead of him, his 2016 Accord exceeded the speed limit on I-91 as windshield wipers swiped away drops of rain. He called to check on his partner. "Where are you?"

"On my way. I'd say about fifteen minutes out. How about you?"

"Almost there. I'll see you soon."

CHAPTER 2

His Honda's headlights shone upon the school's red and white, falcon-logoed sign at the campus entrance. Emergency vehicles lined the road to his right, so Dan parked behind a black and white next to the major crime unit's van. In need of a shot of caffeine, he chugged coffee from the thermos, closed the lid, and placed it back onto the passenger seat. When Dan got out, he saw several students across the street under umbrellas, and he heard crowd murmurs as police instructed them to go back to their dorms.

The detective walked toward the student center main entrance. It was a little past four a.m. as he made his way past two uniforms into the building and through a roomful of empty tables and chairs. One officer pointed to the stairs where Dan ascended up to the second level into the radio station. He encountered a familiar policeman and said, "Morning, Train." He'd been tagged 'Train' because his first name was Lionel. "Were you here first?"

"You got it, Columbo. Nice hat. Victim one is in the air studio, and there's a shook-up student in the room at the end of the hall with the station manager, Ramsey Dale. He's the one with a goatee. Victim two, a security guard, is in the rear stairwell."

Passing a glassed-in recording studio, Dan didn't see traces of blood. He approached paramedics and lead crime scene investigator Kara Mann inside the adjacent air studio where a covered body was on the EMT's transportable bed. "What can you tell me?" he asked Kara.

Her eyes met Dan's. "His name is Gordon Gunderson. His sweatshirt, wallet, and cell are on the chair against the wall. There's a fresh mark on his left arm and an empty syringe on the console. It looks like an overdose, but the guard, that's another story."

Dan slid back the sheet and studied the dark-haired young man. "Where was he when you arrived?"

She pointed. "Right there as you see him. Paramedics said he was slumped over in that chair. They had to get him off to try to revive him but got no response."

Dan took a close look at the arm. "Is this the only needle prick? Looks raw."

"I only see one injection site, and it does appear to be chafed."

The detective studied the room: recording equipment, a control board with several toggle switches, sound monitors, a swing mic, and racks of CDs. He even spotted a relic from the past, a turntable.

Dan stepped back as the crime scene photographer snapped pictures. Spotting a plastic water bottle inside the wastebasket, Dan asked Kara, "You have a glove?"

She handed one to him, and he lifted the item out of the basket, placing it on the console. "Can you bag this?"

"Sure."

"Who's downstairs with the guard?"

"Casey."

The detective moved to the red and white sweatshirt and checked the pockets, finding them empty. He picked up the wallet, opened it, and found a credit card, driver's license, twelve dollars, and a student identification card.

Scotty entered the premises. "What have we got?"

Dan said, "Drugs. His name is Gordon Gunderson. I haven't seen the other victim yet, a security guard, in the stairwell."

"Gunderson? Is this George Gunderson's kid?"

Dan knew the name rang a bell. "If he is, then this is big trouble." He picked up Gordon's cell phone. "Last call and texts were around ten o'clock last night. Interesting. Wonder what this means." He showed Scotty.

4

Cody Wilcox: meet me, same place. I'll have it.

Gordon: Tuesday morning.

Rather than bagging it, Dan placed the phone in his coat pocket. "Let's get a look at the second victim."

As they neared the door to the back stairs, Dan glanced into the room straight ahead and saw two males. "Wait, we have to talk to them."

Dan introduced himself and Scotty to a bearded male. "I understand you are Ramsey Dale." Pointing to the student on the couch, Dan asked, "What's his name?"

"Jason Ritter. He found the guard and Gordon. I think an EMT gave him something."

"We'll be back. We need to talk with him."

The detectives headed to the open door where another patrolman was standing. Seeing the guard's body at the bottom of the landing, Dan said, "Nobody told me it was a female."

The crime scene examiners had set up lights in the otherwise dimly lit, cold stairwell. Splotches of blood stained the concrete landing, the guard's rain slicker, and head. Her blonde hair had streaks of damp red fluid.

Casey didn't wait for the detectives to ask for specifics and looked up at them. "Broken neck, nasty gash on the back of her head, ankle looks dislocated. Her left shoulder as well."

Dan looked underneath the torn slicker where he noticed a badge on the uniform as well as a name sewn on the pocket of the guard's green uniform. "Christine Kole," Dan said. "What do you think?" he asked his partner.

Scotty studied her face. "Early to mid-twenties maybe."

Dan glanced at Casey, who was taking the young woman's fingerprints. "Seems like a needless task, but I know you have to do it."

"Positive identification, legal stuff. It's rare, but I've seen it before where a victim was falsely identified."

Dan noticed a cap several feet from the body as well as a belt around her waist. The walkie-talkie and flashlight appeared to have been crushed. A set of keys were still hanging from the belt. "Have you seen a phone, purse, or any other personal belongings?"

"No. Take a look at these bruises." Casey pointed to contusions on the side of her neck. "I think she might have had a strap around her neck and over her shoulder with some type of purse attached. It may have been ripped from her. That would explain the absence of a purse, phone, or wallet."

Observing the marks as well as the rip on the slicker, Dan said, "You may be right. The killer yanked it off her."

Scotty said, "There should be footprints here and upstairs."

Casey looked at the detectives. "Did you see how many people are upstairs? All with wet shoes? I'm sure there are multiple sets of contaminated prints."

Dan eyed the exit and glanced back at Casey. "The killer had to leave the building this way. You have a flashlight?"

Another officer standing nearby handed his to Dan. Scotty leaned on the bar to swing open the door, and the two detectives carefully stepped outside. The light above the door gave them a limited view. Shining the flashlight on wet grass, Dan said, "There are footprints, but the rain didn't help us, nor do these leaves." He saw a call box mounted to the right of the door and looking up, he noticed a camera. "We need to get the video."

The detectives went back inside. "We'll leave you to finish up here," Dan said to Casey. "We're going back upstairs to see the station manager."

He and Scotty entered the office. Jason was sitting up, wearing a sweatshirt like the one Gordon had apparently worn. A backpack was leaning against the wall, and Dan addressed the student. "We understand you found the guard and Gordon. Can you tell us what you saw when you got here? And approximately when was that?"

With a weary, shaky voice, he said, "I'm on after Gordon, so I got here around ten of three. I hit the buzzer on the call box outside, but Gordon didn't respond, so I entered the code into the keypad and opened the door. The light isn't too good in that stairway, but I saw her. I was scared as hell. I froze, started to freak out, and wondered about Gordon, so I yelled, and he didn't answer. Her bloodied body was just lying there. I hopped over her arm and rushed up the stairs. Gordon's head was on the console, and I shook him, but he didn't wake up." Jason closed his eyes. "I shut the program down and called nine-one-one from my cell. Then I called Ramsey."

"Did you recognize the guard?"

"Kind of. I've seen her once or twice before. I think her name was Christine."

Dan addressed the station manager. "We need to know if any listeners may have heard anything."

Ramsey said, "I can have announcements made during our shows."

"When do you expect to be back on the air?"

"I'd like to get back up as soon as possible after everyone is out of here."

"How many people do you think may have been listening?"

"Hard to say. I'm guessing a few hundred, maybe more. The station signal carries a radius of fifty miles."

Dan handed Ramsey a business card. "Can you run the announcements often and for at least the next three days. I'd like you to have listeners call the Hartford police, specifically my number. Can you do that?"

"Yes."

"I'm sure the news will get out soon, and the media will be all over this. We'll have the local channels put out the same request."

Scotty asked, "Are there cameras in here?"

"Not in here. There are cameras above all the entrances." Ramsey replied.

"We saw the one above the back door as well as the call box."

Ramsey said, "The student center main entrance is locked at eleven p.m. when the building is closed, so after hours we enter through the side door. As Jason stated, you can punch in the code or hit the buzzer."

Dan asked, "Is George Gunderson Gordon's father?"

Ramsey nodded.

7

Dan was familiar with the man. George Gunderson was a wealthy businessman, and having built a financial empire, he was hinting at a run for the governor's seat.

"Has anyone at the security company been notified?" Scotty asked.

"I don't know," Ramsey answered. "I didn't call them, but your officers may have contacted them."

"Who was here when Gordon arrived?" Dan asked.

"That would have been Doreen Patrisi. Her show ended at midnight."

"We need to talk to her." Turning to the student, Dan asked, "How well did you know Gordon?"

He took a breath. "Not well. I'd see him here."

Dan asked Ramsey, "What can you tell us about him?"

"I thought he was a bright student, a journalism major. He loved jazz and always appeared to be respectful, a nice young man. The Sunday night jazz show has been on for a decade, but students come and go. He'd done it for the past thirteen months."

Dan rubbed his unshaven chin. "How many other students do you have doing shows?"

"Twenty-eight. We're on all day and night."

Dan said, "All of them could have accessed the code box and entered the studio. Am I correct?"

Ramsey shook his head. "Yes, but I doubt anyone did."

Dan saw the concern on Ramsey's face. "I doubt it, too, but we'll need all their names."

Ramsey pulled a list from his desk and handed it to Dan.

Scotty asked, "This is an all-resident school, isn't it? I mean, there are no commuter students?"

"True. Gordon was at the Rago residence hall. It's up in the quad."

"Thanks," Dan said. "We're going back into the studio now."

The detectives entered the room. Dan took out Gordon's driver's license and noted the address. "Looks like we get to break the news to his parents. We better get out there."

Scotty said, "We need to verify that address. Are you sure the one on Gordon's license is correct? Do we know if he lived with them?"

Dan nodded. "Wait here. Ramsey might be able to tell us."

A couple of minutes later, Dan rejoined his partner. "That's it. Gordon had a cookout there for the radio station staff last July while his parents were on vacation."

The detectives stepped into the hallway where a heavyset man dressed similarly to the deceased guard, except for stripes on his sleeves, was standing beside a uniform. Dan saw the man staring at Gordon as he was being rolled away, and then peering into the air studio. Breathing hard and visibly upset, he asked, "What happened? My name is Aaron Westland. I manage the security company. I was told a student and Christine Kole are dead."

"Yes, sir." Dan said. "The student you saw on the gurney was Gordon Gunderson. He may have overdosed. Your employee, Christine Kole is in the stairwell. I'm sorry, sir. You can't go down there. It appears she fell or may have been pushed. You'll be able to make a positive identification before she is taken to be autopsied in Farmington."

Westland's face became pale.

"I think you better sit," Dan said. He moved the manager to a chair in the hallway and asked, "We noticed a camera above the side entrance. How soon can you get us the video?"

A cold silence came over Westland. "You aren't going to believe this. Of all the nights. The cameras were disabled late Sunday afternoon because we're upgrading our system and had to cut off the video. They should be back up around noon today."

Dan looked at his partner and shook his head. "Tell me he didn't just say that."

Scotty nodded. "Timing is everything. This is piss-poor."

Dan asked the man for personal information about Christine. Westland stated that she lived with her grandparents, was not married, and had a two-year-old little boy. Dan then told him to stay with one of the patrolmen until asked to identify his dead employee.

9

"Bad enough we have to go tell the Gundersons, but Christine Kole, damn it. Someone has to tell her grandparents, and it can't wait until after we've informed the Gundersons," Dan said.

The detectives walked downstairs to exit the student center. It was getting light outside, the rain had stopped, and the crowd was gone except for one frantic male student in black sweats. The policeman at the door stopped the detectives. "This kid says he's the victim's roommate."

"Really," Dan said.

"I'm Rosario Cruz.," the hyper student said. "Gordon's my roommate. What's going on?"

Dan said, "I think we'd better sit and talk."

Seated in the lounge, the detectives spoke with Rosario, who was alarmed because Gordon hadn't returned. "I usually hear him come in, but he never came back."

Dan explained what had happened and asked the roommate about drug usage. Rosario tucked his head between his knees. "Gordon didn't do drugs. None of us at Rago do. It's not allowed."

Scotty asked. "Who is the residential assistant?"

"Our RA is Kalani Moore."

"She played basketball here a few years ago," Scotty said.

"Good person," Rosario replied.

Scotty placed his hands on the shaking student's shoulders. "I'm sure the news will spread fast. The only thing you can do now is try to calm yourself and go back to your dorm."

The student raised his head and took a deep breath. "I can't believe it," he said as he got up and walked toward the door.

The detectives weren't far behind him, and Dan glanced at his Timex. "Five thirty. Let's ruin the captain's day. I'm sure he's on his way in if he isn't there already." Dan called Syms.

"What have you got?" the captain asked.

"Where are you?"

"Just got to my desk. Why?"

He updated the boss on what they knew, including the fact that Gordon Gunderson was George's son. "We're heading out to break the news. We have to do it now before the media gets this story out. There's always a chance they'll mention Gordon's name." He paused. "Someone needs to get out to Christine Kole's house to inform her family as soon as possible. She lived with her grandparents." Dan knew making a visit to inform loved ones of a death was difficult and best done when two lawmen delivered the news. "We're following protocol."

"Listen to you," Syms said, "following the rules. Got the address? I'll grab Hanson, Landry, or one of Dixon's guys, and we'll go to the residence."

Dan recited it. "Thanks. See you when we get to headquarters."

The detectives got into their cars, and Scotty followed Dan to the Gunderson estate.

CHAPTER 3

Dan never forgot seeing his first dead body, the bullet holes, the pool of blood, and the smell of death. He never forgot sticking his hand into the victim's pocket and pulling out a wallet. He'd only been on the job four days, and worst of all, he never forgot the look in the eyes of the victim's wife upon being informed her husband had been brutally killed. Now, once again, the veteran detective and his partner were about to inform parents of the loss of their young son.

Dan entered the Gunderson address into his vehicle's GPS and headed to the residence while the sun began to rise. He glanced into his rearview mirror to see his partner right behind. Moving steadily down winding, hilly, route 44 slowed by a seemingly never-ending succession of traffic signals, they were making good time.

Chalmers Hill Drive had signs posted on both sides of the street's entrance. One read: Private Road. The other read: No Outlet. Seeing a wooden sign at the base of the driveway that displayed the address. Dan pulled into the tree-lined entranceway, and Scotty's car followed, parking in back of his partner's car. Upon laying eyes on the residence's French style architecture, Dan thought it resembled a mansion in Newport, Rhode Island that he'd toured a few years ago his family…The Elms.

Walking toward the stately home, Dan noticed the wet, impeccably landscaped grounds. The detectives stepped under an arched porch overhang and stood at the double wooden doors. After ringing the bell, a loud bark could be heard as the outside lights came on. They waited and almost a minute later, George Gunderson opened the door. Dan recognized the man from his TV ads and presented his badge. "I'm Detective Dan Shields. This is my partner, Joe Scott."

The businessman was wearing dress slacks and a button-down shirt without a necktie. Dan took him to be about six feet tall with a slight middle-aged belly bulge. The Rottweiler by his master's side barked again. "Quiet, Ollie," George commanded. "What's this about?"

"Is your son Gordon Gunderson?" Dan asked.

George furrowed his brow. "Yes. What's going on?"

Dan took a deep breath. "Mr. Gunderson, there was an incident early this morning at the college radio station." Dan paused. "I regret to inform you that Gordon and a security guard were victims. They are both deceased."

Shocked and yelling at the top of his lungs, the father cried, "Gordon's dead?"

His wife, tall and slender and wearing a purple robe, rushed to the door. "What did you say?"

George turned to her. "Natalie, they said Gordon is dead."

"I'm sorry," Dan said. "May we come in?"

The woman burst into tears, and George was shaking. Dan noticed a large crystal chandelier in the foyer as well as a spiraled staircase to his left. He and Scotty wiped their shoes on the mat inside the doorway.

They proceeded through French doors into a large sitting room. The huge, white-marbled fireplace caught Dan's eye, as did the family pictures above it on the mantle, especially the photo of a teenager in a baseball uniform he assumed to be Gordon.

Dan and Scotty waited until the dismayed parents were seated on the couch and then the detectives sat themselves on Victorian-style chairs opposite the couple. The dog inched toward the visitors. "Ollie, sit," George ordered. The man's face was pale, and he looked as if he'd seen a ghost. He stared blankly at Dan. Natalie clutched a handkerchief and blew her nose, her eyes watering as she nestled close to her husband.

Dan sat forward and looked into George's eyes. "Early this morning, Gordon was found unconscious at the radio station."

Natalie moaned and tears streamed down her cheeks. George held her and was speechless. He closed his eyes, breathed hard, and after a moment, opened his eyes. Frowning, he shouted, "What the hell happened?"

Dan leaned forward. "We're not quite sure yet. Another student disc jockey showed up to do his own show, and he found Gordon inside the air studio. EMTs couldn't revive him. We can't say yet what happened, but drugs were involved. Possibly an overdose."

Natalie tried to compose herself while whimpering, "Oh my God!"

George's face went from pale to red, and he authoritatively barked, "He didn't do drugs. I knew it, that Hispanic roommate of his, Rosario, and Gordon's useless Black girlfriend, Amalia. I know they're involved. Arrest them."

Not responding to the racial rant and without letting George know they'd already met Rosario, the detective asked, "Who are they again?"

Dan could see George's blood boiling. "Rosario Cruz and Amalia Kendrick. I told him not to hang around with those two. I smelled no-good right from the start."

Dan digested those caustic remarks and moved on. "All we know is that there was drug paraphernalia near his body. We're investigating. Please be patient."

Before the detectives could tell the Gunderson's about Christine Kole, George's face changed from red to white. He was sweating and gasping for air as he fell back, his eyes fluttering. Natalie screamed. "I think he's having a heart attack!"

Dan brushed the barking Ollie aside and immediately called 9-1-1.

Less than five minutes later, a Simsbury police officer and two paramedics entered the house. Soon thereafter, George was rushed by ambulance to Woodland Hospital with his sobbing wife at his side.

There was nothing more the detectives could do, so they headed back to Hartford.

▲

The sun began to warm the day as Dan's car approached the three-year-old brick tri-level police headquarters. He noticed the large clock built into the face of the building that read: 7:37 a.m. He also saw the temperature indicator below. It read: 52 degrees.

He and Scotty both pulled into the back lot reserved for police employees. The detectives entered the building through the rear door. The cafeteria was to their left. Other departments on the main level included traffic, booking, administration, community relations, and several other units. Downstairs was the holding tank, once a daily walk-through ritual for Dan, but these days his visits were random. They shunned the elevator and marched up the stairs to the second floor. Passing the records, property/evidence rooms, and robbery division, they entered the detectives' quarters.

After hanging their coats on hooks inside the ergonomic workspace, Dan heard footsteps. The short, raspy-voiced Captain Syms approached them. "Heart attack? What the hell did you say to him? Let's go to my place."

Dan and Scotty followed their boss down the corridor past bathrooms on their left and two interview rooms on the opposite side. Syms' glassed-in workplace had a view of the ballpark across the street that was the home of Hartford's minor league baseball team. A row of bonsai trees sat on the credenza behind his chair. Arranged on his desk along with his computer, phone, in-box, and a pile of papers was his bottle of Aleve.

The captain eased into his high-back, and the detectives sat on the chairs facing the desk. "We'll check the hospital later," Dan said. "How'd it go with the Koles?"

"How do you think it went? No one was here, and Dixon was in his traffic division daily group meeting, so I took Ashley with me."

"Ashley Marholin?" Dan asked. "Haven't seen her since she transferred to Community Relations."

"Guess what? She's engaged, but she did ask about you."

Dan grinned. "Don't they all?"

"All the detainees maybe," Syms said.

Dan eyed the bottle of Aleve on the desk. "Full one?"

Syms picked up the container. "Not for long, I'm sure. You always have something that makes me down a few."

Dan rubbed his stubbly chin. "One thing bothers me. The injection site on Gordon Gunderson's arm was raw, and it was the only one."

"No," Scotty said. "It was the only one visible. He could have had others. We'll have to see what the pathology report says."

Syms nodded. "I agree."

"About George Gunderson," Dan said, "he didn't hide his dislike for Hispanics and Blacks. It's clear he didn't like Gordon's roommate, Rosario Cruz, and he certainly despised his son's girlfriend, Amalia Kendrick, insinuating they're both into drugs and may be responsible for Gordon's death. And we never got to tell him about the female guard, Christine Kole."

Syms rose. "I have to get upstairs to see the chief. He's back to his old self."

"Say hi to Hardison," Dan said.

The detectives headed to their workspace. The open room was free of partitions with eight desks, four on each side of the floor and spaced several feet apart. Half were empty, the others occupied by Dan, Scotty, Luke Hanson, and Randy Landry. Each detective had their own computer, multifunctional phone, storage bins, and trash baskets. Two extra chairs were against the back wall as was a printer and a table. The only windows in the room overlooked the rear parking lot.

The wall outside the workspace contained coatracks and a table that at one time housed a coffeemaker. It had been left empty ever since the Keurig Syms purchased mysteriously broke. The captain refused to replace it, making his crew purchase coffees from the cafeteria. However, there was a water cooler in the room, complete with paper cups.

Dan looked at his partner. "We'll have to see how George is doing at the hospital. I can use some food."

The hulking Hanson and his older, chain-smoking partner Landry entered the room. "You guys look like shit," Luke said.

"Funny," Dan said. "You buttheads know what it's like when you're out half the night. We're going to the caf."

"Caf?" Hanson asked. "Come on, let's go to Blues. It's turning into a nice morning."

"That's not exactly how I see it," Dan said.

They walked the few blocks to the twenty-four-hour diner. Hanson opened the door to the crowded eatery, and they went inside. Blues opened after Connie's Place was torn down, taken through eminent domain by the city in order to refurbish the area. Interestingly, after her diner closed, Dan recruited Connie Costanzo to watch his kids after school, a job vacated by Dan's deceased mother. Blues was larger, but the interior was no match for her diner that had the feeling of a fifty's eatery with red and white checkered tablecloths and quarter juke boxes in each booth.

Several patrons were sitting at the counter while other diners occupied most of the tables. "Hey, I see one," Hanson said. The detectives followed the big guy, and they squeezed into a corner booth. The smell of bacon wafted into Dan's nose. Napkins and silverware were on the table as were the salt and pepper shakers, along with a bottle of ketchup and empty coffee cups. Dan picked up a menu and a familiar waitress came to them with her green pad and pen in hand. "Coffees?" she asked.

"Right on, sweetheart," Hanson said.

She returned with a full pot and filled their cups. "House special, fellows?"

Landry raised his hand as did Hanson.

"Eggs, hash browns, and bacon with wheat toast," Dan said.

"Same here," Scotty said. "Except make mine rye and dry."

Dan began telling their fellow detectives about that morning's events.

"George Gunderson's kid," Hanson said. "That's heavy shit."

Landry uttered, "Sounds like you almost killed him too."

Dan picked up his cup and took a drink. "Gordon appears to have overdosed, but the guard, Christine … I don't think she accidentally fell down the stairs."

Ten minutes later, their server approached the table with hot dishes of food and placed them in front of each detective. "Anyone need a refill?" she asked.

Landry pointed to his cup, and she came back a few seconds later to pour him more coffee.

They finished their meals and headed back to work. "Before we go to the hospital," Dan said to Scotty, "I want to drop in on Ashley."

A

They headed for her department, and she looked up when they entered. "Well, well, I suppose your boss told you he enlisted my help this morning."

"He did. He also told us you were engaged," Dan said.

She held out her hand. "Getting married in June."

"Nice ring. So, I guess it's final. You won't wait for my son, Mike?"

Ashley gave Dan a flirtatious look. "I can't say you haven't tried. Is he still in college?"

Her smile and demeanor always reminded Dan of Phyllis. "A junior." Curious about her fiancé, Dan asked, "Who's the lucky guy?"

"He's not a cop. He's a teacher."

Dan grinned and looked into her eyes. "He must have a name."

"Paul Anderson."

Dan nodded. "I like it. Ashley Anderson, it has a nice ring."

Scotty nudged his partner. "Okay, you two. We need to get to Woodland Hospital. Nice to see you, Ashley."

Dan asked, "Weren't you here a little early today?"

"As a matter of fact, I was. Strange how things turn out. I dropped Paul off at the airport. He's head of the teachers' union, and there's a conference in Washington D.C. today. I got here before six, and Syms collared me as soon as I walked in. It wasn't easy seeing those grandparents."

"I know. Thanks for your help," Dan said.

CHAPTER 4

Woodland Hospital was a familiar sight to Dan. He preferred the view from outside the medical center, rather than from the room he'd occupied several years ago. The scar on his abdomen from the surgical removal of a bullet was a constant reminder of the perils of his job.

Dan parked in the hospital garage in an area reserved for official vehicles, and placed his police placard in the windshield.

The detectives walked up a ramp into the hospital through sliding glass doors. An elevator was to their left as was an emergency exit. With the administration desk straight ahead, they followed the blue line on the floor and approached the clerk. Dan said, "A man named George Gunderson was brought in here by ambulance a few hours ago. Can you tell us where he is?"

The employee checked the database. "I don't see any admittance records. Are you sure he was brought here?"

"Quite sure," Dan said.

The clerk checked again. "He's not registered. Try emergency. He may still be there. Follow the green line on the floor."

"Thanks," Dan said.

As soon as they got to the ER, the detectives stepped back, clearing the way for paramedics wheeling in a couple of shooting victims. Three uniformed officers also entered the room, and Dan tugged on patrolman Dexter Blacker's arm. The officer told him, "Gang shit. This crap has to stop. One of these guys looks serious, lost a lot of blood. The other one is coherent. What are you guys up to?"

"A student and a security guard died at Hartford City College. The student's father had a heart attack, and he was taken here by ambulance a few hours ago," Dan replied.

"What the hell happened?"

Dan started to explain when Dexter cut him off. "Gotta go catch up with the shooting victims. The still conscious one might be able to tell us something. I think they're both headed for surgery."

The ER was always a hornet's nest. Curtains were drawn on most of the cloistered rooms, Dan counted ten, but there were others around the corner where Dexter's victims had disappeared. He saw one unoccupied unit in the immediate area and then spotted a doctor, who was standing with Natalie Gunderson and a young man outside a closed curtained room. Approaching them, Dan asked her, "How is your husband?"

Natalie appeared tired. "He's better. He didn't have a heart attack. It was anxiety."

The approximately five-ten, dark-haired male wearing a blue pinstripe business suit with a loosened necktie said, "I need to know what happened to my brother."

The detectives stepped aside to let a nurse into the next room. Unaware of siblings, Dan said to the young man, "You're Gordon's brother?"

"Yes, I'm Keith."

"We're glad your father is okay." Turning to Natalie, Dan said, "We know how traumatic this is for you, and we're very sorry."

She replied, "The doctors told us he can go home soon. I'm so upset. Where is Gordon?"

"He's at the state facility in Farmington. They'll autopsy him before he can be released."

"I need to sit," she said as she walked toward a chair outside a small room.

Keith followed and Dan asked him, "Can we go in here for a few minutes?" The detectives and Keith went into in the empty waiting room. "We know how tough this is for you and your parents. Are there any other brothers or sisters?" Dan asked.

"No. I'm four years older than Gordon."

"What can you tell us about him?"

"First off, Natalie is my stepmom. Dad has been married three times. Our mother died when Gordon and I were eight and twelve. Then my father married Ellie. They got divorced, and Dad and Natalie have been together for the past five years."

Dan asked, "What was your relationship with Gordon? Did you know his friends? Did he have any enemies?"

"Everyone liked him, and what's this crap about an overdose? An injection? No way."

"How sure are you? It appears he shot up with a lethal dose."

Keith shook his head. "No way he would have injected himself." He paused. "Gordon was paranoid about needles. He'd break into a cold sweat just getting a flu shot. He even passed out at the dentist once. Needles scared the crap out of him."

Dan digested Keith's comments and said, "We didn't have a chance to tell your father and Natalie that Gordon wasn't the only one who died. A female security guard was killed."

"Are you serious?"

"Her name is Christine Kole. Does she mean anything to you?"

"No. Are you saying she and Gordon were involved in something?"

Dan shrugged. "We don't know. It's possible. We have a lot of work to do." Switching gears, he said, "I take it Natalie called you."

"She did. I had just gotten to my office."

"What kind of work do you do?"

"I manage the New Haven branch of Gunderson Financial."

"How often did you and Gordon speak to each other?"

"We talked every couple of weeks or so. Last time was about ten days ago."

"Did he say anything out of the ordinary?"

"No. He said everything was good. We were planning to meet next week."

"His car must still be at school. What was he driving?"

Keith shook his head. "Car? Gordon was a bicycle guy. He managed without a car at school."

"How well did you know his roommate and girlfriend?"

Keith's jaw tightened. "I never met them, but Dad told me about them."

"What did he say?"

Keith shook his head. "Let's say he's not too thrilled with Gordon's choices of friends."

Dan recalled seeing a photo of a teenager in a baseball uniform on the Gundersons' mantle that he assumed to be Gordon but may have been Keith. He asked, "There's a photo of a baseball player in your parents sitting room. Is that you or Gordon?"

"Gordon. He was a pretty good pitcher."

Dan handed the young man a business card. "Go be with your father and Natalie."

The detectives walked back to the garage. Dan removed the placard from the windshield and said, "The college isn't far from here. I want to find out more about Christine Kole, and we need to go to Rago. I want to talk with the RA and see if any of the students at the residence can tell us anything."

▲

Less than fifteen minutes later, Dan's car was in the small lot of the security building. Three other vehicles were there, including a white van with Bulkeley Security painted in bold letters across the sides. An awning with similar markings and a black bear logo hung over the front door.

The detectives entered the one-level brick building. Two uniformed security guards were inside seated at desks, one male and one female. "Can I help you?" the male asked.

Dan displayed his badge. "Is Aaron Westland here?"

"Yes, sir."

The female employee knocked on Westland's door, and the

manager came out to greet the detectives. His silence was deafening.

"I can see you're still upset," Dan said. "Have you spoken with Christine's grandparents?"

Westland said, "They're devastated."

"That's understandable," Scotty said.

Dan said. "We noticed Christine had with her a walkie-talkie, flashlight, and a set of keys. Did she also have a weapon?"

Westland shook his head. "We've never had the need to carry guns here. No, she didn't have one. I know the Motorola walkie-talkie and the flashlight were crushed."

"It also appeared she may have had a strap over her shoulder."

"Christine preferred to keep her wallet and keys in a small purse attached to it. She could have used one of our locked cubbies."

Dan said, "You mentioned her car was here. We'd like to see it."

"It's the green Prius."

"How long has she worked here?" Scotty asked.

Westland thought for a second. "About a year. Maybe a little longer. She's part-time."

Dan looked to both guards. "What can either of you tell us about her?"

The female said, "I liked her and knew she attended community college. I've worked a few shifts with her. She was happy, told a few jokes, and showed us pictures of her little boy."

"She was easy-going," the male said. "I used to tease her about that ugly green car."

Dan nudged Scotty. "Let's take a look at it."

"We don't have keys," Scotty reminded his partner.

"It's not going to hurt to eyeball it."

The detectives approached the vehicle, and Dan reached for the handle on the driver-side door. It opened. "It's actually pretty clean." He popped the center console compartment. "Mints, pen, loose change, Kleenex." He moved the tissue box aside. "What's this?" He pulled out several baggies, each containing pills, and showed his partner. He counted, "One, two, three. Each bag has four pills."

Scotty opened the glovebox. "What the hell? A few more. Six to be exact."

"These look like oxycodone to me," Dan said. "But there weren't any pills at the radio station, on her, or in the stairwell. What the hell happened?"

"Maybe they were both doing oxy," Scotty said. "Toxicology tests will tell us if either one, or both, were on the pills,"

Dan reached down and pulled a lever. "I popped the trunk. Let's take a look."

Inside was a small spare tire, car jack, two blankets, beach chair, an empty pill bottle, and a box of empty baggies. Scotty took the bottle and baggies. "Hold onto them," Dan said. "I'm going back inside. Wait in my car."

Scotty closed the trunk, and sat in the Accord while Dan went into the security office. Westland was still in the reception area and Dan asked, "Do you drug test employees?"

Westland nodded. "They're tested pre-employment, and our company conducts random tests."

"When was Christine last tested?"

"Upon hiring for sure. I don't remember her being subjected to a random test. Why?"

"It's just a routine question." Dan didn't reveal what he and Scotty found inside Christine's car. Knowing the vehicle could be impounded for thirty days before being released, Dan said, "There'll be a tow here within the next twenty-four hours to take the Prius to impound."

"Listen," Westland said, "how can we help you investigate?"

Dan replied, "I appreciate that. If this were a campus robbery, purse snatching, or fight, that would be yours, but this is a homicide, a police matter. If you do come up with something you think will help us, let me know." He handed Westland a business card.

Dan left to rejoin his partner. "These pills are throwing us for a loop. Christine appears to be selling, but to whom? And who was she buying from?"

"Good question. The quad is up the hill," Scotty said.

The detectives approached the residence hall. A red canopy with RAGO written on it was outside the entrance of the four-story brick building.

The lobby was arranged with four squares of chairs and tables, all in the center of the large room. Another seating area with a wall-mounted TV was in the north corner of the room where there was also a fireplace.

The woman approaching them was Kalani. Scotty said, "Hello. I recognize you." After introducing himself and Dan, he said, "You played a great game in the NCAA tournament. Almost upset a number one."

She smiled. "It was a great experience just to get into the tournament. I still dream about us almost being the first number sixteen to beat the best team in the country. We came that close to upsetting Baylor."

Dan asked, "Is Rosario Cruz here?"

"I saw him leave a while ago."

"We know he roomed with Gordon Gunderson. We already met Rosario at the student center."

"It's so hard to understand what happened. Gordon was always very nice."

Scotty asked, "Would you mind if we took a look at their room?"

Kalani got her master keys and walked the detectives to the third floor where she opened the door of room 315. Dan thought it was typical and reminded him of his old room at college. Beds against the side walls, a window at the back wall. Two desks, a mini fridge, microwave, and TV. Glancing around the room, Dan didn't register anything suspicious. "May I look in the dressers and desks?" he asked Kalani.

After a brief search, he found no evidence of drugs. "Looks clean," he said and then asked the RA, "I noticed a few students in the lounge. May we speak with them?"

"Sure."

Inside the lounge were five students gathered in one of the seating areas. Their chitchat was interrupted by the detectives. "Hi,"

Dan said. "Do you mind if we ask you a few questions about Gordon Gunderson?"

The four males and the lone female all appeared to have been shaken by Gordon's death. None were aware of any drug usage by him. They echoed what Rosario had stated that narcotics were not allowed in the residence. It was clear they all had favorable opinions of Gordon as well as Rosario and Amalia.

Dan and Scotty left Rago and headed back to the squad room. "Do you think because drugs are not allowed, there aren't any around?" Scotty asked his partner.

"Not allowed? There not allowed anywhere on campus. That doesn't mean there isn't substance abuse going on." Dan replied.

"True, but we can't get warrants and search all the dorm rooms."

"On the contrary, pal. We can if want have to."

CHAPTER 5

D an volunteered to complete some paperwork and told Scotty to go home. At six-ten p.m., the weary detective left the station. Northbound highway traffic moved at a normal pace and twenty-five minutes later, he got off and drove past the Suffield strip mall. Nearing his cul-de-sac, he passed the church where his two youngest children, Josh, and Kate were baptized. More recently, two years ago, it was where his mother's wake had been. That was Dan's last visit to the house of worship.

He saw his wife's SUV in the driveway, as well as their nanny's Chevy Volt. The front porch light was on, and Dan opened the door of his colonial-style home. Adhering to his usual routine, he wiped his shoes on the hallway mat, removed them, hung his jacket in the closet, and stowed his Smith and Wesson in the specially built compartment. Dan glanced into the hallway mirror, scratched the dark fuzz on his face, and entered the kitchen.

Phyllis came into the room and said, "I'm sure you're tired."

"I'm hungry. Nothing like an early callout to start the day."

"Quite a five o'clock shadow," she quipped.

"Funny. More like a forest. Don't expect a shave at three in the morning."

"What happened?"

Dan hesitated to talk about it. "I'll spare the details. A security guard and a student were found dead at the college radio station. Ever heard of George Gunderson?"

"The name sounds familiar."

"Gunderson Financial. His son was the student. Scotty and I had to inform the family, so we drove out to Simsbury. Quite an estate. Reminded me of The Elms. Anyway, as I was telling them what happened, George Gunderson appeared to go into cardiac arrest. I called for help, and he was taken by ambulance to the hospital. It turns out he had an anxiety attack."

Connie entered the room and said, "Except for the extra chin hair, you don't look too bad."

"Thanks. Are you leaving now?" Before she could answer, Dan said, "I smell something good. Did you make chicken potpie?"

The nanny said, "Yes. We saved some for you. See you tomorrow."

Mail was on the white and gray marble center island. He sifted through the small pile. "Can't wait to pay off this orthodontist. Where are the kids?"

"In the den. Go wash up and shave," Phyllis said.

"I want to hop in the shower. I'll save the shave until morning."

Twenty minutes later, a still scraggly-chinned Dan, clad in a pair of jeans and a New York Giants sweatshirt, came to the table to eat his dinner.

After finishing the meal, he went into the den where Josh and Kate were watching TV. "How was school?" Dan asked his kids.

They each gave the same short response almost in unison. "Good."

Dan glanced at the table in the corner where Connie's 1000-piece puzzle, a Thomas Kinkade jigsaw, Fairyland Bridge was about half complete. The box with the loose pieces was shut. He sat in his recliner, and Phyllis entered the room. She commanded the kids to go upstairs, clean their rooms and take showers as she moved toward the couch. With the children marching out of the den, she picked up a book and sat on the comfy sofa. "You look beat," she said to her husband as she placed her reading glasses on and opened the book. "Why don't you go to bed?"

"I'm okay. I just want to relax," he replied while holding the remote and clicking to ESPN.

A half hour later, a loud snore caught her attention. Her exhausted husband's eyes were closed, and she reached over nudging him. Groggily, he flinched and opened them. "Go to bed. You had a long day."

Dan followed her advice, eased himself out of his recliner, and went upstairs.

Chapter 6

Dan and Scotty had covered a lot of ground the previous day, but they were a long way from solving the deaths of Gordon and Christine. Only an autopsy would confirm that Gordon Gunderson died from drugs, but there wasn't any doubt about the guard being murdered.

Nearing headquarters, he listened to the New York sports radio station. Hearing that Eli Manning might not play this week against the Redskins, Dan flipped to the local news.

Dan pulled into the empty space next to Scotty's white RAV4, already parked in the lot, and started walking toward the rear headquarters door. He saw Landry pacing with a cigarette in his hand while blowing out smoke. "Morning, Dan."

"You almost done?" Not waiting for an answer, Dan opened the door and began walking up the steps when his inner voice started talking to him. He reversed direction and marched down one flight to the prisoner detention area. Unlike the old Morgan Street jail lockup, Dan thought this holding tank was a little too nice for the guests. Approaching the desk of Sergeant Dom Denine, the detective asked, "How's it going?"

"Pretty boring, to tell you the truth. Only have a few." The gatekeeper paused. "But there is one on the other side who says she knows you."

"A hooker or drug addict?"

"Not sure, but her name is Haley."

Dan thought. Haley. Then he uttered, "Haley? Is she young?"

"Go see LaDonne. She's keeping watch over there."

Dan walked to the door of the women's lockup and entered. "Hi, LaDonne, where's Haley?"

"Number four."

"How about letting me in?"

"You can't go in alone. I have to be with you."

Dan shook his head.

"Rules."

Dan rolled his eyes. "Me and rules don't get along too well."

"I've heard, but the last thing you need is to be accused of eying, touching, or saying the wrong word to one of these ladies. They'll have you up on sexual harassment charges. And you do smell good today."

"Eggshells. We have to walk on eggshells these days. I guess I splashed a little too much aftershave on."

"Come on, I'll protect you."

They walked down the concrete floor past two occupied cells, and Dan wondered why those females were locked up. Then he saw Haley sitting on a bed with her head down. Wearing jeans and a purple sweater, the barely five-foot tall, blonde-haired young woman jumped to her feet when she heard Dan's voice. "Haley. What are you doing here?"

LaDonne moved away to talk with one of the other guests. "Let me know when you're done."

Haley Valente was twenty-one, a high school classmate and former girlfriend of Dan's son, Mike. She glanced at the detective and stepped to the iron-barred door. "I got stopped for a traffic violation."

Dan waited for more information, but she was silent. He looked her in the eyes. "Haley, they don't put you here for a traffic violation. What happened?"

She sighed. "Drugs, there were drugs in the car. They weren't mine, honest."

"What kind?"

"Crystal meth."

"Be straight with me, Haley."

"They belong to my boyfriend."

"Where is he?"

She sighed. "On the other side. He said they're mine."

"So why is he here if you're taking the rap?"

Haley lifted her chin. "Because he had a warrant."

"For what?"

"He failed to appear in court for a previous charge."

Dan shrugged. "Is he selling?"

"He was."

"Some boyfriend, Haley." Dan wasn't convinced Haley was being totally truthful. "I'm going to ask you again, Haley. Tell me the truth. Are you doing meth or anything else?"

Her eyes narrowed. "No…well, not anymore. I've been clean for over a year."

"But this alleged boyfriend hasn't been clean?"

"No. He's been trying, but it's hard."

"What's his name?"

"Travis."

"Travis what?"

"McCarthy."

Dan was seething inside. "They're always trying, Haley." She looked away from Dan. "Where'd you meet this guy?"

The troubled young woman sighed. "At school. We both dropped out of college."

"Nice. Where are you living?"

"Home with my parents."

"Him?"

"He rents a room with a couple of friends." Haley began to cry.

Dan said, "I'm going to talk to this so-called boyfriend."

Tears flowed down her cheeks as Dan started to walk away. Before he took a step, she said, "Wait. Travis is my baby's father."

Taking a deep breath, Dan pivoted again and looked at her. "Great, just great. This isn't good, Haley. Do your parents know you're here?"

"Yes. I called them last night."

"Look, I'm sure you'll be arraigned later. I have a lawyer I can get you."

"I can't afford a lawyer."

"Don't worry. He's cheap but good. His name is Hancock Sasser."

She wiped her tears. "How's Mike?"

"He's fine. Still playing baseball at Arizona State. I'll see you later." The agitated detective signaled LaDonne. "We're done for now."

Walking out of the female detention area, Dan went back to Denine. "Where's Travis McCarthy?"

"Number six."

"Let me in."

Walking toward Travis's cell, Dan couldn't help smelling the alcohol that permeated the air. He didn't recognize any of the other detainees and stopped at number six where he glared at an average height, thin male who looked like he didn't own a razor. "Hey, Travis."

The scraggly-bearded, long-haired detainee wearing a black hoodie looked up from his bed. "Who are you?"

"I'm a detective. Your girlfriend was nice enough to send me over here. We need to chat."

"Go away. I'm not talking to no one."

Dan eyed the wise ass's earrings and sneered at him. Raising his baritone voice, the irritated detective growled, "Oh? You will talk to me. Believe me, you'll talk." His warning resonated around the room, and he saw he'd gotten the other detainees curious. Travis remained on the bed, trying to ignore the detective. Dan stared at him. "By the way, I don't think Haley is your girl anymore." The angry detective backed away and exited the tank.

"Done already?" Denine asked.

"Not at all. I have plans for him," Dan said as he headed to his workspace.

Entering the squad room, he strode to his desk and tossed his jacket on the chair. "What's eating you?" Scotty asked.

Dan noticed Landry and Hanson staring at him as he walked to the water cooler and drank a cupful. Landry uttered, "Scotty's right. What bug is up your behind?"

"The jungle. I was down there and had a chat with a couple of guests."

"Let me guess," Scotty said.

"No one you know. Hold down the fort. I have to go see Dixon. I'll tell you later."

Dan headed downstairs to see the traffic division commander. "Captain, how's it going?"

"Uh oh," he said, "what brings you here?"

Dan looked him in the eyes. "Your guys arrested a junkie named Travis McCarthy last night. He's in lockup, and I need to have a private talk with him. Already had one, but I have a lot more to say to him, and I need the asshole's undivided attention. Can you have him brought up to me so we can continue our discussion?"

Dixon tapped his desk and stared at Dan. "Syms know you're down here?"

"No. I haven't told him about this yet."

"Dan, I know this isn't good. What's the deal?"

Dan huffed. "You know, you sound an awful lot like my boss."

"I know your track record." Dixon gritted his teeth. "I'll have Travis brought up there."

"Great."

Dixon called Denine and arranged to have Travis escorted upstairs. "He'll be up in ten minutes."

"I'll be in interview room one." Dan hesitated. "Do you have a piece of paper and a pen I can have?"

Dixon handed him a blank sheet of lined paper and a pen. Dan wrote on the paper. "Do me a favor and cut the closed circuit."

Dixon peered at the conniving detective. "Just what the hell are you planning to do to him?"

"It's going to be a loud, one-sided discussion."

"Damn, Dan. You know I can't do that. He better not be bleeding or have any bruises after your chat."

"Okay, but not a word to Syms."

Dan entered the small brightly lit room and a few minutes later, a guard and Travis entered. The clearly unhappy detainee sat in a chair at the table. After clipping Travis's cuffs to the iron ring on the table, the guard left the room. Dan moved closer to his prey, and in the detective's intimidating manor, he glared into his eyes. "Nice to see you again."

"Back off, Mr. Cop."

The incensed detective barked, "You bastard. You're not leaving this room until I say so. Why the hell are you pinning drug charges on Haley?" Travis was silent, and Dan edged closer to him. "Was it the warrant? How many times have you been arrested for narcotics? I know you missed at least one court date."

"I'm clean."

"Clean, my ass. You're a shit excuse for a father too." Travis looked away. "Okay, you clown. Listen to me, and you listen good! I'm not playing with you. We'll be here all day, if need be, but you're going to tell me the truth." Dan pointed to the sheet of paper that was on the table. "You're going to sign this and take the drug charge. You're going to admit they're yours and get Haley out of here."

Travis shouted, "Hell no, not until she lets me see Joey. Her parents won't let me near the house."

Dan leaned in close to his face. "So that's it? If you ever want to see your little boy, you'll sign this paper!"

The wall phone in the room rang. It was Dixon. "Don't worry," the detective said. "He's still breathing."

"Hold on, Dan. Just wanted to let you know he's got priors."

"I know. Drugs."

"That, and a domestic."

Dan closed his eyes. "Don't frickin' tell me, Haley Valente?"

"You got it."

"Thanks."

Dan's anger rose to a fevered pitch. "Tell me why I shouldn't beat the shit out of you. Haley? You beat her? You bastard!"

"You don't understand!" Travis yelled.

Dan got within a few inches of Travis's nose. "Bet your ass I don't. Sign this admission…now!"

Travis began to shake as Dan slid the paper and a pen closer to the loser.

"Sign it!"

Travis looked up at the fiery detective.

"Sign it!" Dan reiterated.

As if the walls were closing in on him, the detainee, with hands still in cuffs, scratched his name on the paper.

"You ever touch her or anyone else again, I'll be your worst nightmare. Don't forget to plead guilty at your arraignment." Dan opened the door and said, "Take him back," to the uniform who was still standing outside.

When the guard and Travis were gone, Dan entered Dixon's quarters. "How'd it go, Popeye?" the captain asked with a smirk.

Dan shook his head. "You watched." The savvy detective knew the reference was to Popeye Doyle of The French Connection. "Here's his signed statement. He's taking the rap for the drugs. You can drop the charges on Haley Valente."

"The traffic violation still stands."

"Right. She'll pay the ticket. I'm going back down to tell her the good news."

Dixon stopped the detective. "You know, if he has a lawyer and I'm asked for the video, I have to turn it over."

Dan gritted his teeth. "Right, but I doubt that will happen."

Dan's stomach was churning. He'd just gotten Travis to admit to owning the crystal meth, but he was concerned about Haley's well-being.

He returned to the misguided young woman's cell, and she got as close to him as she could. Dan said, "Listen, I just talked to Travis, and he agreed to take the drug charge and not implicate you. You should be out of here in a few hours." Dan hesitated. "And I guarantee, he'll never lay a hand on you again. He says he can't see his baby. What's going on?"

"It' true, my father won't let him near us. Joey is almost two, and Travis hasn't seen him in nearly six months. I actually hadn't seen Travis for a while until yesterday, He's messaged me a few times, swearing he was going to get clean, and he said he was in anger management. I believed him and picked him up so we could talk. I knew he was high, and when was I was pulled over, he tried to hide his crystal meth under his seat, but they found it." Haley began to cry again.

Dan waited until she regained her composure. "Look, Haley. I don't mean to sound like your father, but you have to take charge of your own life. I've seen it before. Please, Haley…no matter what he says, Travis loves his habit more than he loves you. Move on from him. Call me if you need to talk."

With tears in her eyes, she nodded. "I will. Thank you."

LaDonne handed Haley tissues and escorted Dan out of the detention block.

CHAPTER 7

When the detective got to his work area, Scotty said, "You're really hyped. I think you need some coffee."

"Yeah. I just fried a fish."

"Come on, let's hit the cafeteria."

"A shot of scotch would be better."

"Who the hell got you this riled?"

Dan took a deep breath and told him about Haley and Travis. "That bastard got to me. You know, Mike used to date Haley. I'm gonna keep my foot up Travis's ass. Let's get that coffee."

Returning from the cafeteria with hot cups in their hands, Dan heard Hanson's raised voice and saw the downtrodden look on Landry's face. "What are you two sniping at?"

Hanson ran his hand across his forehead and calmed down. "Syms reamed us pretty good and let me put it this way: we're lucky to still have our badges."

"What the hell did you guys do?" Scotty asked.

"Nothing you wouldn't have done," Landry uttered. "We nailed the wrong kid, that's what we did. Except we're sure he's the right kid."

"What are you talking about?" Dan asked as he placed his cup on his desk.

Hanson threw his hands up as if he were about to be arrested. "We got a positive ID on two teenagers yesterday from the victim of a carjacking, who is still in the hospital, and arrested them."

Relaxing his huge arms, he said, "Turns out, one of the juveniles is the mayor's sister's kid. She's all over Hardison, and they were both let out." He took a breath. "Hate this shit."

Landry took a cigarette from his pack of Marlboros. "I need a smoke. I'll be out back."

Hanson stepped to the water cooler and poured himself a cup. He chugged the liquid and crushed the paper cup as if it were his worst enemy, then threw it into the wastebasket. "No one cares about the victim. Those kids should be in juvie."

Dan said, "Go rescue Landry from his bad habit."

Hanson took a deep breath and blew it out. "I can use some air."

Dan nudged Scotty. "Probably not a good idea to barge in on the captain."

"Probably not, but we're going to, aren't we?"

"Finish your coffee and we'll pay him a visit."

"Could be a while. I'm a slow drinker."

"By the way," Dan said, "I heard Manning might be out for the Redskins game."

Scotty, a Patriots fan, grinned and took his last sip. "Those wimps weren't going to win anyway."

"Come on," Dan said.

As soon as they walked in on the captain, Syms looked up at his detectives. "You better have something good to tell me."

Dan grinned. "Don't we always?"

Syms gave him a wry smile. "I suppose they told you."

"Sure did," Dan replied. "Hardison must have gotten an earful from the mayor."

The captain made a complete turn in his chair, stopping momentarily to admire his bonsai trees on the back table. "You realize when he takes shit, we all take shit." The captain stared at Dan, then sat back and shifted his eyes to Scotty. "Guess who I spoke with yesterday."

Scotty thought for a second. "Tom Brady?"

Syms shook his head. "Close. I called Bev."

"Really? It's been a while since I've spoken with her."

"I know. She might be coming back."

Bev Dancinger had been Scotty's partner. The female detective left the force three years ago after having twins.

"Are you serious?"

"She's thinking about it. Hardison also gave me permission to bring another detective on board." Syms leaned forward. "I need you boys to keep this quiet, okay? I didn't tell Landry and Hanson. Those idiots will think they're being replaced, and they just might be. What's going on with Gunderson?"

Dan said, "George is okay. Didn't have a heart attack. It was anxiety. Turns out he had two wives before Natalie and has another son named Keith. We need to talk with them again." Dan proceeded to fill the captain in on what they learned about Christine Kole and the killings.

Syms pointed to the door. "Go back to work. Hey," he said, "the chief is getting calls from the media about the case. They've already been at the campus. Hardison insists there's nothing to tell. The hounds are out there, but they know to keep off the chief's rear end." Syms paused. "And you two get your rear ends out of here.

Walking toward their workplace, Dan said, "I want to see if George and Natalie are up for a visit." Dan picked up his desk phone and made the call.

Keith answered and said his dad was resting and taking time to process the loss of Gordon. "Did you want to speak with my father?"

"Yes, please," Dan replied.

"Hello, Detective."

"Hi, Mr. Gunderson, I'm happy to hear you're feeling better. We'd like to talk with you again as soon as possible."

"If you want to come now, that would be fine."

"Thank you. We're on our way." Dan gave his partner a nod. "Grab your coat."

CHAPTER 8

Their previous venture to the Gunderson residence didn't go as planned. This time Dan hoped to get into Gordon's history and past behavior.

Traffic was light; it only took thirty-five minutes to reach their destination. Dan's car pulled into the circular driveway. Outside one of three garage doors was a black Tesla with the tag KGUND. Scotty said, "I take it that's Keith's car."

Dan took another look at the house. "Wonder what this place goes for. Two, three million?"

"At least."

Dan rang the doorbell, and Keith opened the door with Ollie by his side. The dog wagged its tail and did the friendly shimmy that begged for a stroke on the head. Scotty obliged. "He may be big, but he's a pushover," Keith said. "Come in."

George and Natalie were seated in the parlor, waiting for their guests. Keith settled on the plush blue carpet with Ollie nestling up to him while the detectives sat where they had before.

Looking at George, who was clutching his wife's hand, Dan said, "I couldn't help noticing how much this beautiful house reminds me of a mansion in Newport my wife and I toured a few years ago."

George nodded and cracked a smile. "The Elms. I styled this house like it. We have a summer place in Newport, and I moor my boat there too."

"How big is the boat?" Dan asked.

"Thirty feet. We've taken it to Nassau a couple of times."

Dan didn't need to be reminded that he was simply a working man, so he got to the business at hand. "What do you know about Gordon's friends?"

Keith chimed in, "I already told you he was well-liked."

"I appreciate that," Dan said.

George blurted out, "I'm telling you it's those two, Rosario and Amalia."

Dan calmly sat back. "Are you saying you know they are involved with drugs?"

"Maybe they are. Wouldn't surprise me," George assertively said. "But that self-injection crap is just that. It's crap."

Keith interjected, "Impossible! I told you about his needle phobia."

George cringed. "And why the hell didn't you tell me about the female guard? It's on the news. They said she was found at the bottom of the stairs. What happened?"

"I would have gotten to it, but you had that anxiety attack," Dan said. "We don't know much at this point. And don't believe everything you might hear on the news. We can't release all the details. We're working it, and we'll let you know what we dig up."

"Fair enough, but I still think it's those two."

Dan again eyed the photo on the mantle and noticed one thing about the picture that struck him oddly. Gordon appeared to be left-handed. Filing that information, Dan asked, "Does the name Cody mean anything to you?"

Keith replied, "Cody?"

George gasped. "Cody Wilcox? You bet it does." He let go of Natalie's hand.

Dan could see the man's temperature rising and hoped another anxiety attack wasn't coming. George continued. "That kid is a pot smoking, troublemaking dropout that none of us ever liked. He's my ex-stepson, Ellie Wilcox's son. Lived with us on and off for three years. He's the reason for our divorce."

"How old is he?"

Keith said, "He's twenty-five, a few months older than me."

Dan thought about the text message on Gordon's phone as George sat back and clutched Natalie's hand again. "You stated Cody did marijuana. Any history of narcotics?"

"Christ's sake," George said. "Definitely."

"Any idea where he is?"

Keith stated, "I don't know for sure. We weren't close, but he called me about a year ago. He said he'd had gone to rehab and gotten his act together. He also said he'd obtained his GED and enlisted in the army, having already been in Iraq and was ready for a second stint. He said he wanted to touch base with me and Gordon, but he'd lost Gordon's number and asked me for it, so I gave it to him."

George winced. "What the hell did he need Cody for? It's bad enough Gordon has that damned roommate and girlfriend."

Dan felt the man's racial bias again coming through loud and clear and acted as if he hadn't heard the comment.

The home phone rang, and Keith moved the relaxed Ollie aside and got up to answer it. "Let it go," George said. "Damn newspaper and TV hounds. Six calls isn't enough?"

"Just keep ignoring them." Dan said. "They'll go away."

Natalie asked. "Are you thinking Cody tried to get Gordon hooked on drugs and is somehow involved with the alleged overdose?"

"I'm not saying that yet. We don't know. We would like to find Cody," Dan replied.

"Try Ellie," George said.

Scotty said, "Tell us about her."

George sighed. "Look. My first wife, Angie, who was Gordon and Keith's mother, died when the kids were young. I met Ellie a few years later at a PWP meeting."

"A what kind of meeting?" Scotty asked.

"Sorry, Parents Without Partners. We had one thing in common, her husband died, so we had both lost spouses. It didn't take long for that kid to put a wedge between his mother and me. Eventually, we got divorced, and it wasn't a pleasant separation." He faced his wife. "We're going on six years."

Dan took George to be close to his own age of fifty, and now that he was getting a better look at Natalie, he guessed she could be as many as ten years younger than her husband. She reached for a tissue from a box on the table beside her. "When can we have Gordon taken from Farmington to the funeral parlor?" she asked.

Scotty said, "It's a matter of protocol. After the autopsy, they'll let you know when he can be released. It really shouldn't be too long."

Dan sensed it was time to end the conversation. "We appreciate your hospitality and may want to chat again." Before being escorted out by Keith, Dan took another glance at the photo of Gordon on the mantle.

When the detectives got into Dan's car, he said, "Not only was Gordon afraid of needles, but he was also a left-handed pitcher. I'm sure someone else injected him, and whoever it was didn't know Gordon was left-handed. If the injection was self-inflicted, it would have been in the right arm."

"What about Cody Wilcox?" Scotty asked. "That text."

"We'll take another look when we get back."

♠

A familiar sight greeted the detectives at the rear headquarters door. Landry was puffing away on a cigarette. He coughed as they neared him. "Don't say it," the smoker said.

Dan opened the door. "Wouldn't do any good anyhow. See you later."

He and Scotty walked up to the squad room, and Dan opened a desk drawer, taking out Gordon's cell phone that he had taken from the studio. He opened it and read that text message again. "What does this say to you?" he asked Scotty.

Cody: meet me, same place. I'll have it.

Gordon: Tuesday morning.

"It screams drugs to me."

Dan said, "Cody Wilcox sure can't be in Iraq if he and Gordon planned to meet somewhere. I want to call him, but first I want to check out the criminal database before making the call on Gordon's cell."

Scotty said. "I'll log in." He checked the database and found the name Cody Wilcox. "Hey, get a load of this."

"What have you got?"

"Cody Wilcox. Looks like he was charged with possession of an illegal substance three years ago, but that appears to be his only arrest."

"George said he did narcotics."

Scotty said, "If he had other arrests when he was younger, they may have gone to the juvie scrap pile. You know that stuff is buried."

"True, he may well have had a long affair with addiction." Glancing at Gordon's cell again, Dan saw the texter's number. "Time to call Cody."

"What makes you think he'll answer if he is involved?"

"I don't, but then again, he may," Dan replied as he entered the number.

To his surprise, the next voice he heard was a female's. "Hello," she said. "Who is this?"

"I could ask the same question. My name is Dan Shields, and I'm a detective with the Hartford Police. So, who am I speaking with?"

"My God, what has happened? I'm Ellie Wilcox."

"This is Cody's phone, isn't it?"

"Technically, that's not true. It's my phone. Cody is on my plan."

Dan swayed back in his chair. "Where is he?"

"In Iraq. I bought him a new phone to take with him and took his because mine was broken."

Scotty nudged his partner and said, "Put it on speaker."

Dan said to Ellie, "Excuse me, I put us on speaker so my partner could listen. You say Cody is in Iraq. How long has he been there?"

"This is his second stint, nine months in. Tell me what happened to Gordon and that security guard. It's been on the news."

"It's all a little sketchy right now. All we know is that Gordon was deejaying, and drugs were involved. The guard, Christine Kole, was apparently making her rounds, and they found her body in the stairwell. Has Cody been back here on leave? When did you see him last?"

"Nine months ago, before he was redeployed to Iraq."

"We obviously have Gordon's phone. We saw a text that came from it and we're curious about it."

Dan heard a sigh and a long pause. "It was me. Gordon and I met recently, and we were going to see each other again."

"Do you mind telling me why?"

Dan heard another sigh. "It's a crazy story. You do know Gordon was my stepson at one time."

"We know that. We've spoken with the Gundersons."

Dan heard one more sigh. "Great. I suppose they didn't have kind things to say about me and Cody."

Dan knew she was right but simply replied, "Would you be able come into headquarters to chat?"

"Can we meet somewhere else? I met Gordon at a doughnut shop on Mapleton. We could meet there tomorrow."

"Which doughnut shop?"

"I can't remember the name, but it has a yellow awning."

Dan rolled his eyes. "It's called The Maple. I know it well. How's ten a.m.?"

"That's fine, I'll be there."

"Thank you," Dan said.

"What do you think?" Scotty asked. "Are they having some kind of affair?"

"I'm not going to stretch that far. Let's see what she has to tell us."

"You know, Hampton might be there."

Dan rolled his eyes at the mention of Hampton, his handy car-thief friend. He knew the self-employed car stealer hung out there with his biker pal, Rollin. Hampton had visited the lockup on at least seven occasions, and Dan took a liking to this harmless felon.

CHAPTER 9

Dan was on his way home when his car's info system signaled a call from his son, Mike. "Hi, what's going on?"

"I'm hitting the gym every day after classes. I saw the baseball schedule. Fifty-six games. We open at home with Miami of Ohio on February sixteenth. You must be in the car."

"I'm on my way home. How's school going?"

"Fine."

"How's the coed dorm? You keeping the ladies away?"

"Dad, I'm here for baseball and an education. No time for socializing."

Dan laughed. "Right. Your mom and I went away to college. How many non-socializing girls are you seeing?"

"Okay, old man. There are a lot of nice-looking ones here. If you must know, I've been dating a girl named Rachel."

"That's it? Do tell."

"She's from Tennessee. You won't believe it, but she pitches and plays center field on the women's softball team."

Dan hesitated. "Sounds like you've met your match. You are being safe?"

"Dad, stop."

Backing off, he replied, "Okay, so are you calling to ask for money?"

"No, but now that you mention it, I could use some. I'm thinking about coming home for Thanksgiving. I actually miss the brats."

"Can you? How long is the break?"

"There are no classes Wednesday. I might be able to work something out to come in earlier."

"You want me to fund the trip?"

"Like I said, now that you mention it."

"That depends upon how bad I want to see you."

Mike laughed. "Funny."

Dan decided to ease into the news about his son's former girlfriend. "Mike, I have to tell you something. Remember Haley Valente?" A car sped by Dan on the right and weaved back in. "Idiots," he uttered. "There's a lot of crazy drivers in this world. One just cut in on me. Sorry, what was I saying?"

"You were saying something about Haley. You know I really liked her."

"How come you stopped seeing her?"

"She kind of got involved with an older college crowd. Where'd you see her?"

"Haley was in the women's detention at headquarters."

"What?"

"She got stopped for a traffic violation, and there were narcotics in her car. Did you know she'd been doing drugs?"

"I heard that. It was those friends I mentioned."

Dan held back the Travis McCarthy part of the story. "She dropped out of college and has a baby boy. She and the baby live with her parents, but the baby's father isn't in their life. She asked about you."

"What's going to happen to her?"

"My guess is they'll set a low bail, and she'll have to pay a fine for the traffic violation."

"Wow. When I come home, maybe I'll call her."

"I think she would like that. Hey, mom worries about you, so text her or call more often."

"I will."

"Thanks for the call, Mike."

Dan kept his eyes on the road as he headed into heavy traffic and realized this trip would take longer than normal. Finally, he made it home and noticed his leaf-covered lawn. He knew his backyard was also covered in leaves, and he dreaded the annual raking chore.

Walking into the hallway, he followed his usual routine while hearing Phyllis's voice coming from the kitchen. He entered the room as she hung up the phone. "That was Mike. The kids were happy to talk to him. He told me he just spoke with you."

"He did. Did he tell you about his girlfriend?"

"Yes. He also told me something else. What's this about Haley Valente? Mike said she was arrested, and you saw her."

"True. She's a troubled young woman. I'll tell you later."

Phyllis said, "Josh has karate tonight."

He entered the room wearing a white outfit with a yellow belt tied around his waist. "Hey, Bruce Lee," Dan said. "Can't wait to see what you'll be doing tonight."

"Come on, let's have dinner," Phyllis said. "Meatloaf and mashed potatoes."

"Great. I'll be right back."

Dan reentered wearing jeans and an Arizona State sweatshirt, and sat at the table with the rest of his family, minus Mike. Soon after their evening meal, Dan and Josh were off to karate.

It was twenty after eight when they got home and a little while later, the kids went to bed. Dan sat with his wife in the den. "I'm worried about Haley. Mike said he liked her, but they broke up because she became involved with a group of older friends." After telling his wife the rest of the story, Dan said, "I held back the Travis details from Mike."

Phyllis grabbed her half-read book but didn't open it. "I have to tell you something."

Dan looked at her while furrowing his brows. "Last time you said that you told me you were pregnant."

Removing her reading glasses, she wryly asked, "And what if I am?"

"Then I'd say my vasectomy miraculously reversed itself," he smugly retorted, "or you're having an affair."

She sneered at him and playfully replied, "I'll never tell. Listen, it's Connie. She may be leaving us."

"What?"

"Her sister and brother-in-law live in Florida. Connie is going to The Villages to visit them for a while. She's considering retiring there. They're her only relatives, and she doesn't know if she wants to go through another winter."

"I can understand her reasoning," Dan said while staring amorously into his wife's eyes. "Who will watch the kids after school?"

"I already talked to Joellen. If Connie does move, we're all set. Josh and Kate ride the same bus with her kids, so they can go to her house after school. I'll pick them up."

"I guess you covered that. Did I tell you Beverly might be coming back? Syms talked to her, and she's interested in returning to work."

"The twins are three, aren't they?"

"They are, but she's apparently ready to join up again."

"You boys will have to start behaving with her around."

Dan smiled at his wife. "I'm always on good behavior. Now, about my vasectomy."

Phyllis stroked her hair and flirtatiously winked at him. "You better behave for another hour or so. Just don't fall asleep."

Chapter 10

Victims of violent crimes always bothered Dan. To him there was nothing worse than a dead teenager, a woman subjected to beatings, or other unthinkable acts. The legal system frustrated him. Deep down, Dan wished the death penalty still existed in Connecticut. It angered him that convicted killers merely went to jail and were living off taxpayer money. He also never understood how some families of victims could be forgiving. Dan knew Phyllis still harbored anger toward the man who had shot and killed her father. She was a teenager when the murderer was sentenced to life. Although Phyllis's feelings toward her father's assassin were hostile, she relied on her religious upbringing to keep her from having the same hard-core, eye for an eye mentality as her husband.

Dan couldn't get Haley out of his mind, he'd thought about her all night, especially after Mike said he still liked her. Travis McCarthy was a pain in the detective's neck, and he wanted to find out what happened to the menacing idiot.

As soon as Dan got to the police station, he immediately went to see Dixon. The captain lifted his head, though he appeared to be intently reading a report. "Just following up on Haley Valente and that bastard, Travis," Dan said.

"She went home. After he reversed his plea and took the drug charge, the judge let her go, but Travis is being held on the outstanding warrant. What's your tie to her?"

"It's my son. They went to high school together. He dated her, took her to their prom."

"Mike? He's still at Arizona State playing baseball, isn't he?"

Dan broke a smile. "He is. The season doesn't start until mid-February. Let me know what happens with Travis."

"Have you told Syms?" Dixon asked.

"Not yet."

Dan thought about Dixon's query as he walked to his workspace. Hanging up his jacket, he said to Scotty, "I was down with Dixon. Haley is home, but Travis is still in lockup."

The thumping sounds coming toward them were Syms' footsteps. The detectives were abruptly interrupted by his angry, raspy voice. He pointed to Dan. "In my office…now, cowboy!" Scotty took a step. "Not you, just him," Syms barked.

The detective followed the captain, who slammed his door shut after Dan entered. "Don't bother to sit," the steamed Syms said.

Dan placed his hands on the desk.

"Take those hands off and stand at attention. What the hell kind of shit did you pull with a detainee named Travis McCarthy?"

Dan looked into Syms' eyes and smugly smiled. "Just gave him a little fatherly advice, sir."

The captain retreated to his chair, opened the pill bottle on his desk, shoved one tablet into his mouth, and washed it down with a swig of water. "Don't give me this 'sir' shit. The chief isn't too thrilled about your chat. What the hell was that all about?"

Dan leaned forward and placed his hands on the desk again.

"Back off," Syms said. "Sit if you must, but this better be good." The angered captain wiped his hand across his face. Clearly dissatisfied with his detective's answer, he stared at Dan and gruffly asked, "How many frickin' times are you going to take matters into your own hands? Hardison is livid. You're lucky he's got shit up to his neck with the mayor."

Still standing, Dan said, "Yes, sir. From this point on, I'll be in total compliance with procedures."

Syms pointed a finger at him. "Compliance? You are a lucky-ass detective. That McCarthy dude admitted to the DA the narcotics were his and pleaded guilty, so you're off the hook for your badgering. But don't let it happen again. You got me?"

"Yes, sir."

"Now, you want to tell me who this addict is and what the hell you have to do with the Haley girl? Is she some hooker you know?"

Dan shook his head and calmly said, "Hardly. I know her and her family." Continuing, he told Syms the whole story.

The captain rose. "Get out of here, but I'm warning you. That badge doesn't say anything about job security." The captain glanced at the red light on his desk phone. "Damn, it's Hardison. How bad can this day get?"

Dan said, "I'm leaving." Having dodged a bullet, a cold sweat came over him as he walked back to his partner.

Scotty asked, "What was he mad about?"

"Care to guess? Neither he nor the chief are too pleased with my interviewing techniques. They found out about my discussion with Travis McCarthy. Take a look at your badge."

"Why?"

"Tell me what it says."

Scotty said, "My lucky number, eight-one-seven-seven."

"Nice. Put it back. Syms let me know my badge doesn't guarantee job security. I didn't think it said that on yours either."

With a wry smile, Scotty said, "That's good, Dan. That's really good. It's going to be great having Bev back."

"It is. I'll never forget the day she delivered the babies at the old headquarters. Seeing those twins come out was unforgettable."

"She was early." Scotty grinned. "Forgot to tell you. There's going to be an addition to the family."

Dan squinted. "You frickin' hound. I told you to get a vasectomy. Four kids. Congratulations. Are you done now?"

Scotty laughed. "Maybe."

"Maybe?" Dan asked. "You want five or six?"

Toning down his laugh, Scotty answered, "Did I say Sallie was pregnant? It's her sister in Boston. She's having her first."

Dan shook his head. "Nice, pal, but I still think you should do it."

"We're talking about it."

"Talk won't get you more action. The snip-snip will."

"Christ, you make it seem like a haircut."

Dan brushed his hand across his chin. "Well, you do get a close shave."

"What time do we need to be at the doughnut shop?" Scotty asked.

"Ellie said she'd be there at ten." Dan glanced at his watch. "We should leave here soon."

Dan's desk phone lit up and he answered it. As he did so, the second line blinked as well. He picked up the first call. "Detective Shields."

"Sir, I heard Gordon Gunderson's last show."

"You did. Could you hold a second?" Dan answered the other line. It was another caller who had listened that night. "Yes," Dan said. "What can you tell me?"

The female caller said, "I was listening and after hearing Miles Davis, I think the song was 'Stella by Starlight', the music stopped, and I never heard anything else."

Dan got back to the first caller and her story echoed the other listener. "Thank you," he said.

"Anything?" Scotty asked.

"Not really."

Scotty said, "It's ringing again."

Dan answered the phone and took a statement from another listener. He spun his chair around and said, "Their stories are all similar. They heard music until about ten past two and then it stopped. There was nothing but dead air. Unfortunately, that's all they heard. The station went silent." The phone rang again. "This could take all day."

After two more calls, the lines stopped lighting up. "We better get to The Maple."

Chapter 11

The Maple doughnut shop was more than a little familiar to Dan. He was sure Hampton, and Rollin would be there. As they pulled up to their destination, Scotty asked, "You see that bike?"

Dan took a look at the shiny black motorcycle. " A Harley. I knew it."

Entering The Maple, the aroma of freshly baked goodies and recently brewed coffee assaulted the detectives' noses. Tempting was the array of chocolate frosted and honey glazed doughnuts, as well as the ample supply of other sweet treats inside the glassed case. Dan saw patrons occupying tables to his left and then looked to his right where he spotted Hampton and Rollin in their usual corner nook. Hampton yelled, "Dan! Hey, how's it goin'?"

The detectives approached the two men. "New Harley?" Dan asked the ponytailed Rollin.

"Beauty, isn't she?"

Dan clearly smelled marijuana in the immediate area and suspected the odor likely emanated from the two men now in the company of the detectives. Hampton raised his coffee cup. "I ain't been down to lockup in a while."

"You been a good boy?" Dan quipped.

The long-haired Hampton took a sip and placed the cup on the table. "Yup. I'm out of the business. Retired."

Dan stared into his glassy eyes. "You? Retired? Don't hand me that crap. You just haven't been caught recently."

The ex-car thief motioned with his hand toward two empty chairs while taking another drink of coffee. "Hell no. Serious, Dan. The chop shop got busted. Gone."

Dan declined the offer to sit. "We're waiting for someone. And just what the hell are you doing now?"

Hampton laughed. "This is pretty much it. Not yet forty and waiting for social security and Medicare, but for now I'm on government disability. Not a bad gig, Rollin too."

Dan shrugged, looked at Scotty, and aimed his comments at the two retirees. "We're paying you to sit here and have coffee and doughnuts. It's a great country, isn't it?"

"Checks come like clockwork." Hampton smiled.

Dan eyed his jovial friend. "Okay. What kind of disability do you have? Smells like one that a little weed medicates."

Hampton frowned. "Hearing. I don't hear so good no more. Can't work."

Dan's radar went up. He rotated his head so Hampton couldn't read his lips and softly asked, "You wanna earn a few bucks?"

Hampton instinctively replied, "Whatcha got?"

"I knew it," Dan laughed. "Hearing disability, my ass!"

Scotty tapped Dan on the shoulder. "I think she's here." A dark-haired woman, appearing to be fiftyish, wearing red-rimmed glasses, entered the shop. She had on a short light-blue jacket and was toting a large purse. "That might be her," Scotty said. He waved at Hampton and Rollin. "See you, boys. I think our guest has arrived."

"Hey," Hampton said to Rollin, "didn't we see her here last week?"

The biker scratched his head. "Yeah, with her kid."

"What makes you think that was her kid?" Dan asked.

"They was huggin'," Hampton said. "Suppose it could have been her boy toy."

"Gotta go," Dan said as the detectives approached the woman. "Are you Ellie?" he asked.

"I am."

58

"I'm Dan Shields, and this is my partner, Joe Scott." Dan pointed to an empty table at the opposite side of the shop. "Let's sit there."

They walked past a table occupied by three men, all appearing to be senior citizens, and reached the one Dan had selected. Ellie sat nearest the wall and placed her coat on an empty chair. The detectives took seats on each side of her. "Thanks for coming," Dan said.

Opening her purse, she placed a manila folder on the table. "I can use a cup of coffee."

Scotty rose. "How would you like it?"

"Regular, cream, no sugar, thanks."

A couple of minutes later, he placed the hot cup in front of her, and she sipped the drink. "This is so awkward. First off, George doesn't know anything about me and Gordon."

Dan sat back thinking Scotty was right that she and Gordon might have been having an affair. He knew Ellie saw him glance at his partner, and she closed her eyes for a moment. Reopening them, she shook her head. "It's not what you're thinking. You do know Gordon was a journalism major and wrote for the school's newspaper, right?"

Dan said, "We were told he majored in journalism but weren't aware of him writing for the college newspaper."

Ellie opened a folder and pulled out an article. "You need to see this." She placed it in front of the detectives. "Gordon wrote this after pledging and quitting Delphi. He had a passion for doing the right thing. Politics annoyed him, as did corporate greed and dishonesty."

Dan and Scotty read the document. "Quite a piece. I take it he created a few enemies," Dan said while wondering why no one had mentioned this until now.

"He did, and he was uneasy about staying on campus much longer. He was thinking about going to New Haven College to get into criminal justice. Gordon was exposed to these hazing activities and parties when he was pledging. The fraternity was banned from the college, and two members were expelled from school." Ellie grimaced and sipped her coffee. "Now. You want to know about George, and where I come in."

"Yes," Dan said. "Do you have another copy of the article?"

Ellie slid it to Dan. "Take it."

"It sounds like your relationship with George is rocky."

"Rocky is mild. It's stone-cold nonexistent." She looked into Dan's eyes. "I know Gordon wouldn't have shot up with heroin or cocaine."

Dan nodded. "Look, Gordon apparently injected a deadly dose of narcotics into his arm, but we don't buy it either. We know he was in fear of needles."

"Yes, I think it's called trypanophobia. I once looked it up."

"What about his roommate, Rosario, and girlfriend, Amalia? George is not happy about them."

Ellie took another sip of coffee. "Um…about Amalia. She wasn't exactly his girlfriend. She's Rosario's girlfriend."

Surprised, Dan asked, "Why the charade?"

"You know Rosario is Latino, and Amalia is African-American, right?"

"Right," Dan said.

"Gordon knew his father was racist. He was a good kid, didn't hate anyone. He knew his father would be enraged, so he introduced Amalia as his girlfriend. And Rosario? That was bad enough for George."

"Did Gordon ever mention the security guard, Christine Kole?"

"No, but I saw the name in the news."

"Could they have been connected in some way?"

"He never mentioned her." Ellie took another drink, and then she gritted her teeth. "Exactly what has George told you about Gordon, me, and Cody?"

"He really didn't say much before his near-heart attack," Dan said.

"Heart attack?"

"Not really. He's okay. According to Natalie, it was an anxiety attack. We know you were his second wife. He said your son, Cody, was the reason for your separation."

Dan watched her eyes roll and sensed she was deeply disturbed by what George had said. She rested her glasses on the table. "Let's get this straight. Cody had nothing to do with our divorce. It was Natalie. He was sleeping with that slut right from the start."

Dan eyed his partner and knew they were in for an earful.

"George opened a new branch and hired her to manage it. I knew they were having an affair. I saw texts and receipts. The one that got me was from Victoria's Secret, and he took her to Vegas on a so-called business trip. Some business…monkey business."

Dan and Scotty remained silent as Ellie continued. "I suppose he told you Cody was a bad kid."

"He didn't have a lot of good things to say, and he told us Cody had been arrested on narcotics charges." Dan said.

She took a breath and placed her glasses back on. "True. I do admit Cody was a handful at times and not George's cup of tea. Look, my son did a lot of stupid things, like dropping out of school and hanging around with a bunch of derelicts, but he straightened out after the drug arrest. That was his second brush with the law. He went back and got his GED before enlisting. And Iraq is no picnic."

"We know the juvenile case was hidden," Dan said.

Scotty was writing as fast as Ellie was talking. She took another drink of coffee. "About George: he is corrupt, about as corrupt as they come. I witnessed a few dirty deals. He's wiggling his way into politics, and Gordon knew who and what his father really was, nothing but a greedy and dishonest, power-hungry businessman. His yacht was a quid pro quo gift. Gordon wanted to expose his father and bring down his financial empire. I told Gordon what I knew. I had documents that could do George harm. That's why we met and were going to get together again."

"Do you think George had any idea what Gordon was up to?"

"It's possible."

"But Gordon never told you that his father suspected anything?" Dan asked.

"No, I was hoping to get into that when we met, but we never got the chance to speak again." Ellie's eyes teared up. "I want you to know that I was a good stepmom. I liked Gordon and Keith. Keith was…still is a little distant, but Gordon always called me, sent me birthday and Christmas cards. I did love him as my own." She wiped her wet eyes with a napkin. "I've told you a lot. Believe me, Gordon was a good kid. I should say man."

"I'm sure he was," Dan said. "I know there will be a funeral after Gordon's body is released from Farmington after the autopsy."

"I still can't believe it."

Both detectives stood, as did she. "Thank you," Dan said as he handed her his card. "Call us if you think of anything."

Ellie picked up her purse, put on her jacket, and walked ahead of the detectives toward the exit. As they neared the door, Dan heard Hampton's voice. "Hey. I see that lousy lawyer and his daughter are out."

Dan reversed direction. "Come on," he said to Scotty. The detectives again approached the car thief's table. Hampton was referring to Angelo Biaggio, an attorney with whom Dan had an adversarial relationship. It was this sleazy attorney who put Dan's family in jeopardy, and the resourceful detective had coerced Hampton into stealing Biaggio's beloved Jaguar. The attempt was foiled, but Dan subsequently arrested the lawyer for aiding and abetting a vehicular homicide. It was the lawyer's daughter, Rozalie, who drove the Jaguar and killed a young boy. They were still awaiting trial for that tragic incident. Dan also charged the ambulance-chasing attorney with insurance fraud when he discovered a setup Biaggio had with a repair shop and a doctor. "It's not over," Dan said. "There's another hearing coming up soon."

"He ain't never gonna see jail time," Hampton said. "He got too much money."

Dan bristled at the remark because he knew it might be true. "We'll see about that. He can't buy all the judges." Dan couldn't leave without noting the marijuana. "You know you boys reek of weed."

Hampton grinned, raised his coffee cup. "I think it's the decaf, it's hazelnut. Has an outdoor smell."

Dan laughed. "Okay, stay out of trouble." He and Scotty headed for the door.

Getting back into Dan's car, Scotty said, "Look at that. Ellie's pulling away in a Lexus."

"She said a mouthful," Dan replied as he fastened his seat belt.

CHAPTER 12

Smelling all those doughnuts made Dan hungry. He looked at his watch. "How about lunch?"

Scotty answered quickly. "Sounds good to me. The Burger Joint is around the corner."

As Dan drove toward the restaurant, he recognized the barbecue place where he'd once met Hancock Sasser for lunch. "I hate smoked food. That's where Sasser took me when I almost barfed." The food-sensitive detective couldn't stand the aroma of charred food, so that day Dan dragged out his EpiPen and feigned an attack to get himself out of the eatery.

He saw a metered parking space in front of the restaurant and parallel parked his car. Approaching the meter, Dan checked his pockets and had no change. "Got any quarters?"

Scotty pulled four from his pocket and handed them to Dan. "That should get us an hour. Let's eat."

Dan deposited the coins into the machine's slot, and they headed into the eatery. Two people were in line ahead of the detectives. Scotty nudged his partner and pointed to the bar where there were empty seats. "We can sit there."

They walked over and sat on high-backed swivel stools. A TV mounted in the corner was tuned into The People's Court. "Do you believe the idiots who go on these judge shows?" Scotty asked his partner.

"I think they get paid." Dan got a glimpse of himself in the rectangular wall-length mirror mostly obscured by three shelves of liquor bottles. "Do you think I need a haircut?"

"Do you?"

"Maybe. I'll wait until Phyllis gets on my case."

The bartender/server approached the detectives and took orders. They waited for their food and finally, plates with burgers and crinkled fries were set in front of them. Dan took a juicy bite. "Good," he said. "Did I tell you Connie might be leaving us for Florida?"

Scotty wiped his mouth with a napkin. "No. When?"

"She has family there and will be visiting them. She says she may retire down there."

Scotty drank from his glass of diet Coke. "I kinda still miss her."

"At this point, it's not a sure thing, but I'd bet on it."

The hungry detectives wasted little time devouring their lunches. Dan got off the stool. "I'll be right back. The boys' room is calling."

Returning a few minutes later, Scotty handed him the tab. Dan objected. "Me?"

Scotty smugly laughed. "I did pay for parking."

Dan proceeded to the register, took out a credit card, paid the bill, and drove back to the police station.

⊼

Dan noticed there were messages on his desk phone. There were four. "Looks like we might have a few more people who heard Gordon's show," he said to Scotty. "Want to listen?"

"Sure. I hope someone has helpful news."

After hearing all four messages, Dan said. "It's the same story. Nothing."

Dan glanced at his computer and saw an email from Aki, the chief lab technician in Farmington. "It's the toxicology report."

Scotty peered over Dan's shoulder.

Dan said. "Gordon Gunderson had bad heroin laced with fentanyl."

"What about oxycodone?" Scotty asked.

"Negative. I need to call Aki." Dan picked up his phone and put it on speaker. "Hi, Aki. Thanks for the tox report. What about Christine Kole?"

"Did you look at the second page?"

"Wait." While on the phone, Dan scrolled down the document to take another look. "Sorry, I got it. She had oxycodone. Odd isn't it? One victim had only heroin, and the other had only oxy. What about the syringe? Prints?"

"Talk to Kara."

"I haven't seen anything about the autopsies."

"Arnstein's report is being finalized."

"Anything unusual?"

"No. Just the one needle mark."

"What about the guard, Christine?"

"She had a few welts on her chest and shoulder. Her cause of death was blunt force trauma."

"Has Arnstein released the bodies?"

"Not yet. He will later today."

Dan looked at Scotty and asked Aki, "Can you have him hold them? I want to get another look at Gordon's arm. I also want to take a look at Christine."

"Better get here soon."

"Be right down. We'll see you in about twenty minutes."

Dan opened his desk drawer and pulled out a baggie with what he believed to be four oxycodone tablets. He knew he should have placed them into evidence, but he didn't follow standard procedure. "As long as we're there, I want Kara to test these." He grabbed his jacket. "Get yours. I hope it's not too cold in the freezer."

▲

All suspicious deaths in Connecticut require autopsies performed at the medical facility in Farmington. The freestanding two-story facility housing the forensics lab and morgue was on the medical center grounds diagonally across from the hospital's main entrance.

Scotty opened the door and, knowing the layout of the building, the detectives proceeded to see Aki. Three white-coated analysts wearing latex gloves were busily at work, and Dan caught their attention. "Where's Aki?" he asked.

A female technician pointed to the back room. "In there. I'll get him."

A few seconds later, he came out and greeted the detectives. Dan immediately noticed the ring on Aki's hand. "Been a while," the newlywed said.

"Guess we haven't seen you since the wedding in Kyoto."

Aki shook his head. "What a waste of money. I told you Mayu had a lot of relatives. Over a thousand came to the wedding." He smiled. "I think half of them were named Suzuki. That's kind of like Smith."

Dan quickly got down to business. "The toxicology report has me wondering about the guard. We can't prove anything yet, but it looks like Gordon Gunderson's overdose wasn't an accident or suicide. The guard, we know that's a homicide."

"A nasty one." Aki said. "I told Arnstein you were coming. He's waiting for you."

Dan said, "We're going next door to see Kara first."

The detectives walked into the forensics room and Dan saw Kara at the counter. "What brings you two here?" she asked. "By the way. The prints on the syringe are hard to get. I can't confirm anything."

"What about the water bottle?"

"Ah. There were more than one set of prints on it. All pretty smudged."

"I'm fairly sure those prints belonged to Jason Ritter and Gordon," Dan said. "Ritter told us he put the bottle in the basket."

Dan handed Kara a baggie with four pills inside. "Can you test these? They appear to be oxy, but I want to make sure."

"Where did you get these?"

Dan shook his head. "Let's just say we found them in a vehicle."

Kara took the bag. "I'll test them."

"Can you do it now? We're headed downstairs to see Arnstein."

Kara pointed a finger at Dan. "Check back when you're done in the basement."

"How cold is it down there?"

She chuckled. "Not as bad as the Arctic. You'll be okay."

"Thanks," Dan said.

Pathologist Max Arnstein got up from his chair when they entered his office. "Aki said you want to see Gordon Gunderson and Christine Kole."

"Think we'll be warm enough?" Dan asked.

Arnstein grabbed his white coat. "Where do you think you're going? Alaska? Has it been that long since you were here? It's cool, not cold."

"It is called the freezer," Dan said.

"Only by you guys." Arnstein led the way into the room where he performed autopsies and where the bodies were stored. "See?" he said. "Not so bad in here."

The extremely brightly lit room contained three steel tables absent of dead bodies. Shiny utensils were on the counter that could have come from an operating room or a butcher shop. The hose hanging from a chain above the tables looked like an ordinary backyard variety. Dan got a whiff of chemicals that remained in the air. "Formaldehyde," Arnstein said as he moved to the back of the room where six rows of vaults, four in each, occupied the wall.

"How many are here now?" Dan asked.

"Eight. Not exactly a full house," the pathologist replied. He walked to chamber five, slid out the concealed corpse, and unzipped a gray bag.

Dan read the toe tag with the name Gordon Gunderson typed on it. After scanning the body, he studied the needle mark, took out his phone, and snapped a few pictures. "So, that's the only injection site you found?"

"It is. His body is clean except for the scar on his side. That's from an appendix removal."

"You can put him back," Dan said. Arnstein zipped the cover and slid Gordon back into the vault. "How about Christine Kole?"

The pathologist moved one row over and opened number ten. Scotty positioned himself to one side, and Arnstein unzipped the body bag. The guard's naked corpse was in view, and the pathologist pointed up to her abdomen and rib cage. "I noted the bruise right here, probably from being forcefully pushed. The contusions on her shoulder and neck look like a strap mark, probably a shoulder strap. There's also a gash on her left breast. That could also be from the strap."

Dan snapped a few pictures and said, "Zip her up and slide her back in."

The detectives and Arnstein walked out of the morgue. "Thanks for the show," Dan said.

"Yeah, we had a blast," Scotty quipped.

Returning to check if Kara had tested the pills, Dan saw her zipping up the baggie with 3 pills inside. "They're oxycodone," she said as she handed the baggie back to him.

"Thanks."

Dan knew they had a house call to make. Exiting the facility, he told Scotty, "We have to arrange a visit with Christine's grandparents. I'll call them when we get to headquarters."

A

Dan retrieved the Kole's phone number, spoke with the grandfather and turned to Scotty. "All set for tomorrow, ten a.m. I have to see Dixon."

Entering the traffic captain's office, Dan said, "Got a minute?"

"What's on your mind?"

"Is Travis still here?"

"Hell no. He got bailed."

Dan scowled. "Figures. Who bailed him?"

"All I know is he's out."

"Thanks."

While walking upstairs to his desk, Dan wondered who might have bonded out Travis. His first thought was Haley, but he didn't want to think she'd actually do that. He sat beside Scotty. "Dixon told me Travis made bond. I hope Haley wasn't foolish enough to set him loose."

Scotty huffed, "And why would that surprise you? You know those domestic things are hot and cold."

"I know." Dan nodded. "And they have a kid wedged between them. I'll get my answer tonight when I call her father.

Chapter 13

Dan didn't mind the morgue visit, but he was aware that tomorrow's meeting with Christine Kole's grandparents might not be pleasant. He knew they would be in a fragile state of being, trying to cope with the tragic loss of their granddaughter.

As Dan's Accord pulled out of the headquarters parking lot, he received a call from his wife. "Hi, I'm leaving now. Just got in the car."

"Good," Phyllis said. "I need you to stop at the drugstore to pick up some children's Pepto and Tylenol. Josh didn't go to school today. He has a stomach issue and is running a mild fever."

"Kate okay?"

"She's fine so far."

"See you soon."

▲

Entering the drugstore, Dan made his way to the over-the-counter medications and checked the shelf marked 'antacids' but couldn't find what he was sent for, so he went to Sarah, the pharmacy manager. "Hi, Dan," she said. "I don't recall seeing any prescriptions. Do you need a new set of pens?"

He smiled at her. "No, I think I'm good for a while longer. Josh is sick, and I need some Pepto."

She pointed to the bottom row of a nearby display case. "Over there."

"Thanks. I also need children's Tylenol."

"Next to the Pepto."

Dan browsed the shelf. "Got it. Thanks."

After purchasing the drugs, he called his wife to tell her he'd picked up the requested items.

▲

Dan placed the medicine bag on the kitchen's granite-topped island. Phyllis kissed him. "Thanks."

"I see Connie's gone."

"I told her not to come. I stayed home with Josh. He's upstairs."

Kate waited for her hug, and Dad happily obliged. "Are you okay?"

"Yup."

Dan walked toward the stairs. "I'm going up to change and check on him."

Returning, wearing his favorite jeans and a Giants sweatshirt, Dan said, "Josh says he feels better."

Five minutes later, the pajama clad boy appeared, and Phyllis felt his forehead. "Are you hungry?"

"Yes"

She was sure he had no fever, but still opened the Tylenol bottle, making Josh swallow two tablets with a glass of water.

Dinner was served and soon after the meal was finished, Dan was in his familiar place watching TV. It was a few minutes before Jeopardy when the house phone rang. "Hi," he said to Dave Valente. "I was going to call later."

"Dan, I want to thank you again for helping Haley."

"I tried to get her to realize what she was doing, and who she was doing it with. Travis is bad for her."

"I agree."

"Level with me. She said she has been drug-free for a year."

Dan heard Dave take a deep breath. "She was in rehab, but

Travis came back into the picture a month or so ago, and I can't be sure of what's going on."

Dan sighed. "Haley told me she hadn't seen him until a few nights ago when they were arrested. When I left her, she seemed determined to forget him."

"That's Haley. A little lost at times and not always truthful. Travis is a big problem, but he is Joey's father."

Dan was reluctant to bring it up but felt it necessary. "Haley didn't tell me, but I know Travis was arrested for domestic violence. What happened?"

"They had an apartment for a short time. He came home one night, and I don't know exactly what happened. All I know is that he hit her, and she called the police. I wanted to grab a baseball bat and smack his head off."

"I hear you. I told him I would beat the shit out of him if he ever touched her again."

"Funny thing, you know every so often the old Haley does emerge. She thinks about going back to college."

"One question. Did Haley bond him out?"

"Not that I'm aware of."

"Is she home?"

"She's giving Joey a bath."

"Can you ask her if she bonded Travis? I really want to know."

"I'll ask her. Can I call you back?"

"Sure."

The call ended. Phyllis had entered the den halfway through the conversation. "Was that Dave?"

"Yes." Dan told her about their conversation. "You know something? Mike said he'd like to see her."

Phyllis walked to the bookshelf and took Mike's yearbook from it. She opened it and their prom picture fell out. "Handsome couple," she said when she showed it to Dan.

Dan studied it. "She's still cute. You never know what can happen to them."

"That's for sure. I see a lot of misguided young adults."

Dan thought about the syringe and Gordon's phobia. He realized who better to ask about it than his wife. "I have a question for you."

"You look perplexed."

"I kind of am. If someone has a deep fear of needles, could they pass out at the sight of one?"

"A fear of anything can cause severe changes in mind and physical movement. Why are you asking?"

"It has to do with the Gordon Gunderson case. He was afraid of syringes; more than that, deathly afraid of them. And I'm sure he was injected by someone else, but there was no sign of a struggle. Why wouldn't he resist or put up a fight?"

"It's totally possible that he could have fainted."

Dan winced. "That would explain it."

The phone rang, and Dan answered it. "Dan," Dave said. "I asked Haley about the bail. She said she knew he was out, but she didn't post it. He texted her, and he's tried to call her, but she doesn't answer him. I'm actually getting her a new phone with a different number."

"That's good, but he knows where you live. Can I recommend you and Haley get a restraining order that will keep him from getting near you? If he violates it, you can have him arrested."

"That's a good idea. I think Haley is really done with him."

"Let me know how it goes," Dan said, ending the call.

CHAPTER 14

It was no surprise to Dan that Landry was pacing the parking lot, enjoying another cigarette. "Looks like a nice day," Dan said.

Landry took a puff. "Wait until you see what's in the squad room."

Dan opened the back door and proceeded upstairs where he saw Scotty and Hanson standing at the previously empty table in the corner. "Are you kidding? Syms broke down and got a new coffeemaker?" Dan asked.

Scotty replied, "Yeah, a Keurig and a whole box of K-Cups."

"Don't get the wrong idea," Hanson said. "Blues is still on my agenda."

Dan hung up his coat and pulled a coffee mug from his side desk drawer. As he approached the coffeemaker, he looked toward the captain's office. "Who's that in with him?"

Hanson said, "I don't know, but he was here when I arrived."

Dan made himself coffee and went to his desk. Scotty was right behind him.

"We're outta here," Hanson said. "Landry and me will be you-know-where."

Minutes later, the captain's door opened, and he walked out with a tall man who wore a tan sport coat. Dan took him to be in his late thirties, about the same age as Scotty.

"Where are Hanson and Landry?" Syms asked. "I suppose they're at the diner."

"You got it," Dan said. "They left a couple of minutes ago."

Syms introduced Malvin Jones to the detectives. "Mal is transferring from Waterbury. He'll be on board soon. We have to get up to Hardison and finalize the paperwork."

Syms and Mal exited the room, and Dan moved closer to Scotty. "We should be at the Koles in an hour."

▲

Scotty insisted on driving, and they headed to the address given to them. "That's it, the yellow ranch with the wrought iron fence," Dan said. He checked out the single-family house, the shrubs, the unattached one-car garage, and a gray Honda Civic in the driveway as they approached the front door.

Scotty rang the bell, and a short, thin, white-haired man, appearing to be at least seventy, with a cane in his left hand opened the door.

Dan displayed his badge and asked, "Are you Christine Kole's grandfather?"

"That's right," the man replied.

"My partner is Joe Scott. May we come in?"

"I suppose."

Scotty asked, "And your name, sir?"

"Henry." He pointed to his wife who was seated in a brown cushioned chair that appeared to be well-worn. She placed her knitting needle, and ball of yarn on her lap and peered at the detectives through her thick glasses. She motioned the men toward the couch. "Sit," she softly said.

"How are you both doing?" Dan asked.

The old man gritted his teeth. "You ever lose a grandchild?" He took a few steps, each with the walking stick hitting the floor as he stepped toward his rocker chair. "She's been with us for the past three years."

"We've spoken to Christine's employer. I believe the manager spoke with you."

Mr. Kole sat in his rocker, and his head bobbed as he spoke. "Westbrook did contact us. The fact is, Christine had gone back to community college and later took the weekend security job, but she also worked a couple of days a week at the veterans' hospital."

Dan heard the baby stirring and looked at him. "Beautiful little boy."

"Thank you," the grandmother commented, her eyes teary.

Dan asked, "Was Christine ever married?"

The grandfather bristled at the question. "No," he brusquely said.

Dan digested the cold response to his question and knew the grandfather didn't want to talk about the baby's father. "Mr. Kole, I can see the baby's father is a sore subject. Where is he, and may we have his name?"

His wife remained silent as the grandfather huffed and said, "She doesn't know who the father is." He hesitated. "Christine had a rough time after her parents, our son and his wife, died in a car accident five years ago. She was twenty-one and moved in with a girlfriend. They were bartenders and that led her to drinking." He grabbed a handkerchief. "She had a lot of male friends, if you know what I mean, and one of them got her pregnant."

"That's okay," Agnes spoke, her voice weak. "She came to live with us and got off the liquor on her own, and we have Mason. Christine had been trying to save money to get her own place."

Dan took a few seconds before he asked, "Can you tell us if Christine was on any medications?"

"She had headache pills," Henry said.

Dan was curious. "Do you know what she took?"

Agnes said, "She has a bottle in her room."

"Would you mind getting it for us?"

The grandmother got up, and slowly walked to Christine's room, returning with two prescription bottles and a few baggies, each with four tablets inside.

Dan looked at the pill containers. "OxyContin, thirty tablets." He noticed the fill dates. One bottle was empty, and the other was near-empty. "Are there any others, perhaps in the kitchen or bathroom?" Dan asked.

"I think I did see one in the medicine cabinet," Agnes said.

"May we see it?" Dan asked.

The woman retrieved the full one, and handed it to Dan.

"What's going on?" Henry asked.

"We're not sure," Dan said. "Would you mind if we took the bottles and the bagged pills? They may mean nothing, but we're still investigating her death as well as Gordon Gunderson's."

"Take them," the grandmother said.

The little boy began to stir in the playpen. Dan said, "We'll be on our way. Thank you for allowing us to visit. By the way, Christine's Prius was impounded, and you can get it in thirty days. Also, Christine will be released from the state medical center soon. They will call you so you can arrange a funeral."

The Kole's looked at each other, then the grandmother spoke with her voice cracking. "We're going to have her cremated." She pointed to the mantle above the fireplace. "We want her right there."

The detectives got into Scotty's car, and Dan said, "Interesting. OxyContin, oxycodone…. Same thing. Different doctors and different pharmacies."

"Well, we know one thing," Scotty said. "She didn't appear to be getting the pills off the street; she had legit prescriptions. The headache excuse may be just that, an excuse to have the medication prescribed. Do you think she was selling them to save up for a place?"

"Could be, but who did she sell them to? We need to find out. How many different doctor's names are on those bottles? We have three here and you have the one we took from the car. That makes four. I want to call at least one of the doctors who prescribed the pills to find out if Christine did in fact have Migraine issues. Was she ever tested?"

"Maybe we should call them all."

▲

It wasn't long after the detectives got back to their workspace that Dan placed the prescription bottles on his desk and looked at one. "Doctor Piscatelli." He called the number listed on the bottle and after holding for a few minutes, the Ophthalmologist spoke with Dan. When the conversation ended, Dan said to Scotty. "He diagnosed her with having severe ocular migraines and prescribed the pills, but he was unaware that she had seen other doctors who had also written prescriptions for the medicine. Obviously, she took the pills for her headaches, but Christine got addicted to them. I'm calling doctor number two, Patel."

Scotty took two of the containers. "I'll check these doctors."

After speaking with the eye doctors, Dan and Scotty knew the prescriptions were indeed legit, and that Christine played the game well.

Dan peered down to Syms' office. "Time for us see the captain," he said.

The detectives approached their boss. Dan said, "You need to hear this."

Syms grabbed his Aleve and gave Dan his undivided attention. "I'm listening."

Not bothering to sit, Dan said, "Christine Kole was on oxy, and we've confiscated prescription bottles and more than a dozen baggies. She was selling, but we don't know who her customers were." Dan proceeded to fill in the captain on their morgue visit as well as their chat with Ellie Wilcox.

Syms' phone rang, and he said, "I need to take this." Dan and Scotty moved toward the door. "Don't go. Sit."

The captain answered Bev's call as the detectives listened. He smiled broadly. "That's great, can't wait." Syms ended the conversation and stared at his detectives. "Fantastic! She's coming back! Bev will be here as soon as she gets day care worked out. She's lucky her husband works from home." The captain pivoted to the back table. "Got a couple of new bonsais. What do you think?"

"Nice," Scotty said.

"They look good. You're a fine daddy," Dan said.

Syms rolled his eyes. "Go back to work and send your comrades in here."

Dan informed Landry and Hanson that the captain needed to see them pronto. Minutes later, the two detectives came out with Landry holding a warrant. "Unbelievable," he said. "It's time to make an arrest."

"Slow it down," Dan said. "What are you talking about?"

"The mayor," Landry said. "That no-good nephew of hers that we got our asses reamed for. We're arresting him and his friend. Apparently, the mayor and the chief had a long talk, and she told him to go after the juveniles." Hanson paused. "By the way, Syms told us about Bev and Malvin Jones. I guess he was the guy we saw in with him."

"That was him and if you hadn't rushed out to the diner, you would have met the man." Dan said. "He's about your height but appears to be younger and a whole lot better looking than you."

Hanson sneered at Dan. "Right, old man. We gotta go."

After watching Landry and him them leave the room, Dan turned to Scotty. "How do you feel about school?"

"What?"

"I'm thinking we should go back to college tomorrow."

Chapter 15

Dan thought about Gordon Gunderson, and he remembered what Ellie Wilcox had said about Delphi, so he read that article about the fraternity again. Upon reading it, he realized Reed Barbour and Gregory Melrose were the two students who had been expelled from school and they might well have had a score to settle with Gordon. He jotted down the names Reed Barbour and Gregory Melrose. He then wrote the names Doreen Patrisi, Jason Ritter, Rosario Cruz, Amalia Kendrick, and Ramsay Dale on the same piece of paper. He looked at the squad room clock above the water cooler. It was quarter past eight, and Scotty was late. Wondering where his partner was, he called him. "Where are you?" Dan could hear traffic.

"On my way. There's a rollover on ninety-one. I'm clear, should be there in about ten."

Landry and Hanson entered the workspace. Not bothering to remove his jacket, Hanson said, "We got them, the nephew, and his friend, but my guess is they'll make bond this morning and be let out. You know how that goes. I gotta take a piss."

When Scotty finally arrived, Dan said, "I made a list of people we need to see." He showed it to his partner.

"Who first?"

Dan thought for a second. "Ramsey Dale. Then we can scoot over to the administration building. They should have addresses and phone numbers for Barbour and Melrose. I'd like to set something up with Rosario and Amalia, and we need to speak to Doreen Patrisi.

How about calling Rosario while I talk to Ramsey?"

The detectives got to work with their self-assigned tasks and as soon as Scotty completed his chore, he stood at his partner's desk. Dan had just hung up his phone and looked at Scotty who said, "Rosario and Amalia have a full day of classes as well as lab. He asked if they could meet us tomorrow. They can be at the student center around eleven thirty."

"That's fine," Dan replied. "Ramsey said he'll be at the station all day. Let's go."

▲

The detectives entered the busy student center and made their way to the radio station where the glass door marked with the station's call letters on it was shut. Scotty rotated the handle, but the door remained closed.

Dan noticed a buzzer and pressed it. A few seconds later, he heard a click and the door unlocked so he turned the handle, and they went inside. Ramsey Dale was standing in the hallway awaiting them. "Pretty crowded downstairs," Dan said.

Ramsey replied, "It's like that every day."

Dan glanced into one of the two glassed-in studios and briefly watched a red-haired female, wearing a headset. The door was closed, and he couldn't hear anything, but it was clear she was speaking into a mic. They walked past the studio where Gordon had been found, and Dan noticed two male students inside sitting at different microphones. They also wore headsets. With the door ajar, he heard folk music coming from the studio as they entered Ramsey's office.

Dan said, "Thanks for announcing our plea for listeners to call us. We got several calls, but no one heard anything."

"Should we continue to make the announcements?"

"It won't hurt to continue for a few more days. We need to talk with Doreen Patrisi. I believe you us told she was here just before Gordon," Dan said.

"Right. She left a little after midnight."

"How do you know she left then?"

"Ask her. She's in the recording studio doing PSA's. I'll get her." The station manager walked down the corridor and returned with Doreen who sat beside Ramsey. "These are the detectives investigating the deaths of Gordon and the security guard, Christine Kole."

"Hi," Dan said. "I know this is tough, but as we understand it, you were here when Gordon came in to do his show."

"That's true. I let him in."

"Was he alone?"

"Yes."

"Did he seem nervous, edgy, or was he normal?"

"He was fine. He told me it was raining. I had about ten minutes remaining on my show. Gordon took over at midnight, and I left after calling security for an escort back to my dorm. That was maybe five minutes later."

"Is that what you normally do, call an escort?"

"I do. We're encouraged not to walk alone at night."

Dan asked, "Who was it that walked with you?"

"A guard named Watney. It was raining, so he took me back in his car. I didn't know what happened until later that day."

"Thank you," he said. "You can go back to what you were doing."

Dan noticed a rack on the back wall and drew Ramsey's attention to what he saw. "Are those tapes?" he asked.

"They're audio recordings. That's a library of our shows."

"Gordon's show was taped?"

"Yes. It's on an audio disc. I probably should have mentioned that. I'll make a copy."

"How soon?"

"I'll run one off as soon as Doreen is done recording public service announcements. It should be an hour or so."

"How often are the announcements aired?" Scotty asked.

Ramsey explained, "DJs are to run at least two per hour, as well as give the required station ID every thirty minutes."

"Wait," Dan said. "Are all those messages taped?"

"No. There are also announcements typed on cards that the DJs read. They can play a recorded ID, although we prefer them to be live."

"So, we may hear Gordon's voice either between songs or every half hour?"

"It depends on whether he chooses to play the recordings or read the messages. You should hear his voice when he breaks in to tell the listeners what songs he aired or is airing."

Dan said, "We expect to be on campus for a while. Call me when you get the audio copy done, and we'll pick it up."

Scotty asked, "Do you have Jason Ritter's cell number? We want to talk to him again." Ramsey took out his phone and read it to the detectives. "Thanks," Scotty said.

Ramsey escorted his visitors to the door he'd opened for them, and the detectives walked downstairs into the noisy student center. They exited the building, and Dan shook his head while eying several vaping students. "They don't get it. It's still smoking."

"We did stupid things when we were their ages," Scotty said. "I remember doing a little weed. You can't say you didn't do some."

"Like you said, we all did stupid things. I want to check out Doreen's alibi that she was escorted back to her dorm. I know she's believable, but it can't hurt to check it out. As far as we know, she was the last person to see Gordon alive."

"Wrong," Scotty said. "The killer was the last one to see him breathing."

A quarter mile down the road, Dan parked at the security facility. They were greeted when entering the building by the same two guards they had seen previously. "Would you like me to get Mr. Westland?" the female asked.

She got up as Westland entered the room. "What have you found out?" he asked.

"Nothing concrete," Dan said. "I have a couple of questions. We were at the radio station, and a female student named Doreen Patrisi told us a guard named Watney drove her back to her dorm around twelve fifteen a.m. the night of Gordon's death."

"That wouldn't be unusual," Westland said.

"Was Watney the only other guard on duty besides Christine Kole that night?"

"Yes."

"Did he also do rounds that night?"

"No. He was here while she was out. They alternate on their shifts."

"So, Watney wouldn't have had a reason to go to the student center, other than to pick up Doreen Patrisi?"

"Right. He was here when I got here, then I went to the station."

"How sure are you he was here the entire time?"

"What are you asking?"

Dan eased back. "It's only a question. Would you mind if we speak with him?"

"He's off for a few days."

"Do you have his number?" Westland recited it to the detectives. "Thanks," Dan said as he and Scotty moved to the door.

Their next stop was the administration building where they obtained the information on Reed Barbour and Gregory Melrose they needed. However, they were unable to find out anything about Delphi or its members because the fraternity had filed a lawsuit regarding its ousting. Barbour and Melrose were the only two expelled from Delphi and the college.

"I'm going to check in with Ramsey. Hopefully, he'll have our audio disc," Dan said. He called the manager, who informed him there was a problem with the duplicating machine. Shaking his head, he told Scotty, "The recorder is on the fritz. It should be fixed later this afternoon. We'll be back tomorrow to speak with Rosario and Amalia. We can get it then."

They got into Dan's car, and he said, "I haven't forgotten about Watney." He took out his cell and attempted to contact him. Watney's phone rolled to voicemail, and Dan left a message. By day's end, the security guard hadn't called back.

CHAPTER 16

It was Friday morning, and Dan saw Syms walk to the Keurig to make himself a cup of coffee. The captain took his coffee black and picked up the full cup. Then he pointed to Scotty with his empty hand. "Follow me."

"Me too?" Dan shrugged.

Syms nodded. "Okay, but I want to talk to him."

The detectives followed their boss, and he invited them to sit as he placed his cup on the desk. Taking a drink and then putting the cup back down, he said, "Pretty good, isn't it?"

Dan had no idea where this conversation was going until Syms addressed Scotty. "Are you enjoying the free brew?"

Scotty nodded. "Sure."

"Know what's missing, Muffin Man?"

He closed his eyes and reopened them. "Oh no, I quit baking a while ago." At one time, Scotty supplied the crew with his homemade muffins. But since Sallie had their third child, he abandoned the kitchen.

Syms leaned forward. "May I strongly suggest that you and Sara Lee get baking again? Bev will be back on Monday."

Scotty smirked. "We do love Bev. I'll do it for her, but I'm not making it a regular thing."

Syms smiled. "We'll see. At least it's a start."

"And what kind of start is that?" Dan asked. "Are you giving him back to her?"

"You afraid to lose him?" Syms barked. "And you be quiet," he said to Scotty. "Bev and I discussed it. She will be a floater. She'll help whomever she can, and that includes you boys."

Dan changed the subject. "We were at the campus yesterday, and we're going back to speak with Rosario and Amalia."

Syms pointed to the door. "I hope college teaches you something."

⚹

The student center was as bustling at eleven twenty-five. It occurred to Dan they knew what Rosario looked like, but they hadn't met Amalia. Dan scoured the room and lamented, "Those were the days. Four years of hanging out in places like this." He kept looking around. "Reminds me of my days in college. There's a lot of talent here."

Scotty jabbed his partner. "Talent? Is that what you called the coeds at North Carolina? I know you and Phyllis met there. So, she was talent?"

Dan side-glanced his partner, grinned, and wryly said, "Damn right. Best looking girl on campus. And I know where and when you met Sallie. How can I forget that day? When you saw her standing at the copy machine inside that real estate office, your face was as red as her hair. I still can't imagine what she saw in you."

"Thanks. Prettiest woman I ever laid eyes on. I'm surprised I was able to talk."

"Me too." Dan noticed a couple of students enter the building. "That's Rosario, and I assume that's Amalia with him."

They wore matching sweats, and both carried backpacks. Moving toward them, Dan said, "Hi." He looked at the pretty girl whose cornrowed hair rested below her shoulders. "You must be Amalia."

"Yes," she said.

"Nice to meet you. My partner is Joe Scott, but we call him Scotty."

Scotty pointed at Dan. "You don't want to know what we call him back at headquarters."

Rosario directed their attention to the rear right corner of the room. "It should be a little quieter over there."

They followed him to a seating area partially hidden by two tall plants. The students set their backpacks down beside their chairs as they all took seats. Scotty got out his notepad, and Dan wanted to break the ice. "Scotty and I were just talking, and I was saying how nice this campus is. I have a son at Arizona State University on a baseball scholarship, and that's the only other campus I've been to in quite a while. What are you majoring in?"

Rosario said, "We both have academic scholarships. My major is genetics."

"I'm studying pharmaceutical sciences," Amalia said.

"That's great," Scotty said. "Good luck. Chemistry wasn't one of my strong suits."

Dan leaned forward. "Tell us about Gordon." He looked at Amalia. "We know his father thought you were his girlfriend. As a matter of fact, I think he still does, and he's less than thrilled."

Rosario said, "You should have seen his face when he saw me and found out I was rooming with Gordon."

"I can imagine," Dan said. "So, to further infuriate him, you three decided to pretend Amalia was his girlfriend."

"It was Gordon's idea," Rosario said. "I know you were in our room. Kalani told me you came to the residence hall."

"We did. We didn't disturb anything," Dan said. "Did you know about Gordon's stepmom, ex-stepmom, Ellie Wilcox?"

"Kind of. I know Gordon went to meet her at a doughnut shop. He borrowed my car. His bike is still here. Keith didn't bother to take it when he came to pick up Gordon's things."

"Do you know why he met Ellie there?" Dan asked.

Rosario replied, "Gordon majored in journalism and wrote for the school paper. He said he was seeing her for a story he was working on."

A few students passed by and took seats nearby. Dan pulled his chair a little closer toward Rosario and Amalia. "Tell us about Delphi."

Rosario shook his head. "That's a bad story. It's no secret who Gordon's father is, and it's no secret they have money. The fraternity came after Gordon to pledge."

Dan watched Amalia's face become sullen as Rosario continued. "He lasted about a month before dropping out. He'd been subjected to hazing and witnessed barbaric stunts three other pledges endured. Gordon took pictures of them the next day. A couple of them had bug bites so bad from being sent naked in the woods, they were in the infirmary for two days. Gordon knew he needed to quit the fraternity, so he did."

Amalia suddenly burst into tears. "Amalia, are you okay?" Dan asked.

Rosario put his arm around her and said, "There was a party that Gordon went to with lots of booze, pot, and other stuff."

She sobbed and cleared her eyes, obviously trying to regain her composure, she uttered, "Gordon had gotten drunk, but my roommate, Trish, she was raped."

"I'm sorry," Dan said. "Did she report it?"

"No," Amalia replied. "She was scared and embarrassed, and she got pregnant that night. She doesn't know who raped her. She thinks someone slipped roofies into her drink." Rosario slid his arm back, and Amalia wiped her eyes on the sleeve of her sweatshirt. "Gordon felt so bad because he brought her to the party, but he was drunk and didn't know what happened until the next day. Trish left school and went back to New Hampshire. Everyone thinks her mother is ill, and her father can't take care of her."

Dan could see pain written all over Amalia's face. "Did Gordon stay in touch with her?"

She sighed. "Trish shunned him. She didn't understand how he could take her to the party. Need I say more?"

"We know two members were expelled," Dan said. "Do you know Reed Barbour or Gregory Melrose?"

Rosario clasped his hands and leaned forward. "Those two were the ringleaders. I heard they brought in drugs and booze, and they were responsible for the hazing rituals."

Dan asked, "Do you know if they and Gordon had any contact after the Delphi article was published?"

"I don't know; he never said. I do know he was scared and thought about transferring out of here," Rosario said.

"That's what Ellie Wilcox told us."

"Those animals!" Amalia spoke loudly, and Dan saw more than pain, he saw anger in Amalia's eyes.

Scotty tried to calm her. "I can see you are very upset. Do you want to take a break?"

Amalia took a deep breath. "I'm okay."

Scotty's voice seemed to soothe her. "You mentioned Gordon brought Trish to the party. Were they dating?"

"Yes." Amalia sighed and raised her chin.

"I hate to ask you this, but you said your roommate was impregnated that night. Were Gordon and Trish having sex?" Scotty asked.

Amalia breathed deeply. "They were. She swears he always wore a condom. She had to have gotten pregnant at the frat house."

"Do you think it could have been Barbour or Melrose who raped her?"

Amalia began shaking. "She thinks she may have actually been raped by more than one guy. I don't know. She said she remembered hearing two voices when she woke up naked in one of the bedrooms."

Dan sensed Amalia had enough, so he decided to stop the interview and looked at both students. "Thank you for meeting with us. Go get something to eat."

"We will," Rosario said. He held his girlfriend's hand as the students picked up their backpacks and walked toward the canteen.

Dan's cell rang, and he answered it. Ramsey Dale said, "I have the audio."

"Great, I'll be right there. I'm inside the building."

Five minutes later, Dan walked back downstairs with the disc.

As they were getting ready to leave, they got a break.

"That's Ritter," Scotty said. "He just walked in." The detective engaged the student. "Hi, Jason. Can my partner and I talk with you? It will only be a few minutes."

They found a few empty chairs and sat in a semicircle. "Hi again," Dan said. "We spoke with Ramsey and Doreen a little while ago."

Jason took off his backpack and set it on the floor by his feet. "I can't sleep well."

Dan asked, "Have you seen a counselor?"

He shifted in his chair. "I've thought about it."

"Listen," Dan said as the young man's leg began to twitch. "We need you to tell us again what happened when you entered the building."

"I saw her, the guard. It was just like on TV. There was blood, and I knew she was dead. I thought about Gordon, who was in the studio, and climbed the stairs. It was obvious he was dead. I was dazed and called for help." Jason put his hand on his knee as if to stop it from twitching. His eyes widened.

Dan asked, "And nothing looked out of place, no struggle or anything unusual, except for Gordon slumped in the chair?"

"No. It was so surreal. I just saw the needle and the water bottle next to him."

"And you placed the bottle in the wastebasket."

"I guess so. Like I said, it was so surreal. I remember calling for help and waiting until they showed up."

"Are you going up to the station?" Dan asked.

"Yes. I want to tape a segment for my next show."

"We won't keep you," Dan said. "Have a good day."

Jason picked up his backpack and walked toward the stairs as the detectives exited the building.

Dan and Scotty returned to the police station with the audio of

Gordon's show. Eager to hear it, he said, "Hope you like jazz." Then he inserted the disc into his computer.

They listened to see if they might hear something, like a voice or a couple of voices. Scotty forwarded the audio to the first music lull, the twelve-thirty a.m. ID. A three-minute taped PSA followed, and then Gordon was on the mic running down the aired songs from his playlist. After that, there was more music. He repeated the process every half hour. Expecting a two-thirty a.m. break, the music stopped at twenty minutes after two, and there was no sound at all. They continued listening to the silence, and at two-fifty, there were two clicks.

"What are those clicks?" Scotty asked.

"Play that back again and turn up the volume." Listening closely, Dan said, "I hear them."

Scotty looked at Dan. "Just clicks, no voices."

Dan got up, walked to the water cooler, and drank a cup. He made his way back over to Scotty. "This case has a lot of moving parts. We have a dead student, a dead security guard, heroin, oxycodone, and now a rapist or two. The only one or ones who appear to have a motive when it comes to Gordon are the Delphi students. And let's not forget, we don't know what we have with George Gunderson and Ellie Wilcox. If George Gunderson knew his ex and son intended to torpedo him, who knows what he is capable of doing to save the family empire."

"I can't see him offing his own son," Scotty said. "I guess it's possible."

"And Christine Kole may have simply shown up at the wrong time and became a second victim." Dan reached for his jacket. "Let's call it a week." He then grabbed his cell phone. "Before I go, I want to give Watney one more try. This time, I'll tell him it's urgent." Dan punched in the guard's number, and he answered. There was a lot of background noise. "Where are you?" Dan asked. "Why haven't you returned my texts or calls?"

"I'm in Times Square with my buddies."

The sounds of loud jackhammering made it difficult for Dan to hear Watney. He yelled into the phone, "I need to know where you were after you dropped Doreen Patrisi off at her dorm."

Watney began to explain, but Dan heard every other word. "It's a little tough to hear," Dan said. "When will you be back?"

"Sunday night."

Still talking loudly, Dan said, "I'll call you again on Monday." He put his phone in his pocket. "Watney is in New York City with friends. I could barely hear him with all the construction noises in the background."

"I'm surprised Syms didn't hear you shouting."

The captain rushed toward Dan. "What the hell are you yelling about? I think my bonsais started to shake."

"Relax," Dan said. "I was trying to talk to the security guard, Watney. He's in Manhattan and with all the background noise, we could hardly hear each other. I'll have to contact him when he gets back home."

Syms blew out a breath. "I'm glad Hardison couldn't hear you."

Dan pivoted toward his partner. "Let's get out of here."

CHAPTER 17

When Dan got home, he heard voices coming from the den. Entering the room, he saw Phyllis and the kids gathered around Connie as she set the final tile into her puzzle. He placed his hands on the nanny's shoulders. "Very good, congratulations." He kissed Phyllis and hugged the kids.

Phyllis asked, "How about ordering pizza?"

"Fine with me." He tapped Connie again. "Are you staying?"

"I'm in. No pepperoni. It seems to give me heartburn."

"Sausage?"

"Fine."

Dan picked up the den phone and called in an order for a large pie. Phyllis and the kids went to the kitchen to set the table.

Connie looked at him with daggers in her eyes. "You like your wife, don't you?"

"Of course, I do. Why are you asking?"

"I'll tell you a little secret. I've been around here a while, and she's as good as it gets."

Dan smiled. "Agreed."

"So why don't you do something nice and take her out to dinner…and not somewhere cheap."

"You know, you do remind me of my mother. Any suggestions?"

"My favorite place is always Skolar, and I suggest you buy her roses. I'll sit tomorrow night. You make reservations."

"I will later."

Connie stayed behind and Dan saw daggers in her eyes. "Will? You better pick up that phone and do it right now," the assertive nanny commanded.

Dan did as his beloved second mother ordered: he looked up the restaurant's number and made reservations for seven p.m.

"That's a good boy," Connie said. "Now go get the pie."

They joined the rest of the family in the kitchen. "I'm going to pick up the pizza. Josh, are you coming?"

The two males still residing at the Shields' home got into Dan's car. During the return ride, Dan asked, "How about helping me tomorrow? We have to rake and bag leaves."

Josh wriggled his nose. "Do I have to?"

"Mike's not around, so you're up. It won't be too bad."

"Yes, it will," Josh replied, seemingly reluctant to agree to help.

As he pulled into the driveway, Dan said, "You don't have a choice. Believe me, it won't be that difficult. Take the pizza."

Josh carried the box to the table, and Phyllis divvied up the first round. Soon the pizza was gone. Before Connie went home, she whispered to Dan, "Flowers. Don't you dare forget."

He grinned at the nanny. "Are you sure you're not my mother? See you tomorrow."

Connie left, and the kids went off to watch TV. Dan was alone with his wife. He hugged her and looked into her eyes. "Have I told you lately how much I love you?"

She squinted and stared at him. "What are you up to?"

"I made reservations at Skolar for tomorrow night. Connie is sitting."

"Really?" she said with a surprised look. Her eyes welled up, and she kissed him. "I love you. I better get my hair done. Maybe a new dress."

Dan thought, I knew this was going to cost me big time.

⚓

Saturday morning, Dan enlisted Kate to help out as well. He and the two kids raked the yard with the father doing the lion's share of the work. They stacked several bags of leaves by the side of the garage while Phyllis was at the hair salon.

The happy father rewarded Josh and Kate by taking them to McDonald's for lunch. When they got home, Phyllis was there, her dark hair now with a hint of red and cut short.

Dan smiled broadly. "I love it."

"Thank you. Would you like to see my new dress?" He hadn't noticed the bag that was hung on the closet door.

"Surprise me later. I need a haircut."

"I was going to mention it. Go."

Returning home with his hair neatly trimmed and a bouquet of pink roses in hand, he called out to his wife. "Where are you? I need you in the kitchen."

She entered the room, and he slid the bouquet from behind his back and handed the flowers to her. Tearing up, she hugged him tightly. "They're beautiful."

Three hours later, Connie arrived. Dan and Phyllis were dressed and ready to have a romantic dinner. "You look lovely," Connie said to Phyllis who had on a sexy blue dress. She shifted her eyes to Dan, eying his navy pin-striped suit. "You too, handsome. Nice haircut."

▲

They were seated in a cozy corner of Skolar with a candle lit in the center of the table. Sconces on the walls glowed, dimly setting a romantic atmosphere. They ordered wine and browsed the menu. Minutes later, their long-stemmed glasses were filled with Merlot, and the server wrote down their dinner selections.

Dan began to reminisce about college and how fast time had gone by. "I remember the first time I laid eyes on you in the student center. I knew I had to meet you."

Phyllis sipped her wine. "You weren't too bad. I forget who said it in a movie, but you had me from hello."

Dan drank from his glass. "You could have fooled me. I sure worked hard to impress you. And I didn't know how much you hated football, but you let me take you to our school's games. And I don't think I kissed you until our third date."

The server placed Dan's steak in front of him and set a plate of salmon before Phyllis. "Enjoy," he said.

They slowly savored their dinners. "Yeah, I was waiting. I never thought you would." Phyllis said.

"Well, the wait was worth it."

She raised her glass, as did Dan. "Yes, it was."

Dan finished his wine while glancing at her cleavage. "You're the best."

"See something you like?" she flirtatiously asked.

Dan grinned and whispered, "I think we should get out of here as soon as we're done."

"What about dessert?"

He smiled broadly at his petite, beautiful wife. Staring into her hazel eyes, he said, "I'm looking at it."

Phyllis wryly responded, "Well, at least you're buying me dinner first. Can we have coffee?" She winked. "You are buying, aren't you?"

Dan grinned at her. "I'd pay a million bucks, dear."

"You better remember that the next time you want action," Phyllis said demurely.

After they finished their coffees, Dan paid the bill, and the happy couple left the restaurant.

When they got home, Connie was on the den couch appearing to have dozed off. She sat up, yawning. "Everything good here?" Dan asked.

Connie yawned again. "Fine. How was dinner?"

"Fabulous," Phyllis said.

"Josh and Kate went to bed an hour ago."

"Thank you so much for sitting," Dan said. "Are you okay to drive home?"

"Yes, I'll be home before the late news."

Soon after Connie left, Dan and Phyllis slid under the covers to complete their enjoyable evening.

▲

Phyllis had made pancakes for the kids who were enjoying breakfast. Dan, wearing a pair of sweats under his black bathrobe, smelled the flapjacks as he made his way to the kitchen. "Morning gang," he said.

Phyllis poured him a glass of orange juice, and he whispered to her, "Last night was incredible."

She smiled and whispered back, "Can't wait to do it again."

"I don't have a million bucks." Dan grinned and continued to whisper, "You better give frequent flyer points."

She placed a stack of pancakes on a plate and placed it on the table. "Don't wolf them down," she said as Dan poured maple syrup on them.

Josh and Kate finished theirs and were excused from the table while Dan ate his breakfast. "I suppose you'll be watching football later," Phyllis said.

"I will, unless you get rid of the kids for the day."

Dan spent the afternoon relaxed in his chair watching the Giants. Near the end of the game, Mike called. "Hey," Dan said. "How's it going?"

"Good. What's happening there?"

"You escaped a dirty job. Josh, Kate, and I raked yesterday."

Dan heard Mike grunt. "Yeah, I really loved that chore."

"How's everything? You want money?"

"You know, you always ask me that, and I'll never say no. I used the credit card you gave me to buy a mini fridge for my room. The one that was here broke."

"I hope there's something other than beer in there."

"Water."

"Does Rachel like water?"

"Dad, stop."

"Okay." Dan huffed. "Giants are losing twenty-four to seven, two minutes left. I suppose you want to talk to Mom and the kids."

"Yeah. Thanks, Dad."

Dan relinquished his time to the rest of the family.

After the game, while eating dinner, he realized Halloween was a day away. "You guys all set for tomorrow night?" he asked his kids.

Phyllis said, "We're all candied up. Trick or treat."

Dan asked Josh, "What are you dressing as?"

"Michelangelo."

Dan gave him a blank look. "An artist?"

"Boy, are you out of touch. No. A mutant ninja turtle," Phyllis said.

"Right," Dan said as he looked at Kate. "How about you?"

"I'm going as Anna."

Dan again had no clue. Phyllis chimed in, "The princess from Frozen."

Dan grinned. "I knew that. I guess I'll handle giving out the candy."

Chapter 18

There was no hiding the Giants' latest loss. Dan knew he was likely to get a ribbing from Scotty. As he approached his workspace, he saw his partner staring at him. "Don't say it," Dan warned.

"Okay. But you do know the Patriots won."

"Thanks. You've made my day."

Peering into Syms' place, Dan recognized Bev. "She's back!" He moved toward the Keurig. "You made muffins."

"Bev already grabbed a couple. One for her, and one for the captain."

Dan made himself a coffee, took a blueberry muffin, and set it alongside the mug on his desk.

The captain's door opened and Syms, with Bev by his side, approached the detectives.

"Don't look so happy, guys." she said.

Dan replied, "I see you've already staked your claim to a muffin."

"Think you can handle having me around again?"

Hanson laughed, "You got baker boy back."

"We really missed you, Bev, "Landry said. "Not to mention the muffins."

"Save me one," Syms said as he turned toward his office and took a few steps.

Dan asked, "Do you have pictures of the kids?"

"On my desk. Take a look."

Dan and Scotty both eyed the photos. "Adorable," Dan said. "How's day care these days?"

"Expensive. At least my husband can handle the job most of the time."

Bev settled into her workspace, and Dan nudged Scotty. "Get that audio of Gordon's show."

Scotty retrieved it from his desktop and looked at Bev. "This is Gordon Gunderson's last show. What do you know about the case?"

"Only what I've read and seen on TV."

Dan moved his chair closer to her and brought her up to speed. "How about doing us a favor? We've heard the show. Take a listen and tell us if you hear anything unusual."

Dan's desk phone rang. Seeing the name Sasser, he picked up the call. "Hancock? What do you want?"

"Nice to hear your voice too, my friend. I have some interesting stuff for you."

"Like what?"

"Oh, it's good. How about dropping in?"

"What are you driving these days?"

"What the hell do you think? Shiny black Cadillac." He paused. "And don't you let that Hampton anywhere near it, or I'll make sure you spend time in the tank with him."

"Funny. We ran into him and Rollin the other day. And damn you, Sass. Is that any way to talk to an officer of the law?"

Dan heard Sasser laugh. "Only a handpicked few. It's a short list."

"How about tomorrow?"

"How about now? And bring your partner."

"Can't now, Sass. We're busy."

"So am I. Only have a small window today, and you're gonna want to hear this crap."

"Sass, you know you have a way about you. We'll see you in a little while."

Dan rotated to his coworkers. "That was Sasser."

"Hancock? What's he up to?" Scotty asked.

"Come on. We won't know until we see him. He says it's important."

⚙

The always dapper Hancock Sasser had done a complete turnaround in recent years. At one time, every criminal in town hired the once opiate-addicted attorney. His office was five miles from police headquarters. When Dan's car neared the place, he thought the small building looked different. "They painted it, and that's a new awning and sign." Dan saw a Cadillac in the spot reserved for the attorney and parked beside the expensive car. "He trades them like they are baseball cards.".

The detectives entered the building, walking into a newly redecorated waiting area with Salvador Dali-like pictures on the walls, four chairs, and the most striking addition of a female secretary. Sasser, whose door was open, yelled, "Check in, please."

Dan waved his hand at him. "Have it your way."

The young woman said, "I'm Chantel. Go in. He's told me about you gentlemen."

"Thanks," Dan said. "And how did you get so lucky to work for him?"

She smiled. "Uncle Hancock knew I needed a job."

"Hey!" Sasser yelled. "Leave my niece alone. Step on in, boys."

The slick lawyer sat with his alligator shoes resting atop his desk. Dan looked around the room. "Did you hit the jackpot? New stuff…And I know that black Cadillac isn't exactly used."

"You might say I've had a run of good cases. Have a seat, you two. And there's cameras in the lot. Saw you pull in."

"Okay," Dan said. "Wipe the silly smile. Get to it. What the hell is so important?"

Sasser placed his feet under his desk. "Biaggio, that's what."

"What about him? We know he's bonded out, and another hearing is coming soon."

"Soon? Like last week."

"What happened?"

"His criminal defense attorney is attempting to get the insurance fraud charge dismissed."

"Figures," Dan said.

Sasser rapped his hand on his desk. "The aiding and abetting charge was changed to accessory after the fact. Rozalie is on the hook for negligent homicide with a motor vehicle. They'll both likely get a thousand dollar fine and six months in jail, but it's no sure thing they'll serve. I suspect they'll get suspended sentences with probation."

"Nice system, isn't it?" Dan commented.

The attorney leaned forward. "Wait. It's not all bad. I'm representing the Ibanez family. They're suing for wrongful death."

"Say that again?"

"You heard me."

Dan shook his head. "How the hell can they do that? Didn't Biaggio give them fifty grand and have them sign a Hold Harmless Agreement?"

Sasser put his hand to his chin. "Well, not exactly. Biaggio was smart. He knew they didn't read English very well and his thugs had them sign the agreement, but there was never any exchange of money referenced. I brought the argument to Judge Harper and told him the document was signed under duress and explained about the money. He said that part would be hard to prove. And to make matters worse, the Ibanez's never deposited the money. As it turns out, they spent some on Javier's funeral and burial, and sent the rest to her family in Cuba." He paused. "The fact of the matter is that Rozalie was driving her father's Jaguar when she struck twelve-year old Javier, killing him. She fled the scene, and the dirty bastard Biaggio sent his henchmen to the Ibanez's house and convinced them to sign that agreement. Bottom line is there's no way to prove Biaggio gave them any money. That's the point, so now I've convinced the Ibanez's to sue for wrongful death. We're going for ten million. That's a case the court will entertain."

Dan said, "You do have a devious mind. What's your cut?"

Sasser looked into Dan's eyes. "Now, come on. I do deserve a piece. Justice will be served." He pointed his ring finger at Dan. "Me? A devious mind. Look who's talking, Mr. Detective who doesn't exactly follow police protocol."

"Okay, Sass. We're leaving now." Dan pivoted around and extended his hand to Sasser. The attorney smiled and shook the detective's hand. "Good job," Dan said. "Let us know when you go to court."

"Sure thing, buddy. It could be a while. You know the system."

"We'll have to tell Hampton about your new car."

"No way…if I see that dude, he's going for a long ride to prison."

Dan grinned. "Nothing to worry about. He's retired."

"Retired? You telling me he has a bankroll or some kind of annuity?"

"Somehow, he and his running mate, Rollin, got on government disability, and we're funding their retirement."

Sasser plopped down in his chair. "Great country."

The detectives exited, and Dan addressed Chantel. "It was nice to meet you. The decorating must be your doing."

"Exactly." She winked.

"Very professional. Have a nice day."

"You too, gentlemen."

The detectives got into Dan's car. "How about that guy?" he mused.

"Like you keep saying, he's a piece of work."

⚐

Dan and Scotty returned to their workplace. Seeing the disc of Gordon's show on Bev's desk, Dan asked, "Did you listen to the entire show?"

"I skipped through some music. Other than the announcements and IDs, I heard a couple of clicks near the end. The good news is that I know what those clicks are. That's the control board. Each channel, as well as the volume, has a button. I think those noises are the controls being shut down. I did a little radio in college."

Scotty said. "Jason did say he shut down the station."

"I remember," Dan said. He then eyed Bev. "Do tell about your radio days."

"It was only my senior year, but I did have to get my FCC license. I hosted an hour show once a week on books. I'd interview students about what they read. We'd discuss certain books and why they were good or not so good."

"What's your favorite?"

"To Kill a Mockingbird."

Scotty said, "Great movie. Gregory Peck."

Bev shook her head. "Figures."

Dan got back to business and went to his workstation. "I have to call Watney." He keyed in the number on his desk phone and the security guard answered. "Hi," Dan said. "This is Detective Shields. How was Manhattan?"

"Crazy, best city ever. We took the train back last night."

"Listen, I want to make sure my documentation is correct. Doreen Patrisi told us you picked her up at the radio station and drove her to her dorm around twelve fifteen."

"I did."

"Where did you go from there?"

"Back to the office."

"We know the cameras were out that night. As we understand it, you didn't hear what had happened until Westland contacted you."

"That's right."

"Why is that? Emergency vehicles arrived around three-fifteen a.m. Were you sleeping?"

There was silence. After a few seconds, Watney said, "Please don't tell my boss. I was playing a video game, Minecraft."

"You were so engrossed that you didn't know what was occurring?"

"I guess. Look, Westland can't find out. Please don't tell him."

Dan shook his head. "I won't, but I'd advise you not to do that anymore. Westland said you and Christine alternated rounds when you worked together. How well did you know her?"

"I knew she had a drinking issue at one time, and she has a little boy. I never saw her drink or smelled alcohol on her. She was an okay person."

Dan was curious. "Did you ever hang out with her?"

"No, I have a girlfriend."

"Did she ever try to sell you pills?"

"Pills? What kind of pills?"

"Oxycodone."

"No. I do remember she said she took medication for headaches, but I assumed she meant extra strength Tylenol or something like that."

"Thanks." Dan said. "Have a good day."

The call ended, and Dan told Scotty and Bev what Watney told him.

Bev still had the audio disc and handed it to Dan. "It's all yours. I'm not sure that's why I came back. Can't wait to get called out."

Dan gave her a whimsical smile. "Sure. How's two a.m. sound?"

"How's going home sound? Halloween…candy night," Bev said. She pivoted to Scotty. "I'll be expecting more muffins in the morning."

Scotty shook his head. "Fat chance. A Snickers bar, maybe."

Dan said, "Unless you'd prefer a Kit Kat. Come on, let's go make a few kids happy."

CHAPTER 19

Dan had mixed emotions about Halloween. He had shared his nightmarish story with Phyllis, but he never told his children. It happened in his hometown, Winston-Salem, when he was ten. Costumed as the Lone Ranger, he and two friends, who lived next door, went trick or treating, and they all had plastic pumpkins filled with candy…real bars of Hershey as well as other desirable chocolates. The boys started walking home in the dark, and when they rounded the corner of their street, two costumed bullies came out from behind bushes and demanded their goodies. Dan was the first to protest, and he was shoved into the bushes, his candy falling to the sidewalk. He survived with a few scratches, but one of his friends was beaten, robbed, and badly hurt. That friend ended up in the hospital with broken ribs and a fractured arm. He recovered, but the thieves wearing white sheets were never identified.

This memory hit him every Halloween, and it gave Dan and Phyllis reason to not let their children go trick or treating without supervision.

The outdoor porch light was on when Dan walked into his house. A wicker basket of candy was on a hall table inside the door. "Looks like we're ready," he said. Striding to the kitchen, he saw dinner already on the table, and Josh and Kate were in their outfits. "They ate," Phyllis said. "It won't be long before the doorbell rings."

He looked at his children. "Don't get too much candy, or I'll have to arrest you."

That remark didn't draw a response from either child. Phyllis said, "We'll be going in a few minutes."

"Do you have to?" Josh asked. "I'm old enough."

Phyllis said, "Maybe so but your sister isn't, and I don't want you running off with your friends." Dan started eating while Phyllis, Josh, and Kate headed for the door. "We'll see you later."

Less than two minutes after his family left, the bell rang. Dan abandoned his half-eaten dinner and walked to the door. Opening it, he heard those magic words: trick or treat. Two elves and a little penguin held their bags out, and he dropped candy in each one. That was the start of a seemingly endless parade of gremlins, monsters, superheroes, and other characters the detective was clueless about.

It was a little after eight when Phyllis returned with Josh and Kate, their bags nearly full to the top. "I see you made out like bandits," he said.

"Yes," Phyllis said. "Now we have to sort it out and get rid of the junk."

Dan showed her the near-empty basket he'd been in charge of. "Almost gone. Good thing I haven't seen anyone in a while."

"You can turn off the light and go watch TV," Phyllis said.

"I want to see what Michelangelo and the princess got." He observed the candy haul his wife had emptied into two bowls. "Nice. You guys will be seeing the dentist soon." Dan went into the den, sat in his recliner, picked up the remote, and tuned into the Monday night football game while Phyllis made sure the kids took showers and dressed for bed.

She later joined her husband in the den to read while he watched the game. Dan began to doze off, clinging to the remote, but snapped to attention when the phone rang at nine fifty-seven p.m. Answering it, he heard Syms' raspy voice. "You sleeping?"

"I was. Now what?"

"Shooting at a club called Stackpole on Worthington Ave."

"How many?"

"Dixon said one, possibly two. Call Scotty."

He placed the receiver back onto its base. "I have to go. There was a shooting at a club. I need to call Scotty."

Yawning, he started to dial his partner's number, then stopped, remembering what Bev had said. "She couldn't wait for a callout." He phoned the female detective and got up from his chair. "Looks like Halloween isn't over yet," he said to Phyllis.

"You called Bev?"

"She asked for it."

Dan went upstairs, splashed his face with water, wiped it with a towel, and went back down to get his weapon and coat from the closet. This call reminded him of how much he detested Halloween, but he had no choice and headed to the crime scene.

Chapter 20

Not knowing what he was going to encounter, Dan pictured a bloody mess with at least one body on the floor. He looked at the speedometer that read eighty-three and slowed down, realizing what had happened had already happened.

Three blocks from Stackpole, he saw flashing lights and a few seconds later, his car came to a stop behind a squad car. A shot of adrenaline hit him as he approached the door where two uniforms were standing. "Kara here?" he asked.

"Yup. Go see the show," one of the officers replied.

Dan went inside. Taking a quick look around, he noticed a few tables out of place but no broken bottles or signs of a fight. Patrons in costumes were standing in a corner to his right while a few others were seated at tables. The crunching noise beneath his shoes as he walked were peanut shells strewn all over the barely visible hardwood. To his left, beer bottles and mugs lined the counter, and a large TV above the bar that was tuned into the Packers-Bears game.

He spotted Bev kneeling, observing the body on the floor next to the bathroom. A dart board was on the wall above her, as well as several small holes where arrows had badly missed their target. Bev looked up at Dan. "You got your wish," he said to her. "What is this place, a peanut farm?" He knelt beside Kara, scanned the corpse, and took pictures on his cell. "What the hell? Batman? Is there another victim? Syms said there might be two?"

"No. This is it. Halloween. Anyone wearing a costume got a free drink," Bev said.

Kara added, "Patrons heard two shots, but I only see one entry right above the heart."

"The owner of this place is standing at the bar," Bev said. "His name is O'Malley. He said everyone scattered when the shots were fired."

"Anyone identify the shooter?" Dan asked.

Bev pointed to the witnesses. "According to a couple of them, the shooter suddenly appeared from a spot near the front of the bar, fired a couple of shots, and ran out."

Kara had removed the victim's mask, revealing a nearly bald Caucasian male. "What do you think? Fiftyish?" Dan asked.

"Looks about right," Bev said.

Dan rotated the man slightly and reached into his pants pocket, pulling out a wallet. "Chester Hadlyme, fifty-three. This license expired two years ago." He counted the money. "Nine bucks. Robbery certainly wasn't the motive." Dan looked to the costumed patrons. "Did they give you a description?"

Bev gave Dan an evil look. "Go talk to them. I'll tell you this...they're all pretty soused."

Dan walked on the shells to approach the inebriated men. One of the drunkards had his head on a table, and there was no mistaking the snoring. The detective got a heavy whiff of alcohol as he took out his pad and pen. "Alright, gentlemen. Who saw the shooter?"

Slurring his words, a witness dressed as a circus clown said, "He had on a ski cap, and nylon stocking."

Another teetering man with charcoal covering his face, still holding a beer bottle mumbled, "I just come out of the can." He burped. "We was in there pissin', me and Batman, but he was still pissin' and when he came out it was bang, bang. I think I crapped my pants."

"What did the gunman look like?"

Another witness in a Darth Vader outfit and seemingly not as inebriated as the others said, "He was tall, thin, wore a ski hat and a stocking on his face."

"White, Black?"

"Couldn't tell because of the stocking."

"What about his hands. Did you see the gun?"

"Happened too fast."

Dan took a few crunchy steps and approached O'Malley in front of the bar. "Was the victim a regular customer?"

O'Malley shrugged. "He's been here, but he's usually bumming cigarettes and trying to scrounge up change. I guess he knew he'd get a free one tonight. Only thing I know is that he stays at the shelter down the street and tells a few good jokes."

"Was he alone tonight?"

"Yes."

"Did you see the shooter?"

"Briefly. He came out of nowhere. I don't think he was in here for more than thirty seconds."

"What did you see?"

"He wore a ski cap and was dressed like a bank robber."

"What exactly do bank robbers look like?"

O'Malley smirked. "I mean he had a stocking over his face."

"What about the gun, his hands? Could you tell if they were white or black?"

"I'm not sure. He was gone in a flash."

Dan looked around the place again and stared at the drunkards, who were getting louder. "How about tossing them out?" Dan hesitated. "On second thought, I don't want them out in public, nor do I want them driving. Let them sober up here. One guy is asleep anyhow. Can you make coffee?"

"Way ahead of you. Got a pot in back."

"Do you have video in here?"

"No. I've thought about it. I guess I'll get on it now."

Dan shrugged. I should have known. Why me? Why do I get all the places without cameras? He proceeded back to Bev and put his pen and pad back into his pocket. "No cameras in here. Figures."

"The shooter fired from the front of the bar," Kara shared.

"There should be casings near there, under the nut shells somewhere."

Dan was behind Bev as they headed for the front door. She stopped suddenly. "I see a shiny object on the floor," She bent down and swept peanut shells aside. "It's a bullet casing."

"Good eyes." Dan knelt and took a look at it. "I'll get a bag from Kara. Looks like a thirty-eight."

Dan obtained an evidence bag and glove from Kara, placed the shell inside, and gave it to her.

Upon exiting the crime scene, Dan told Bev, "According to O'Malley, the victim was homeless and stayed at a shelter down the street. Chester Hadlyme. His name is a little eccentric, isn't it?"

"Kind of classic," Bev thought. "Two towns heading toward Saybrook."

Dan said. "Wonder if his father's name was Clinton Hadlyme?"

"That's rich."

"Yeah, well, I can't see going to the shelter now. It's late. Let's hit the place tomorrow."

CHAPTER 21

Dan got home at one-fifteen a.m. He stayed awake for another hour, replaying the night's events. Finally, after having a glass of milk and a mini-sized Milky Way, he went to bed. As quiet as he thought he was, he awoke Phyllis.

"How bad was it? I heard you come in."

"Routine, one victim…his name was Batman."

"Batman?"

"He was dressed as Batman. I'm glad Halloween is only once a year. Go to sleep. I am."

▲

A few hours of rest seemed more like a catnap, and Dan dragged himself out of bed; the nightstand clock read 5:25 a.m. He knew he had a long, hard day ahead of him, so he hopped into the shower and readied himself for work, downing a bowl of Wheaties before leaving the house an hour later.

Landry was standing the station back door puffing away. "Hanson here?" Dan asked.

"Not yet. I'm waiting for him. You up for Blues?"

Dan stared into Landry's eyes. "Seriously, you're smoking an awful lot lately. You know you should have quit a long time ago."

"You guys are all a pain in my butt. Get off it."

Dan watched Bev pull into the lot and waited for her.

"Hey, sunshine," Landry said. "This guy is pretty grouchy today."

"So am I. We were out last night, and to make matters worse, the twins kept me up."

Landry extinguished his cigarette. "What happened?"

Dan explained as they walked upstairs to their desks. Landry sat waiting for Hanson while Dan and Bev hung up their coats and walked into the captain's office. Syms was staring at his computer, then looked up. "Who is the dead guy, and what's the story?"

Dan said, "A man named Chester Hadlyme, fifty-three."

"No one could identify the shooter," a weary Bev said. "It was costume night, and the killer was wearing a ski cap and stocking over his face."

Syms glared at Dan. "I told you to call Scotty. You called Bev?"

"Looks that way, doesn't it?" Dan said. "I have to hit the boys' room. I'll be right back." After relieving himself, he exited the lavatory and saw Scotty, who appeared to be heading to the Keurig. "Hey, I saved you a good night's sleep."

"You what?"

"Hold the coffee. Come with me."

They entered Syms' office. "What's going on?" Scotty asked.

"Halloween night was no fun for us," Dan said. "Me and Bev went to a club shooting." He eyed Bev. "She said she couldn't wait to get back in action, so I called her." Dan continued until Scotty and Syms heard everything the detectives learned about the killing.

"You guys can go now," Syms said.

The three detectives lined up at the coffeemaker. Dan said, "Bev and I have to get to a homeless shelter this morning to check out the victim."

Back at their desks, Dan drank from his cup, and turned to the female detective. "The bar owner described him as a bank robber, nylon stocking on his face. Hopefully, someone at the shelter can tell us about the victim."

"I'm thinking we won't get much more than we got last night," Bev said. "What was the motive? The guy had no money."

"There's a lot of crazies out there. We don't know if it was premeditated or if some nut with a gun just doesn't like Batman," Dan said. "I'm going to see if the incident report is done."

Dan had taken a few steps when he heard Syms frantically shout, "Holy shit! Dixon just called me. We have another dead Batman."

"What?" Dan asked as he faced the captain.

"Yes. They found another Batman shot dead behind the Worthington Avenue Diner on the next block up from the club. Get down there."

Bev pointed at Scotty. "How about you taking this one?"

▲

It was eight twenty-five a.m., and a brisk forty-three degrees. Dan and Scotty made their way to the crime scene and arrived to see black and whites cramming the diner's lot. The eatery's large neon sign was brightly lit, but the yellow tape, the police presence, and the closed tag on the front door kept patrons away. The detectives were led to the rear of the diner where an employee had discovered the victim behind one of two dumpsters.

Dan walked toward the dead man and asked a policeman, "A name? And don't say Batman."

"No, sir. He hasn't been identified, but the employee who found him recognized him as a customer. He says the guy always ordered ham and eggs. The manager's name is Burt Ryland. He's the heavyset guy behind the counter."

Dan approached Kara. "You as tired as me?" she asked. "One shot. Entry was right side of the head below the ear. I'm guessing he's been here all night."

Dan asked, "Close range?"

"I'd say so," Kara said. "There's no wallet, phone, or any form of ID. All we have is a Caucasian male. I hope to get a match on his prints." She handed the detective a crinkled ATM withdrawal slip. "This was in his pants pocket."

Glancing at the piece of paper, Dan uttered, "A thousand buck withdrawal."

Scotty eyed the receipt. "Three nineteen p.m. this afternoon."

"Yesterday afternoon," Dan said as he placed the slip in his pocket. "Let's talk to the manager."

As the detectives approached him, Dan looked around the diner and observed the waitstaff: four waitresses sitting in a large booth, not knowing when they might be put to work. Dan showed his badge and asked Ryland, "What can you tell us?"

"Not much." The manager called over the employee who discovered the body.

Dan said, "We heard he was a regular. A name?"

The employee replied, "Yes, sir. He's here two or three times a week, but he was quiet. Just ordered, ate, and paid with a fifty. Always sat at a table in back and didn't like anyone around him."

"Was he here yesterday?"

"I don't think so. I remember seeing him a few days ago."

"Alone?"

"No, he was with a female. She had coffee, fruit, and a yogurt."

"Can you describe her?"

He put his hand to his chin. "Average height, dark hair, Asian…a butterfly tattoo on her ankle."

Dan asked the manager, "Did you have any Halloween night specials, I mean like customers wearing costumes?"

The manager replied, "We had meal specials, pumpkin squash, and pies. That kind of thing. I don't recall seeing any outfits."

"I'm going to chat with the kitchen crew," Scotty said.

Dan glanced over at the rest of the chatting waitstaff and questioned them, but none had meaningful information. Scotty returned and said, "Not much from the kitchen help."

The detectives went back outside and took a closer look around. A trail of blood ended at a point in the driveway, and there were tire tracks in a slightly muddy area off the pavement. "I don't think he died here. I think he was shot somewhere else and deposited here," Dan said.

"I think you're right," Scotty said. He pointed to heel scuffs extending from the edge of the driveway to the dumpster. "These marks indicate he was dragged. Probably from a car. Maybe the crew can get tire tracks."

Dan wondered if these two Batman killings were related or if they were two separate incidents that happened to involve men coincidentally dressed in Batman suits. He pointed to a camera in the corner of the building. "I saw that before. I hope it was working. We need the video. What are the odds?"

"With our luck," Scotty said. "Slim to none, but I'll go see the manager and ask for it."

Dan waited, taking another look at the victim before the corpse was removed from the scene. A few minutes later, Scotty, holding a disc in his hand, returned. "Got it."

"A miracle," Dan said. As soon as they got into his Accord, he said, "You know, Stackpole and the homeless shelter aren't too far from here. I'm gonna call Bev and tell her we're going to the shelter to find out what we can about Chester Hadlyme."

Before he could pull away from the diner, Scotty held the video up. "Chester is at the morgue, and he isn't going anywhere. How about taking a look at this, and then you can head to the shelter with Bev?"

Dan nodded and drove to the police station.

Chapter 22

Anxious to view the video, the two detectives approached Bev. "Tell me about Batman two?"

"A little more gruesome than Stackpole," Dan said. "It appears that this one was killed somewhere else and dropped at the rear of the diner."

Scotty placed the video on her desk. "This may solve the second Batman killing. We don't have the victim's name, so Kara will have to process the fingerprints."

Dan pulled out the ATM receipt. "This was in the victim's pocket, an ATM withdrawal slip. It looks like he took out a thousand dollars yesterday."

Bev inserted the disc into her computer. The video started, and at one thirty-six a.m., a car came into view stopping at the end of the pavement. A tall, thin male wearing a ski cap got out, opened the back door, and dragged a costumed body out. "That's gotta be him, the shooter at Stackpole," Dan said. "Witnesses told us he wore a ski cap and was tall. Hard to tell if he's got a stocking on under the cap."

"Pretty dark," Scotty said, "but look at those mag wheels."

Bev zoomed in. "Is there someone else in the car? Look at the passenger side."

"They're moving. It's definitely a person," Scotty said. The driver got back in and drove away. "I can't tell the make. That's the problem these days; they all look alike. My fifty-seven Chevy, you knew it from a mile away."

"We'll have to check with Kara later," Dan said. "She may have a name for us." He asked Bev, "Do you think we'll look out of place at the homeless shelter?"

Bev laughed. "Me maybe, but not you, although you did shave."

Dan shook his head and grinned. "Okay, let's do it."

Leaving Scotty behind, the male-female duo headed to the shelter.

Driving to their destination, Dan asked her, "How's it going so far…like you remembered?"

"Like riding a bike," Bev said. "Can't wait to fire my gun."

Dan laughed. "And just when did you do that? I know when I last fired mine."

"At the range. Never had to use it for real. Now that I'm back, I have to requalify. Syms set it up for tomorrow."

Dan drove slowly down the street, looking for the shelter. Bev said, "I think that's it. The old building that appears to have, at one time, been a church."

After parking the car, they walked up ten steps and opened one of two thick metal-handled wooden doors. Inside were more than a dozen men. A few were seated around a table playing cards, some napping, and others chatting while getting ready for a meal in the soup kitchen to their left. Dan thought they varied in ages, but similarly clad in old worn clothes, most had long hair and were unshaven. At least they were able to shower, sleep and eat here.

Dan and Bev were approached by a woman. "Are you looking for someone?" she asked.

"We're detectives." Dan said. He asked, "Do you know a man named Chester Hadlyme?"

"Yes. Why? Has something happened?"

Dan said, "Last night, there was a shooting down the street at Stackpole. A man we believe to be Chester Hadlyme was shot to death."

The woman, who wore a white apron around her waist, gasped. She was silent for a moment. "Oh my God, I have to sit." They walked to a corner where the woman set herself down in a wooden chair. "What happened?"

"We've just started investigating," Dan said. "All we know is that he was at Stackpole, dressed in a Batman suit, and someone shot him. May I ask your name?"

"Mary Alice Jeter." Her jaw dropped open. "Chester, poor Chester. He had the outfit on yesterday and was parading around making jokes. He probably left here around seven thirty last night. It's the same one he had last year."

"Did he have family?" Bev asked.

"No. His wife died a few years ago, and then he lost his job and house, and wound up here. We missed him this morning at breakfast, assuming he'd passed out on a park bench or something."

"I take it he's been found on park benches before?" Dan asked.

"Yes, but he was a harmless man."

"Do you know if he had issues with anyone, or if anyone might have wanted to harm him?"

She looked at Dan. "No one. He had a good heart."

Dan wanted to get positive identification of the victim and held his cell phone. "I'm going to show you a picture. It's a little gruesome, but I'd like to know if this is Chester Hadlyme."

Mary Alice looked. She grimaced and began to sob. "That's Chester."

Bev tried to comfort her as two kitchen helpers appeared, both females wearing aprons. Mary Alice regained her composure. "It's Chester…he's dead."

The detectives had a positive ID but didn't have a motive. Dan looked around the room. "May we talk with everyone else here?"

"Go ahead, but we all liked Chester."

An hour later, the detectives departed. Mary Alice was right, and Dan wondered who and why anyone would kill this man. Once inside his car, he made a U-turn, and Bev asked, "Are you thinking what I'm thinking?"

"I might be. You first."

"Was Chester Hadlyme a victim of being in the wrong place at the wrong time?"

"Bingo. I think the Batman at the diner was the intended victim but for some reason, the killer got the wrong guy. Hadlyme, unfortunately had on a Batman outfit. I think the shooter knew his intended victim would be wearing a Batman costume, and he thought he knew where he might find him, but he was wrong. Dead Wrong!"

⚓

As soon as they got back to headquarters, Dan grabbed Scotty and the detectives went to see the captain. The senior detective made sure they were all on the same page.

Syms tapped his desk. "Thanks for the update. By the way, Hanson and Landry are at the railroad station. There was a mugging, homicide. From what I understand, it was an elderly woman who had gotten off a train."

"Oh no," Bev said.

The trio of detectives went to their workspace and Dan called Kara. "Listen," he said, "Bev and I visited the homeless shelter and got a positive ID on Chester Hadlyme. Did you find any other bullets?"

"We dug out a shot from the wall. It went through the dart board."

"What about the one that didn't miss?"

Kara hesitated. "Don't ask me. You know the routine. Arnstein will pull it when he does the autopsy. He'll also have the one from the second Batman."

Dan sheepishly replied, "Right. Any results on prints from Batman two?"

"Not yet. I'll let you know."

"We're going to follow up on the bank slip. I'll get back to you if we find out anything."

CHAPTER 23

Hanson was standing at the coffeemaker and Dan said, "Hey. How about making me a cup?"

The big detective pointed down the hallway to Syms' office. "Landry's been in there ever since I got here, this is my second one this morning. I don't know what's going on with him. He's lighting up more than ever. Scotty and Bev aren't here yet."

Hanson made Dan a cup and they walked to their desks. Hanson said, "We have a couple of good pics of the suspect who mugged and killed that old lady at the train station. Her name was Margaret Krasinski. I want to get the photos on TV and hope someone comes forward. All we know is that she got off the train and was waiting for a cab. We have her phone, and it turns out she was on her way to see her father who is in an assisted living place. His birthday is today…ninety-two."

"Where's she from?" Dan asked.

"Stamford. Margaret was sixty-nine, a widow with no kids. We went to the nursing home and spoke to the caretakers. The saddest thing is that they don't think her father would have known who she was. Dementia."

Dan heard Landry's lumbering footsteps coming toward him and Hanson. "I need a cigarette. I'll be back," the chain-smoking detective said as he grabbed a pack of Marlboros from his desktop and strode purposefully toward the back door while sidestepping Scotty.

"What's up with him?" Scotty asked?

"I'm going out to have a talk with my partner," Hanson said.

"Where's Bev?"

"I think she's at the range," Dan said. "She has to requalify." He got up. "Let's go see Syms."

"Now?"

"Right now."

They stood at the captain's desk and neither detective said a word. Syms crossed his arms. "Somebody want to talk?"

"What's up with Landry?" Dan asked.

Uncrossing his arms, the captain said, "Nothing's up. He just wanted to chat. Anything wrong with that?"

"It does seem unusual," Scotty said.

Syms leaned forward, stared at Scotty, and pointed at Dan. "Now I know you've been around him too long. And it's not like you to be asking dumb questions. I suppose you two have a story to tell me."

Dan eyed the bonsais. "Your little trees look good."

Syms sneered at him. "Get out of here."

Back at their workspace, Dan's cell rang, and he read the caller ID. "It's Gunderson." Reluctantly, he answered the call. "Mr. Gunderson. How are you and Natalie?"

"We're fine. My ex, Ellie, called to find out when Gordon's funeral will be. She wants to attend. I can't stop her, but she told me she met you someplace and had a long chat. What the hell did she tell you?"

"We wanted to know more about Cody and his relationship with Gordon."

George's ire was evident as he said, "Is that all? I got the feeling she said things about me that aren't true."

"Like what, sir?"

"I'm not sure. You tell me."

Dan seethed at George Gunderson's hostile tone and asserted, "You sound a little paranoid."

"I'm not paranoid. I just don't want you talking to her."

"Why is that?"

"Listen, if you talk to her again, you'll hear from my lawyer. You just find out what happened to Gordon and stay out of my personal life."

Dan had enough of the angry man's attitude. "You listen, George. We have an active investigation, and we need to go wherever the trail leads us. If it involves people you don't like, so be it."

George backed off. "Okay, okay."

"When is Gordon's funeral?" Dan calmly asked.

"Day after tomorrow."

"Do you mind telling me where, so we can pay our respects?"

George gave Dan the name of the church and cemetery. "You don't have to come, though I appreciate the gesture."

"We'll see. Have a nice day."

"What was that all about?" Scotty asked.

"He isn't pleased we talked to Ellie Wilcox and wants us to stay out of his business. Gordon's funeral is Friday. Stay here. I have to tell the boss."

As soon as he entered the captain's office, Syms grumbled, "What now?"

"George Gunderson called me, and he's not happy we spoke with his ex. He told us not to see her again. What's that tell you?"

Syms leaned forward, picked up his pills, twirled the bottle in his hand and asked his ace detective the same question, "What's that tell you?"

Dan placed his hands on the desk. "It tells me he doesn't want us to find out what skeletons are in his closet. You know we will."

"Be careful," Syms said.

Dan went to his partner, who had the ATM receipt in his hand. "Let's see what we can find out about that. The bank should be able to tell us the name on the account, and I'm sure they can pull up a video of the withdrawal."

"According to the slip, this branch is on Frankland."

▲

Dan saw the drive-up ATM as he pulled into a space in front of the bank. He and Scotty entered the lobby where another cash machine was against the wall. They walked past the tellers toward an open door in the right corner where a young male in a dark suit, sitting at a desk, stood. Dan displayed his badge. "May we talk with you?"

The wooden nameplate on the desk read: Eric Tyson, Manager. He invited the detectives to sit, and Scotty pulled out the creased ATM receipt, handing it to the banker. "Would you be able to tell us who made this withdrawal?"

"Why are you asking?"

Dan explained it had to do with a crime that was committed. Tyson said, "You know, I'm not supposed to do this without a court order."

"Right," Dan replied. "We need to know immediately. That person's life may be in danger."

Tyson nodded. "I can tell you it was made at the drive-up machine." Turning to his computer, the manager brought up the transaction and tracked the withdrawal. "The account is in the name of Ahn Lee."

Dan looked at Scotty and then asked the manager, "Ahn Lee. Female?"

Tyson said, "Sounds like it. Let me look at the personal info." A few seconds later, he said, "Yes."

"What else can you tell us about her? Address, phone number?"

The manager picked up a pen, wrote the woman's name, address, and phone number on a notepad, and handed the sheet of paper along with the ATM receipt to Scotty.

Dan said, "I assume there is a video of the transaction. Can you retrieve it so we can view the withdrawal?"

The manager rose. "Come with me." He led them to a small room and flicked on a light. The detectives moved to his left as he engaged a recorder/player and prepared to run the video from that day.

Dan said, "I want to watch it from the time just before the car pulls up to the machine."

"Let me see the time again."

Scotty showed Tyson the receipt, and the manager set the video. They watched a car pull up to the ATM a few seconds before the withdrawal. The driver's window rolled down, and a male slid a card into the machine. Dan noticed a pair of dice hanging from the mirror and a female in the passenger seat. "She looks Asian. That might be Ahn Lee."

The man keyed in numbers and took the thousand dollars as well as the card and receipt from the machine. Dan asked Tyson, "Can we get a copy of the video?"

Ten minutes later, the detectives got back into Dan's car with the copied disc. Scotty looked at the piece of paper the banker had given them. "Her address is 1427 Jeffers Street."

Dan took out his cell. "Read me that phone number." He punched it in as Scotty recited it. The phone rang and immediately went to voicemail. "Interesting. It's a male's voice on the recording. It just says, 'leave your name and number.' Fasten your seat belt. We're going there now."

Dan slowed his vehicle as they approached the two-family dwelling. Scotty said, "That's it, the brown one."

Dan parked close to the driveway, and the curious detectives walked up four creaking porch steps. "It says Lee on the mailbox to the right," Scotty said.

"There's a 'For Rent' sign on the upstairs unit's door," Dan said.

Scotty rang the bell to the first-floor apartment. "I don't hear any activity inside."

Dan peeked into the window where curtains were half drawn. "There's no sign of anyone being here. We'll have to try again."

They walked down the driveway that had a wire fence separating the yard from the neighbor's house. "No car," Scotty said. "But that pit bull on the other side of the fence doesn't seem to care for us. Tell it to quit barking."

"No, thanks. Kind of reminds me of Syms."

Chapter 24

It wasn't an uncommon sight to see Landry in the parking lot with a cigarette in his hand and a cloud of smoke spewing from his mouth. This chilly day Hanson had his hands in his jacket pockets and his head looking skyward. "What's with you today," Dan asked.

Hanson looked at Dan. "He's not here."

"Who's not here?"

"Landry. Let's go to the caf."

"Okay, what's up?"

"Come on, I need to talk to you."

They walked into the uncrowded dining area. "Grab a coffee," Hanson said. They both purchased drinks and then sat at a table. Dan unzipped his jacket as Hanson put his hands around his cup. "It's not good." The big detective took a swig and looked at his comrade. "We had a long chat. I knew something wasn't right with him, but Landry's a tight-lipped guy."

Dan had a sinking feeling Hanson would say something about the cigarettes. "What are you telling me?"

Hanson took a gulp of coffee. "You know he's been smoking a lot, and his coughing has been getting worse." There was a pause. "He's starting chemo in two weeks. Syms arranged to have him on medical leave, so he'll be covered."

Dan noticed the dour look on the detective's face. Hanson tapped his cup. "He couldn't even be straight with me until last night. You know he hasn't had it easy. He was an orphan, made it around from foster home to foster home, and never really had parents." Hanson took another gulp. "Never had kids and when his wife died ten years ago, he had no one…except us. He's a loner, and I understand that. He's afraid to get close to anyone. The amazing thing is how he ever kept on this side of the fence. He's a good cop."

Dan picked up his cup and drank some coffee. "I don't know what to say."

"There is nothing to say, and none of us could have done anything to help him. You saw. It was him, his cigarettes." Hanson spread his hands on the table. "Right now, he wants to be left alone, but I have to check in on him despite his objection."

Dan closed his eyes and wiped his forehead. "My God."

"Yeah, and the last thing he wants is us to feel sorry for him."

Dan was nearly speechless. "My heart is in my mouth."

Hanson shook his head. "Been with him forever, twelve years. He broke me in. We both came up from domestic violence units, him long before me. That's why we usually get the domestics. Met his wife a couple of times. She was a nurse, had breast cancer. It was always on his mind; that's why I never got his smoking. I think he always wanted to be with her."

"Think positive. He is starting treatment."

"Drink up," Hanson said. "I have to get over to the TV station with photos of the guy who killed that old lady. They should be able to enhance the images."

Dan finished his drink and stood, then placed his hand on Hanson's large shoulders. "You're a good man, Luke. I see how hard you're taking this."

"Thanks."

"Have you told Scotty or Bev?"

"No. You're first in, besides Syms."

With the weight of the heavy news on his mind, Dan headed to the squad room and looked at Landry's empty desk. He then walked to the captain's office. Syms looked up. "Now what?"

Dan nodded. "You knew about Landry."

Syms leaned back. "I did. He told me a while ago. I had to get his leave approved."

Dan shook his hand at Syms. "So that's the reason you hired the new guy."

"Nice deduction. Bev's a better shooter than any of us," the captain said, quickly changing the subject. "She got a perfect score at the range."

"That doesn't surprise me," Dan said.

Syms eyed his detective. "Let me see when the last time you qualified was."

Dan said, "I was just leaving. Do let me know. Do you want to tell Scotty and Bev?"

Syms turned toward the window and Dan saw a tear in the captain's eyes. "Why don't you do it. I have to see Hardison."

Dan was at his desk when he heard his partner. "A little chilly today." Scotty said.

"That's an understatement," Dan replied. "Have a seat. I need to tell you something."

Scotty hung up his coat and sat beside Dan. "It's Landry." Dan told his partner the sad news and an hour later when Bev showed up, he repeated the story to her.

As the shocking news began to wear off, the detectives focused on their job. Dan was glad to have Bev back, knowing her computer skills far exceeded his, and asked Scotty to give the ATM receipt to her as well as the personal data. "How about checking out Ahn Lee?" Dan asked.

Bev read the name and address and proceeded to search the criminal data base, which took only a few seconds. "Here we go. She's no angel."

Dan and Scotty peered over Bev's shoulders. "Interesting," Dan said. "Twenty-eight and two arrests for solicitation."

Bev printed the file that included Ahn's photo, and Scotty retrieved it. "She's a working girl, and it wouldn't surprise me if Batman two was her employer," he said.

"More like a pimp?" Bev suggested.

"By the way," Dan said, "Should we call you Annie Oakley?"

She grinned and pointed her finger at him as if it were a gun. "Perfect score."

Dan said, "I want to see the videos again, both the diner and the bank."

He retrieved the videos and Bev inserted the one from the diner into her computer. They took a closer look, studying the vehicle of the suspected killer. "It's a silver Maxima," Scotty said.

"The mag wheels do look like the ones on the car at the bank. Run the other video," Dan requested.

She switched to the bank video. "That looks like the same car to me," Scotty said. "A Maxima."

Dan's desk phone rang, so he picked up the call. Kara was on the line. "AFIS has matched the prints. Batman two, his name is Spencer Gaddis, forty-six, with a history."

"What kind?"

"Look him up. He's done time."

"Thanks."

Dan relayed Kara's message to Scotty and Bev. They finished reviewing the videos, and Bev entered the name Spencer Gaddis into the criminal data base. "Take a look," she said.

Dan read the rap sheet aloud. "Seven years at Cheshire for trafficking and selling illegal substances. He got out eight months ago." Dan stepped back. "Well, he's dead now. He was better off in prison. Ahn Lee. Time to hit her place again."

CHAPTER 25

Approaching the light at the corner of Worthington and Jeffers, Dan braked when the signal changed to amber. When it was red, the crossing light began counting down, and he saw a woman with a leashed dog that had a vest across its body. "That shepherd is a Fidelco dog in training," Scotty said.

"It is," Dan said as the dog and trainer made it to the other side. He kept watching, and the car behind him beeped twice.

"Light's green," Scotty said.

The Accord rounded the corner onto Jeffers and parked in front of Ahn Lee's place. Dan glanced into the window of the house. "We may be in luck. I see a light."

The detectives walked up the noisy wooden steps again, and Scotty rang the bell. They waited for nearly two minutes, and no one answered. He rang it again, and no one came to the door. There were no sounds coming from inside, so Dan pounded on the door. "I know there's someone in there," he said. He knocked again but still no answer.

"She might have a customer," Scotty said.

"We'll find out soon." Dan knocked one more time and shouted, "We're Hartford police, and we need to talk to you. Please let us in, Ahn. We know you're home."

Dan heard footsteps and finally, the door opened. An Asian woman dressed in pink silky sweats opened the door. "What do you want?"

"We have a few questions, and then we'll be gone. May we come in? You are Ahn Lee?" Dan asked.

She nodded, and the detectives identified themselves. They entered her living room. She directed them to two chairs opposite a couch, all surrounding a glass table. Dan spotted an empty ashtray with a pack of cigarettes on an end table and noticed a suitcase leaning against the wall separating the kitchen and hallway.

Ahn was on the couch with her legs curled under her and, not wearing socks, a butterfly tattoo on her ankle was clearly visible. She reached for a cigarette and lit it.

Dan looked into her deep brown eyes. "What can you tell us about Spencer Gaddis?"

She puffed her cigarette. "Why do you ask?" she replied with a slight accent.

The savvy detective took her answer to be defensive, so he attempted to ease into the gist of the chat. "Where are you from?"

She sat forward. "Seoul."

Scotty chimed in. "How long have you been here?"

"Three, almost four years."

Dan hesitated but asked, "What brought you here?"

"Family."

Dan decided to get back on point. "So again, where is Gaddis?"

Her eyes shifted from left to right. "I haven't seen him in a few days."

"You know he's dead, right?" Dan gave her a cold stare.

She nodded and took another puff. "I heard. That's got nothing to do with me."

Dan knew he had to play hardball. "Look. We know you were with him a couple of nights ago. We know you were at the bank with him when he withdrew a thousand dollars."

"So?"

"So? The money was from your account. Want to tell us about that?"

Her cell phone was on the glass table, as was a closed hardbound notebook. Her phone rang and she appeared to be ignoring the call.

"You can answer it," Dan said.

She didn't move. "That's okay. They'll leave a message."

"Let's not play games." Dan sat forward. "We know you've been arrested twice for prostitution, and Gaddis did time at Cheshire for trafficking. Is that what this is about?"

She protested, "So, I work for a living."

"And what did Gaddis do?"

"If you must know, he stayed here…well, not all the time."

"Where else was he staying?"

"I'm not sure. He moves from place to place."

"Why is that?" Dan asked. "How many other girls does he have?"

She puffed the cigarette. Dan looked at her again as she exhaled. Ahn took a deep breath. "Damn bastard got me pregnant."

"You have a kid?" Dan asked.

She hesitated, then said, "No. He found a doctor, and I had an abortion."

"Who killed him, and why was he dressed as Batman?"

She tensed up, shifted her posture, and crossed her legs. "I don't know. I don't know who would have killed him. I'm afraid."

"Whose Maxima was that at the bank? It's the same one that dropped your dead friend, Gaddis, off at the diner."

"I don't know whose car that was. He started driving it last week. He may have swapped his Audi."

"That was you in the Maxima when Gaddis's body was dumped at the diner, wasn't it?"

"I was here all night. I had a date."

"Would your date's name be written in that client book by your phone?"

Her phone rang again, and she ignored it.

"Looks like you have a couple of customers to call back," Dan said. "Tell us, Ahn. Who are you afraid of? Who are you protecting? Your pimp is dead."

She got off the couch. "I think you two should leave now."

Dan asked, "Are you going somewhere? I see that suitcase."

"That's none of your business. I might be going on vacation. Now get out."

"Have it your way," Dan said as he handed her his card. "Don't lose this. Call me if there is anything else you need to tell us."

She walked the detectives to the door.

"What do you think?" Scotty asked when they reached the Accord.

"I don't buy her story. When we get back, I want to have Dixon put a BOLO out for the car. I know we don't have a plate number, but I want to get a description of the car down to him. Late model Maxima, silver, mag wheels, shaded license plate. Anything else?"

"Don't forget the dice hanging from the mirror."

Chapter 26

It was Friday and Gordon Gunderson was to be buried in a few hours. Sitting with Scotty in Syms' office, Dan said, "We have to go to Gordon Gunderson's funeral. You know, sometimes TV gets it right. Killers do often show up at their victim's funerals. There's a church service in Simsbury, but I'm more interested in seeing who is at the Granby cemetery, so we should get out there around ten."

"Have fun, boys."

▲

Dan utilized his GPS to navigate to the burial grounds and drove down the winding road to the gravesite. He parked across the way from a tent and chairs that had been placed there. A pile of dirt and open hole were centered under a canopy. Trees, absent of leaves, seemed to serve as guardians of the dead.

A few minutes past ten, a procession of vehicles came toward them. Dan looked back to see a black limo and hearse, followed by a long line of cars. "Here they come. Let's wait until the clergy and the Gundersons get out and make their way to the grave."

"I see Ellie's car," Scotty said.

The Gundersons began walking alongside a clergyman and took positions at the grave. Two black-suited men opened the hearse's back door and rolled the casket out. Six pallbearers, all wearing gloves, carried the wooden container to the open ground hole. The detectives walked toward the tent as mourners exited their vehicles and did the same.

Dan looked at clouds forming and buttoned up his coat. Standing a few rows back, he surveyed the crowd. "I see Amalia and Rosario. Ellie is near the tree to the left."

Scotty said, "I see Ramsey Dale."

"Must be a couple hundred people," Dan said. "I'm going to go stand by Ellie. Why don't you go to Amalia and Rosario? Keep a lookout for anyone who might be acting strange."

After making his way to Ellie, Dan whispered to her, "Were you at the church?"

With a handkerchief in her hand, she said, "I was."

"Did you speak to George or Natalie?"

"No. I sat far back, but I know they know I'm here."

Dan silenced himself and slowly moved away while scanning the crowd. It appeared several students and friends of Gordon were there. He assumed most of the other people were George's employees and those close to the family. Observing a man wearing a black raincoat who was holding his phone up, appearing to take pictures, Dan wandered over to him. "Sad, isn't it?" the detective whispered. "How did you know Gordon?"

"We played baseball together in high school. He pitched and I caught."

Dan didn't get bad vibes from the man. He thought if anyone knew Gordon was left-handed, it would be this young man. "I hear he was a pretty good southpaw."

"You got that right."

"When was the last time you saw him?"

"About a year ago."

Dan threw out a little bait. "You knew he did drugs, didn't you?"

"Are you serious? Not him. Hell, no. Our coach would have kicked our butts if he even caught us with a beer. Besides, I know his father would have grounded him for life."

The young man snapped a photo, and Dan asked, "I'm just curious. Why are you snapping pictures?"

"I'm sorry. I'll stop. I'm sending them to my brother. We were all on the baseball team. My brother lives in California."

"Getting chilly," Dan said as he stepped away from the man and walked slowly toward Scotty, Rosario, and Amalia.

The service ended, and Gordon was lowered into the ground. "Let's beat the rush out of here," Dan said. "Did you notice anyone suspicious?"

"No, but I did see you talking to someone with a camera."

"He's a person who went to high school with Gordon. They were teammates. He was the catcher, and confirmed Gordon was left-handed. He was taking photos for his brother who couldn't be here. He's not a person of interest."

▲

Upon returning to headquarters, Dan told Bev about the funeral. When his desk phone rang ten minutes later, he was surprised to hear Ellie Wilcox's voice. "Hello, Detective Shields. After the funeral, I went to say a few words to George and Natalie. He railed at me and told me not to contact you again. I looked for you, but you were gone. We need to talk."

"Would you mind coming to the police station?"

"I have to gather a few things together. I can be there in a couple of hours."

"Do you know how to get here?"

"I do. It's near the ballpark."

"Right. Come in the front entrance and tell the officer at the counter you're here to see us."

Turning to his partner, he said, "Ellie Wilcox wants to talk to us again. She'll be here in about two hours. Let's get a bite in the cafeteria."

It was ten past two when Dan got a call letting him know Ellie had arrived. "She's here," he said to Scotty. "I'm going down to get her."

"I'll be in interview room one."

"Get some water."

Dan returned with their guest, again toting the large purse, and they entered the interview room. Other than a tiny hidden camera tucked in a corner of the white-walled enclosure, a six-foot table with hand restraints, three chairs, and a bottle of water, there was nothing else in the cozy quarters.

Ellie set her bag on the table and draped her coat over the back of a chair. Scotty asked, "Would you like some water?"

"Thank you," she said as she sat.

The detectives took seats opposite her. "You sounded frazzled," Dan said.

She placed her glasses on the table, opened the tote, took out a manila folder, and set it down. "I can't believe how he ordered me not to talk to you again. Like he was the gestapo. That may have been his biggest mistake."

Dan sensed she was about to drop a bombshell.

Ellie spread a few documents on the table. "Here we go," she said.

"Tax returns?" Dan asked.

"Five years. The five we were married. Fraud, all of them."

"Wait," Dan said, "but you signed them too."

She waved her hands. "Oh no, I didn't. These are his. We filed separately. That was his idea because I had Cody. Good thing. And there's more. He laundered money through his company, and he was in cahoots with a couple of inside traders. I have names and documents."

"Does he know you have these?"

"He sure does, but he thinks he can silence me with threats."

Dan had a sinking feeling. "What about Gordon?"

"Gordon knew, but I hadn't had a chance to show him these."

Dan rubbed his forehead. "Do you think George thinks Gordon had these documents?"

She sighed. "He might have known."

Dan didn't want to let himself go there, but he had to. "If George thought Gordon had these, as well as the other documents, do you think he would in any way—"

Before he could finish his question, Ellie uttered, "Have Gordon killed?"

"Yes," Dan said.

"I don't know. I can't say yes, and I can't say no, but it's possible. It's also possible that Keith could have done it."

Dan's jaw dropped. "Why him?"

Ellie blurted out, "Can't you see? He's his father's clone."

"Whoa," Dan said. "That's a big leap. I thought he and Gordon got along."

"That depends on how you define getting along. They spoke with and visited each other occasionally, but they never saw eye to eye."

Dan said, "As of now, we don't have anything to link either Gunderson to Gordon's death. We do have a couple of other possibilities, including the fraternity members who were expelled from school."

Ellie sighed again as she gathered the documents and placed them back inside the tote. "I'd like to go now."

Dan asked, "Do you feel you need protection?"

"It's a heck of a question. Just know that if anything happens to me, you know who to go after."

"Scotty will see you out," Dan said. "Please call us anytime."

"Thank you," she said as she put on her coat.

As soon as Scotty reappeared, he said, "She's really unnerved."

Dan looked at his partner. "Let me ask you something. Do you really think George is stupid enough to do what she implied?"

"You mean have Gordon killed?" Scotty shrugged. "It's happened before."

"That's for sure." Dan blew out a breath. "You know, the one thing that's crazy is Keith. Think about this. He did say he talked with his brother, and if Gordon were to let anyone into the studio other than Jason, it would have been Keith. And how perfect was that injection to deflect suspicion? Keith knew Gordon hated needles. He also knew Gordon was left-handed, so to force a syringe into his left arm would have made it appear that whoever did it didn't know Gordon was left-handed. So that would eliminate Keith."

"It's a good theory. But how did he know the cameras would not be working? Was it dumb luck or had someone told him?"

"Good question. We know Keith claimed he was in New Haven when Natalie called to tell him to meet her at the hospital, but we can't verify where he was. He could have been close by."

Captain Syms appeared in the detective's workspace. "How did the meeting with Ellie Wilcox go?"

"You'd better sit," Dan said.

Syms pulled up Landry's empty chair, and Dan summarized the conversation. "You think there's a chance George Gunderson had his own son killed?"

"I don't know," Dan said. "If the Menendez brothers could kill their own father, who's to say any father couldn't have his son killed? We can't rule anything or anyone out at this point, and that includes Keith. We need to see if he has an alibi."

Syms got up and headed back to his office. "I'm packing it in. I'm outta here until Monday."

Dan said, "And my phone will be off the hook."

"Scotty said. "About Keith."

"Right," Dan said. "I'm calling him right now, and he better have a good alibi." Upon reaching Keith's office, Dan heard a recording that the office was closed until Monday and advised leaving a message. "The office is closed. I didn't want to leave a message. We'll have to call him first thing Monday morning."

Chapter 27

Aside from another Giant's loss, Dan's weekend was uneventful. The talk with Ellie Wilcox gave him a lot to think about. The squad room clock read 9:10 a.m. and Dan said to Scotty, "That message I got Friday said Gunderson Financial opens at nine a.m. today. He picked up his desk phone. "I'm calling and hopefully Keith will be there."

Dan was glad to hear a live voice. "Gunderson Financial," a woman said.

"Hi. This is Detective Dan Shields. May I speak with Keith?"

"Speaker," Scotty said.

"Hold on. I'll put you through."

"Hello," Keith said.

"Good morning, Keith. This is Dan Shields. I'd like to ask you a couple of questions."

"How are you making out with Gordon?"

"We're following a couple of leads. Would you mind telling me where you were that Sunday evening and early Monday morning?"

"Are you accusing me?"

"No, Keith. I'm documenting the file. Where were you?"

"It sounds to me like you are accusing me."

"I'm not accusing you, and if you have nothing to hide, you will answer my question."

"Okay. I was out Sunday night with my girlfriend at a club in New Haven. We left there around midnight, and I stayed at her place. I was there until about seven, then came here, and Natalie called me from the hospital."

"Fine," Dan said. "What club was that?"

"Frog Lounge."

"Would you mind telling me your girlfriend's name?"

"Melody Trainor. You want her number?"

"If you wouldn't mind."

Keith recited it. "Call her. She'll verify my story. So will the bartender at the club."

"No need to call her. I believe you. Have a good day." The conversation ended.

Scotty asked, "Do you believe him?"

"Do you?"

"I do. There was no hesitancy and no rehearsed story."

Dan got up. "I believe him, but I still want to check it out with his girlfriend." Not wasting time, he phoned Melody Trainor who echoed everything Keith had said. "It's solid," Dan said to Scotty.

His thoughts switched to Ahn Lee and the car. Dan knew she was the key to the Batman killings, but she wasn't going to give up the shooter. "Ahn Lee is playing turtle with us, and cracking her shell isn't going to be easy."

Bev entered the squad room. "I had to drop the twins at daycare. How's it going?"

"Great," Dan said.

Their brief conversation was interrupted when Dan picked up a call from Dixon. "We got the Maxima." The traffic captain's next words stunned the detective. "It's burned out."

"What? Where?"

"The Meadows."

"We'll be right down." Dan motioned to Scotty. "Good news and bad news. That was Dixon; they found the car in the Meadows. It's been torched." Eying his partner, he said, "Let's go."

Dan drove to a desolate part of the city that had become a land of empty warehouses with an abandoned bowling alley. As his Accord rolled across railroad tracks onto an ignored road full of potholes, gray smoke filled the air, and even with the windows shut, Dan could taste the smell of burning tires, and metal.

He stopped behind a couple of black and whites, and the detectives walked toward the smoldering Maxima with tall, wet grass dampening their shoes. Stepping past a fire truck, Dan noticed the remains of two other previously abandoned automobiles several yards beyond the burnt metal of the Maxima. Dan coughed as he approached an officer. "It's hot," the uniform said.

The firemen, having extinguished the blaze, packed up hoses and took their big red machine away from the scene. The detectives and two policemen inched closer to the hot metal with Dan keeping his hands close to his sides as he peered in. "It's gone. Totally."

Scotty, with his wet shoes, stepped around the car. "One ball of metal, but those mags aren't completely gone."

Dan coughed again and took pictures. "We can match those wheels to the video, and that will tell us if it's the same Maxima. There doesn't appear to be any evidence of a body having been inside the car. The smoke is beginning to eat me up." Scotty rubbed his eyes as Dan moved toward one of the policemen. "Hopefully, the VIN number will be readable when it cools down."

Nearing his car, Dan said, "Don't get in." He popped the trunk and pulled out a beach towel. "Wipe your feet." Scotty dried his shoes, and Dan followed suit.

He drove away from the melted metal and heard the roar of a train as his car neared railroad tracks. Red lights flashed on both sides of the road before he could drive across the tracks, and the long arms of the protective gates came down. "A freighter," he said. "This could take a while." Slowly, the huge tanker cars passed before them. "Hey, thanks for not mentioning you-know-what."

"The Giants?"

"Yes, them. They lose in every way possible. Crazy, they had this game won and missed a lousy thirty-yard field goal. They can't beat the Eagles to save their lives."

"I know. Look at it this way: they did beat the Patriots in the Super Bowl. That's one of my worst days. They ruined a perfect season. Not one loss until then."

"That was some game. It's not the same Giants team now."

"They'll be back."

Dan smirked. "I hope it's in my lifetime."

The last train car passed, and the gates pulled up. "I have a bad feeling about Ahn Lee. I want to check her place."

Nearing the house, he slowed his car to a crawl, inching it forward. He saw an Audi when he glanced down the driveway. "What the hell? Didn't she say Gaddis had an Audi?"

"She did."

"Take a look in the driveway." Dan backed up and parked. Stepping onto the porch, Scotty rang the bell. But she didn't answer. Dan peeked into the window, the curtains blocking most of his view. "The suitcase is still there, and I hear music."

"She could be on the job," Scotty said.

"So are we. Ring it again."

Scotty did, and she still didn't appear. "She's not coming out."

"Damn it. You could be right; she may be earning her keep."

The detectives stepped off the porch onto the sidewalk, and Dan peered down the driveway at the Audi. He took out a pen and pad as he got close enough to jot down the plate number. Then he took a picture with his phone.

As he headed back toward Scotty, he stopped. "I don't like it. Whoever is in there with her may be a client, or he may be a killer. We need to get in."

The detectives stepped back onto the porch, and Dan banged on the door. "Ahn, we need you to let us in." He banged louder, and the music faded. A couple of minutes later, Ahn, clad in a short silky bathrobe, opened the door.

"What do you want now?" she asked. "I was taking a bath."

"Are you alone?" Dan asked.

"Yes. I was in the tub."

"Are you telling us the truth? Whose Audi is that in the driveway?"

"Mine."

Dan didn't like that response. "Can we come in?"

"You smell like you've been to a fire."

"We sort of were. I'll get to that."

She moved toward the couch and picked up a cigarette and lighter, then sat in such a way that her robe rode up, revealing intimate body parts the detectives weren't expecting to see.

Dan repeated, "The Audi. Is it really your car, or is it Gaddis's? It wasn't here last time."

She lit the smoke. "I let a friend borrow it."

Dan asked, "A friend? You let a friend borrow it? That's Gaddis's Audi, isn't it? But you said you thought he traded it for the Maxima."

"I don't remember."

Dan stared into her lying eyes. "Well, that Maxima is a piece of scrap metal. It was torched. That's where we just were. I suppose you don't know anything about that."

Her hand shook as she put the cigarette out. "I have an appointment. I have to go now."

Dan heard a shuffling noise coming from another room. "Did you say you were alone?"

"I told you to leave."

Again, Dan didn't like the hostile response. "Have it your way this time, but if we have to haul you in, our next chat will be at our place."

The detectives got into the Accord. "I know someone was there, probably in the bedroom," Dan said.

Scotty mused, "Ahn said she was taking a bath, She never said she was taking it alone."

⚔

Upon returning to headquarters, Dan placed his smoke-laden jacket over the back of his chair, and Bev said, "You both reek. How bad was the car?"

"Gone. I'm hoping the VIN is salvageable," Dan said as he sat.

Syms appeared in the squad room. "Man, you two smell like a barbecue joint I know."

Dan smirked. "Yeah, I know that place. It's really that bad?"

"Bad? Both of you, get out of here. Come back in the morning when you're clean."

Chapter 28

The smoke stench was baked into his jacket. Dan pulled into the garage and upon exiting his car, he quickly removed the pungent outerwear, placing the coat on a hook next to a rake. "Hi, dear," he said to his wife. "I left my coat in the garage because it reeks of smoke."

"Smoke? Cigarette smoke? You're home early."

"More like fire. We had to check out a torched car and were exposed to the lingering smoke. You're early too."

"I had a cancelation. Go take a shower and change. You smell too."

"Okay. I can take a hint."

Phyllis pointed a finger at him. "That wasn't a hint, dear. That was a no wash, no dinner."

"I'll drop the coat off at the cleaners in the morning."

Dan obeyed his wife. He came back after showering and had dinner with his family. "Have you heard from Mike?" he asked his wife.

"I was thinking of calling him."

Soon after the meal was over, he called his older son on the kitchen phone and put him on speaker so Phyllis and the kids could participate. "Hey. How's it going?" Dan asked.

"It's all good."

"Hi, Mike," Phyllis said.

"Hi, Mom. I think I'm going to be able to come home for

Thanksgiving. I'm working some things out."

"When you have your itinerary, let us know," Dan said.

"I will. How is Haley? I'd really like to see her."

"Actually, I was going to call her father later," Dan said.

"I have to run," Mike said. "I'm supposed to be at the library."

"Okay," Phyllis said. "Call us. Love you."

"Hey, we didn't get to talk," Josh said.

"I know," Phyllis replied. "You heard Mike. He had to go."

Dan said, "I'm calling Dave."

"Let me know what's new."

Dan went into the den, picked up the phone next to his chair, sat and called Haley's father. "How's everything going?" he asked.

Dave said, "Better. Haley is doing well. Working at the mall and taking care of Joey."

"Glad to hear it. What about Travis?"

"We haven't seen him or heard from him. I did what you advised and got that restraining order."

"Good. Sounds like she's on the right track. Hope you don't mind my checking in?"

"We appreciate it, Dan."

"By the way, Mike may be coming home for Thanksgiving. He'd really like to see Haley."

"That would be great. I'll tell her."

"Maybe it would be better if you didn't mention it. I think it would be quite a surprise for her to hear from him. There's still a possibility he won't be here."

"Okay, I won't say anything. Let me know if he does come home."

"Take care, Dave."

Phyllis joined her husband just as he ended the call. "What did Dave say?"

"Haley's okay, and Dave knows Mike might be coming home for Thanksgiving, but I suggested he not tell her. He agreed."

"Have you told Mike everything?"

"Not yet. I will when I pick him up."

Chapter 29

Dan's first stop this day was the cleaners. He'd shoved his odorous coat into a green garbage bag to keep the smell off his clothes as well as the car's interior.

Arriving at headquarters, he began to climb the stairs to the squad room, but that little voice in his ear was talking to him, so he reversed direction and walked down to the holding tank.

"Hey, Dan," Denine said. "You back to your old habits?"

"Not really. Anyone I know in the house today?"

"There's only two."

Denine unlocked the door, and Dan started walking down the concrete floor. Approaching the third cell, he couldn't believe his eyes. He'd seen Hampton in captivity several times, but Rollin was another story, one he'd have to hear. "Rollin. What the hell happened?"

Still wearing his Harley jacket, the detainee stood at the barred door. "They got me with weed. Can't believe it. My new bike got a taillight out. Believe it? They stopped me. A bike with a busted light."

"Tell me about the weed."

"That? A misunderstanding."

Dan shook his head. "Okay, Rollin. What kind of misunderstanding? You had to have a few grams."

"Man, I did have a few grams. Well, I guess it added up to a little over an ounce, but it's not mine…not all of it."

"Exactly how much over?"

"Two ounces."

Dan put his hands on the bars. "Two?"

"One for me and one for Hampton."

Dan pulled his hands back and glared at the detainee. "Rollin, I know his list of arrests. What's yours?"

"Never." He hesitated and paced back and forth. "Once or twice, but not here."

Dan tapped on the bars. "You want to tell me a story or not?"

Rollin blew out a breath. "Okay. I had a couple of pot busts in Poughkeepsie a few years back. Nothing big. I did six months for possession."

"Christ's sake, Rollin. You know you can get a year or more, and that's a first offense. If you get lucky, you could get a fine. I think it's a thousand bucks, but you could get both."

"I got a good deal on this batch, and if it had been only a few minutes later, Hampton and me would have split it. Now it's gone. I need Hampton to get my bike."

"Did you call him?"

"Yeah, but they haven't told me where they took it."

Dan backed away from the cell. "Good luck," he said as he exited the room.

When he got upstairs, he eyed his desk phone. "I have to call Sasser."

"Hold it," Scotty said. "Biaggio?"

"No. Hampton, I mean Rollin. He's in lockup."

"Rollin? What's he here for?"

"Marijuana. He got stopped on his Harley and had more than enough to get arrested." Dan called the attorney.

Sasser asked, "Dan, what's up so early?"

"I need a favor." There was silence. "Are you listening?"

"I'm here, but I'm sure I'm not going to like this."

"You remember Hampton?"

"Oh, no," Sasser moaned.

"Just listen. His buddy, Rollin...he's here on a drug charge. He had a couple of ounces of weed, but he's got priors I never knew about. Can you represent him at his arraignment?"

Sasser raised his voice in protest. "Are you nuts?"

Dan matched the attorney's tone. "Maybe. You want your Cadillac?"

"Are you freakin' nuts?" Sasser repeated.

"Stop saying nuts. You know I'm allergic. Just do it, okay?"

Dan heard Sasser take a deep breath. The attorney lowered his voice. "Damn you. It's a good thing I like you, Dan. I'll be there. You keep Hampton away from my car."

"Let me know what happens with Rollin and Biaggio."

"Right. Have a good one."

As soon as he got off the phone, Syms appeared with Malvin Jones. "It's official, Mal is with us starting right now."

"Welcome aboard," Bev said. "You can take the desk next to me."

Dan said, "Watch out, Annie Oakley is a deadeye with a gun."

"And Dan is pretty sharp with his tongue," Bev quipped.

Hanson was quick to engage the new detective. "Feel like making an arrest?"

Mal said, "That's why I'm here. What have you got?"

"A warrant for a guy who mugged and killed a sixty-nine-year-old woman at the railroad station. I had help from the local TV stations. They put out photos of the suspect."

"I'm ready."

Hanson and Mal left the room, and Syms looked at Dan and Scotty. "You boys smell fresh as a daisy."

Bev chimed in. "Daisy? I wouldn't say that. Ivory soap, maybe."

Dan was ready to get back to business. Between the Hartford City College murders, Haley, the killing of two Batmans, and getting Rollin out of trouble, there was a lot of work to do. He said, "Ahn Lee knows more than she cares to tell us. I'm sure we interrupted her while she was servicing a client. Bath or not, there was definitely someone there, and she wasn't exactly dressed to go shopping."

Scotty cracked a smile. Referring to her buttocks, he said, "Yeah, you saw as much of her as I did."

"Can you get her on prostitution?" Syms asked.

"Maybe for her own protection, but I don't want to go there yet."

As it neared noon, Dan said to Bev, "It's time we took you to Blues."

She got up. "Took? As in a date, lunch is on you?"

Scotty nodded at Dan. "You sure have a way with words. Are you treating me too?"

"Nice. As I recall, I paid for the burgers. I think you owe me one."

Bev said, "You two can figure out who's paying while I'm in the ladies' room." When she came out, she went to her desk, and grabbed her purse. "Figured it out yet?"

"We'll see," Dan said. "Let's go."

Upon entering the packed diner, Dan found Hanson and Mal sitting in a large booth. "I thought they went to make an arrest," he said as he led Scotty and Bev toward their comrades.

Hanson said, "Didn't expect to see you guys here."

"I could say the same thing," Dan replied. "I thought you were out rounding up a suspect."

"Done," Hanson said. "Took a couple of uniforms with us and as soon as the guy opened his front door, we nabbed him. He's being booked now."

Their server approached the booth. Bev, Scotty, and Dan ordered from the menu; the males went for sandwiches with fries, and she opted for a salad.

Dan looked to Mal. "Tell us about Waterbury."

"Seven years homicide, three on the fugitive task force before that. Nineteen murders behind me. Actually, twenty-two…three are unsolved."

"Those are always tough to explain to victims' families," Scotty said. "I still have a couple that bother me."

"What made you want to come here?" Dan asked.

As the lunches were being placed on the table, Mal said, "My

154

wife took a job as the nurse manager at Woodland Hospital almost a year ago. Commuting from Waterbury got to be an issue, so we sold our house and moved to West Hartford. Our son and daughter are in high school."

Dan took a bite of his BLT and said, "Good to have you with us. By the way, you'll be visiting Woodland on a regular basis."

After finishing their lunches, Dan picked up Bev's check. "I got it."

▲

Dan was at his desk and heard his phone. It was Dixon. "You're in luck. They got the VIN number off the Maxima and contacted DMV. It's registered to Lorenze Poole."

"Who the hell is he?"

"Good question. Find out."

Dan hung up and said to Bev, "The Maxima belonged to a Lorenze Poole."

She entered the name into the criminal database. "Here he is, gentlemen."

Dan and Scotty looked at the computer screen. "He might be our shooter," Dan said. "Six-two, one seventy-five."

Bev printed the rap sheet that also indicated Poole had done six years at Cheshire for illegal drugs and trafficking. "Same shit as Gaddis," Dan said. "I'm guessing this is the guy Ahn Lee is afraid of but won't give up."

"What about the Audi?" Scotty asked.

"We should run the tag," Dan said.

"Give me the plate number," Bev said. A few minutes later, she handed Dan a piece of paper. "It's registered to Spencer Gaddis."

"Ahn lied to us. I knew it." Dan was worried. "She may really be in trouble. I think we should get over there. I know I told Syms I didn't want to get her on prostitution yet, but it may be the only way to protect her. We need to do it now, right now."

Chapter 30

Fifteen minutes later, they were at the light at the corner of Worthington and Jeffers. Dan raced his Accord through the yellow signal and drove down Ahn's street. He hoped his intuition was wrong but feared he was right. Was she in danger? Was she there? Was she abducted or worse yet, was she dead?

Parking in front of the house, he and Scotty quickly got out and looked down the driveway. "I don't see the Audi." Scotty said.

They raced up the steps, and Dan rang the bell. Waiting, he uttered, "Come on, Ahn." He rang it again but got no response.

"I don't hear anything," Scotty said.

Dan moved to the window and peered through a slit in the closed curtains. "That suitcase isn't there. Let's go around back."

They hopped off the porch and rushed toward the rear entrance. As they hurried down the driveway, they were greeted by loud barks coming from the same dog they'd encountered previously. Approaching the back door, Scotty said, "Hold it. What are those red spots on the steps?"

Dan looked down and followed the path of droplets. "There are a few more on the driveway." He proceeded up to the back door and peered into the kitchen through the door's glass panes. The door was locked. "We have to get in." Dan bent his elbow and aimed it at the pane closest to the deadbolt.

"What are you doing?" Scotty asked. "You aren't going to bust the glass."

156

"You have a better idea? We need to get in there. I am doing this," Dan said, his elbow thrusting into the glass. He carefully reached his hand through the hole to avoid being cut by jutting edges. "Got it," he said as he opened the door.

The detectives stepped inside, avoiding the shards on the floor. There were more red drops on the hardwood, and carpet. "Blood," Scotty said.

"Damn it, I knew she was in deep trouble."

Scotty stepped down the hall toward the bedroom. "Shit. There's blood in here. The bed is covered with it."

Dan went in. "He killed her. Poole killed her and carried her out."

"I don't see blankets on the bed. He may have rolled her up and put her in the Audi."

"That's my guess. We have to be careful and not touch anything, and we have to get CSI out here." Dan called Syms and told him what they discovered. "He'll get Kara's crew to come as soon as possible."

"You were right. We are too late," Scotty said.

Dan walked toward the living room. "I want to check her client book. If we're wrong about Poole, her last customer may have been the last person here." Checking the table where he'd seen the log, he didn't find the book. "Damn it. The suitcase is gone too."

Scotty inched his way into the kitchen. "There's a drawer of spoons, forks, and knives. If he stabbed her, he could have used one of these knives. I didn't see a weapon anywhere."

The detectives headed to the back door, and Dan bent down. Seeing a roll of paper towels on the counter, he said, "Hand me those towels." He took them from his partner and swept the glass into a corner. "We may as well check out upstairs."

They stepped onto the porch, and Dan used his elbow to smash the window of the door to the upstairs apartment. Again, he reached in and opened the door. They avoided the glass and marched upstairs. The apartment door was unlocked. "Christ," Dan said. "Someone was using this place. That 'For Rent' sign on the front

157

door was bogus."

They checked out the abode. "No one leaves a TV like that in a vacant apartment, and the heat is on," Scotty said. "I wonder if Gaddis or Poole was up here?"

"I don't know. That bed doesn't look like it was slept in, but it does have bedding."

"There's some food in the fridge," Scotty said.

"Let's get back down and wait for the crime scene unit."

The detectives waited on the front porch, and Dan paced back and forth. Finally, he watched a police vehicle as well as the crime scene van pull into the driveway. The detectives led them to the back door. Kara said, "As I understand it, there's no victim."

Dexter Blacker got out of his car. "What happened here?"

"We can't say for sure," Dan said, "but there's a lot of blood that suggests there was a murder, and the victim we believe to be Ahn Lee may have been taken out through the back door and placed into an Audi."

Kara followed the detectives, and Scotty pointed to the trail of blood as they carefully went inside. "Watch out for broken glass," Dan said.

As always, Kara carried gloves and evidence-gathering items. Scotty led her down the hallway, and they carefully stepped into the bedroom. "Bloody sheets and a nightie," he pointed out.

Dan said, "We have no weapon. My guess is it wasn't a gun, more likely a knife, and we do know there's a drawer full in the kitchen."

The photographer began taking photos, and Kara asked the detectives, "Are you guys staying or leaving?"

"Leaving," Dan replied. "When you're done here, I think you should go upstairs. It's open."

"What's upstairs?"

"An apartment, but we think the killer might have been up there. We have to get Dixon to put a lookout for the Audi," Dan said.

As the detectives were leaving, Dan asked his partner, "Don't you find it odd that the back door was locked?"

"Not necessarily. Some automatically lock," Scotty said as he took a closer look at the hardware. "But this isn't one of them."

"Why would the killer come back to lock the door?" Dan wondered.

"Beats me."

"Come on, we need to start knocking on doors," Dan said. "Maybe a neighbor saw or heard something. I want to grab Dexter."

The uniformed officer joined the detectives. "I'll go across the street," Scotty said.

Dan said, "I'll start to the right where the dog is. Dex, you take the other side."

The three lawmen began their quest to find a witness. An hour later after knocking on several doors, Dexter, Scotty, and Dan met at the black and white. "Anything?" Dan asked.

"Nothing," Dexter said. "Only thing is that most people know there's a lot of guys coming in and out of here."

"That's no surprise," Dan said.

"Same thing for me," Scotty said.

Dan added, "I got a little from next door. The dog was barking at around two a.m. this morning, and the neighbor woke up. She looked over here; it was dark and no lights, but she heard activity and saw someone get into a car and drive it out of here. She couldn't tell if it was the Audi. I asked if she heard any voices, screams, or anything else, but all she heard was her dog and the car."

Kara's crew was exiting the house, and Dan approached her. "We have DNA, and prints, but that's about it. Time to call it a day," she said.

"That's for sure," Dan replied. "We'll be talking."

Chapter 31

Dan and Scotty were in with Syms recapping the events of yesterday. Dan said, "Before we even got there, I had a feeling something might have happened to her. Everything indicates she was stabbed to death, and my guess is Poole. We need to find him and the Audi that belonged to Gaddis."

Syms leaned forward. "Without a body, it's hard to prove anything. As of now, you have a lot of blood, no weapon, and no body. It's possible she's alive."

"True," Dan said, "but I doubt it."

Syms added, "And you don't even know if it's her blood."

"Kara will be able to tell us. I need to see Dixon and have him put out a search for the Audi," Dan said.

"Okay, get out of here."

Scotty went to his desk while Dan visited Dixon to give him a detailed description of Gaddis's Audi. The traffic captain assured Dan a BOLO would be issued.

Dan got back upstairs, and his thoughts wandered to the Stackpole and diner killings. "You know what? We don't have a ballistics report on the two Batmans."

"Are you sure?" Bev asked. "You're not great at checking your mail."

"I know I haven't seen one. Maybe Arnstein never sent the slugs over for analysis. I'm calling him." The pathologist answered, and Dan asked, "Max, you did remove the bullets from the Batman victims, didn't you?"

"I sent them for analysis. Didn't you get the report?"

"I didn't see one. Thanks. I'll call over there."

Dan rechecked his mail and found the report Avery Wells had sent a few days ago. "I got it. The bullets removed from both victims were thirty-eights. We know both victims were shot with the same caliber weapon but, without the gun, we can't say they were shot with the same one." He turned to Scotty. "Let's pick up the evidence and get it to the property room."

▲

The ballistics testing facility was located near the forensics lab in Farmington. Dan and Scotty entered the single-story building and went to the firearms testing room. Avery Wells said, "Haven't seen you two in a while."

"True. Max Arnstein told us you still have the slugs from the bodies of Chester Hadlyme and Spencer Gaddis. We need to get them placed into evidence," Dan said.

Wells said, "I'll be right back. You'll need to sign for them."

A minute later, Wells handed Dan the bagged shells, and the detective signed for the evidence.

Driving back to headquarters, Dan's phone rang, so he touched the car's info screen. "Hey, Sass. What's up?"

"You in the car?" the attorney asked.

"Yeah. How'd you make out with Rollin?"

"Me? I made out okay. Him? That's another story. He might be going away for a year or two or three."

"What about bail?"

"Hampton was there. He says he'll have put up five grand."

"What about Biaggio?"

"He's creeping me out. I swear there's a car following me." Sasser cleared his throat. "I might need a favor."

Dan had an idea where Sasser was going with his request. "What kind of favor?"

161

"Get them off me."

"What makes you think I can get his goons off you?"

"That thing in your pocket."

"My EpiPen?"

Sasser huffed. "Your badge and that gun on your hip might be handy. Haul them in or something."

"How the hell am I supposed to do that? I can't barge into Biaggio's office or his favorite restaurant, Cefalu and arrest them for what? Are you filing a complaint?"

"I'm talking to you, Dan. You have your ways."

Dan was silent for a few seconds. "Damn you, Sass. Let me think about it, but unless they do something stupid. I don't think there's much I can do."

"Stupid? They already have done something stupid. They're following me, and I don't want to see his boys' asses in my rearview mirror or anywhere else."

"Settle down. They'll go away when they realize you can't be intimidated."

Dan heard Sasser sigh. "Maybe so, but they're playing a good game."

"I'll talk to you later."

"He sounds skittish," Scotty said.

"So am I."

"What are you thinking?"

"I'm thinking Sasser should get back on drugs."

They arrived back at headquarters, delivered the tagged bullets to the property room, and went to their workspace. Bev said, "Did you get them?"

"We did," Dan replied. "Just put the bullets in evidence."

CHAPTER 32

There was nothing more annoying to Dan than a ringing phone, and there it was again. He stared with malice at the nagging machine on his desk while glancing at the caller ID and knew this wasn't going to be a pleasant conversation. He eyed Scotty, then Bev, rolled his eyes and spoke. "Mr. Gunderson, how are you this morning?"

" Fine. It was kind of you to come to the cemetery."

"It was a nice service."

"What's going on? Have you tracked down the killer of my son and that guard?"

Dan calmly said, "It's still an active investigation. We don't have a suspect yet."

George's tone soured. "You don't have a suspect? I told you about those two, Rosario and Amalia. And why the hell did you call Keith and his girlfriend?"

Dan rolled his eyes. "I don't expect you to understand everything we do. It was routine police work, and why are you pointing your finger at Rosario and Amalia? We've already talked to them."

"Talked? Talked? That's it? I'd advise you to check out Rosario."

"How so, sir?"

"You call yourself a detective? Check his record, and I don't mean his grades."

"It sounds to me you've already done that."

"Damn right, I did. Drugs, he's an addict."

"How do you know he's an addict? That's a pretty harsh allegation."

"Damn it. I have sources. The kid's father, same name, was a dealer, went to jail several years ago. And I'm not done checking that Black bitch, Amalia."

"I appreciate the help. Let us handle the investigation."

"Really? Go get Rosario."

Dan abruptly ended the conversation. "Have a good day, sir." He sat in his chair and threw his head back.

Scotty turned to his partner. "What was that all about?"

"Rosario Cruz. Gunderson says he's an addict. He said the kid's father, whose name is also Rosario, was a dealer. I'll look him up. If he's got a record, we'll have it."

"I'll do it," Bev said. She engaged her computer. "Rosario Cruz, forty-eight. Looks like a long list of narcotic arrests. He's at the Enfield prison."

"Any hit on the student?"

"No, but if he was underage at the time, it's probably the same juvenile game, and the records are hidden."

Dan sat forward. "I find it hard to believe Rosario or Amalia had anything to do with Gordon's death. The dorm room was free of any type of drug substances and paraphernalia. He also appeared to be clearheaded. No telltale signs of drug abuse, but we have to talk to him and Amalia again, if for no other reason than to get George Gunderson off our backs. It seems he's doing his own investigating and won't rest until he proves it was Rosario and Amalia who were responsible for Gordon's death."

Bev said, "I'm entering Amalia's name into the database." She hit the keyboard and searched. "Nothing comes up."

"I didn't expect there to be anything." Dan took out his cell and attempted to reach Rosario but had to leave a message. "He's probably in class. I'm sure he'll call back."

"We don't know where Ahn Lee is either," Scotty said.

Dan got up and wiped his brow. "A couple of things bother me about Ahn Lee's apparent murder. I still can't understand why the back door was locked. Think about it. Who carries someone wrapped in a blanket out to a car and comes back to lock the door? Also," Dan continued, "that suitcase bothers me. It was gone. If she's dead, why take the suitcase? And when was the last time you remember a stabber taking the bloodied weapon with them?"

Scotty raised his brows. "Are you thinking it was staged?"

Dan bristled at the possibility. "Don't tell me she's smarter than we think. Don't tell me she set that apartment up with blood spatter. Don't tell me she and Poole set this whole charade up."

Scotty shrugged. "Spatter? I'd call the drops in the driveway and on the steps spatter, but what we saw in the bedroom was more like a splash. It smelled death to me."

Dan ran his hand across his forehead. "Where the hell are they? The Audi is the only lead we have."

Scotty said, "I hope we don't get a call about another torched vehicle."

Dan's cell rang, and he saw it was Rosario. "Hi, thanks for the callback. We would like to talk with you and Amalia again. We have a few things we want to run by you."

"I was just with her. When?"

"When are you available?"

"This afternoon. We can meet in the residence lounge."

"That would be okay, but we'd like to have you come down to headquarters where it will be private."

"That's the place near the stadium, right?"

"Right. Park in front, come in, and ask the officer at the counter for me. How does one o'clock sound?"

Rosario hesitated. "Can we make it one-thirty?"

"Sure. See you then."

As soon as he hung up, Dan said, "They'll be here at one-thirty." He looked to Bev. "It might be a good idea if you talk to Amalia."

It was quarter past one and Dan had placed bottles of water in the interview rooms. They waited patiently and ten minutes later a call came from downstairs. Dan headed to the main lobby to greet his visitors. Rosario and Amalia wore matching City College jackets. Her purse was riding on her shoulder, and they took the elevator up to the detectives' quarters. Dan pointed to room one. "Rosario, you go in here." He walked Amalia a few steps further to the second room. "This nice lady is Detective Bev Dancinger. I'd like you and her to talk while Scotty and I chat with Rosario." Amalia entered the room, and Dan shut the door. Then he backtracked to room one where Rosario was seated across from Scotty. "I like your jackets," Dan said as he closed the door.

"Thanks. They're not cheap."

Dan nodded. "I know. I've paid for my son's college clothes. The water is yours if you want it."

Rosario grabbed the bottle, twisted off the cap and took a drink. Dan proceeded with the task at hand. "You know about the injection into Gordon's arm. Did you say you never saw or knew him to do narcotics?"

"He was clean. I know he was."

"How do you know?"

"I know drug users when I see them."

Dan nodded as Rosario seemed to confirm what George Gunderson had said. "And that's because you did drugs yourself, isn't that true?"

Rosario looked away from Dan, appearing embarrassed to admit he had. He moved his head and looked at the inquiring detective. "How did you know?"

"Look, we know more than you think. How long did you do drugs and what kind?"

Rosario winced. "I was fourteen, on crystal meth for eighteen months. I went to rehab. I haven't touched anything since my junior year in high school."

"Tell us about your father."

Rosario fidgeted. "He's in jail. I haven't seen him in two years. He was an addict and sold the stuff. I lived with my mother, as I do now when I'm home. So what's that got to do with me?"

"I didn't say it did," Dan replied. "But you have knowledge of drug usage, needles, and other paraphernalia. Why didn't you share this with us before?"

"Do you think I had something to do with Gordon's death?"

Dan studied Rosario and placed his hand on the table. "No, Rosario, we don't. We only needed to set the record straight."

"What about Amalia?" the student asked. "Why is she here? She never did anything bad in her life. Neither did her parents."

"I appreciate that," Dan said. "I'll go get her, and then you can leave."

Scotty stayed with Rosario while Dan went next door. "How's it going ladies?" he asked.

Bev said, "Good."

"We're done," Dan said while eying Amalia. "Let's get you two back together so you can go back to school."

The students were reunited. "I'll take them downstairs," Scotty offered.

"Thanks for coming," Dan said.

Bev and Dan went back to the workspace. "What did you find out?" Dan asked.

Bev grinned. "Smart girl and as nice as could be. We talked about her roommate, and Amalia teared up but was happy that Trish is doing okay."

Dan said, "Amalia is the real thing. Rosario is a product of a drug-addicted father, who is in prison, and a good mother. I believe he's on the right road."

Scotty returned. "What do you think?" he asked.

Dan extended his arm out as if he were throwing a dart at the wall. "George Gunderson can kiss my behind."

Chapter 33

It wasn't uncommon for detectives to be working more than one case at a time. The myth that most homicides were solved within 48 hours was just that…a myth. The fact was few were debunked within that time frame. Leads often resulted in the arrest of a suspect within 30 days, but most homicide cases took months and longer to resolve. And then there were those that never come to resolution.

Weeks had elapsed since Gordon Gunderson and Christine Kole were killed, and there wasn't a solid lead on a suspect or suspects. The detectives were no closer to finding Ahn Lee and Lorenze Poole, who they suspected was the killer of the Batman's. Halloween had long passed, and Thanksgiving was fast approaching.

George Gunderson was still in his head, but Dan's old nemesis, Angelo Biaggio's was about to wipe Gunderson's name from the detective's memory.

It was nine thirty a.m. when Sasser called. The attorney was ranting. "Will you slow down? I have no idea what you're saying," Dan said.

Scotty nudged his partner. "What's going on?"

"Sasser is livid."

Sasser shouted, and Dan heard him say, "All four of my tires were slashed." The crazed attorney kept yelling, and Dan had to interrupt him to gain control of the conversation. "Sass. Sass, get a hold of yourself. Take a breath. What the hell happened?"

Sasser quieted and Dan heard him take that breath. "My car, my Cadillac. The tires are flat as pancakes, and it was broken into. Right here where I park it. They swiped my Ray-Bans. God damned Biaggio."

"You didn't hear anything?"

"Chantel noticed it when she came in. I didn't hear shit. Sons of bitches, good thing I installed cameras. I already saw the bastards. Same assholes who have been following me. I think they saw Chantel coming and sped away."

"Sass," Dan said, "hold tight. We'll be right down."

"Bring a bottle of vodka...make it two."

"Jesus, do you have any Xanax?"

"No, but I can get some narcotics."

"Stay put. We'll see you in ten minutes."

Dan heard him huffing. "Make it five."

The detective grabbed his coat. "Come on," he said to Scotty. "I've never heard him so incensed."

"What happened?"

Dan explained on the way there. Thirteen minutes later, they were at Sasser's office. He was pacing the area back and forth, and the rattled attorney's Calvin Klein suit was wrinkled. He pointed to his flattened tires. "See?"

"Flat alright," Dan said.

"I'm waiting for a tow truck. Dirty bastards."

"You said you have a video."

"I do."

Hearing a truck approaching, Dan said. "I think the tow is here."

Minutes later, the Cadillac was up on the flatbed being transported to the tire shop. They went inside where Chantel was standing at her uncle's desk. "He's been cuckoo for the past two hours."

"I see," Dan said. "Where's the video?"

Still frenzied, Sasser asked, "Where's the booze?"

"You know what?" Dan gestured with his hands. "Sit your ass down and take a few deep breaths before you have a heart attack, and I have to call an ambulance."

The irate lawyer heeded Dan's advice and soon regained his composure. Chantel brought her uncle a glass of water, and he drank it. He took a breath and in a slightly calmer state, he motioned the detectives to his computer. "Here's the video."

Dan didn't have to look twice. "Vincenzo and Pug."

It didn't take long for Sasser to become incensed again., "Biaggio's thugs, right?"

"Yup."

"I'm gonna kill them. Those mothers are going to their graves."

The antsy Sasser stood, and Dan waved his hand at him. "Sit down."

"What are you gonna do?" Sasser asked.

Dan thought for a few seconds "It's time to rattle Biaggio." The fast-thinking, revengeful detective said, "Biaggio's prized possession is his Jaguar. He may not have it much longer."

Scotty said, "You can't."

"Oh yes, we can. We're going to the doughnut shop."

Sasser broke a grin. "Hampton?" The lawyer pointed at Dan. "Brilliant! You shoulda been a lawyer."

"One more thing," Dan said. "You know Dixon, right? Call it in. I want this incident on record. He'll send a couple of uniforms out to write up a report."

Dan couldn't be sure if Hampton would be in on stealing Biaggio's Jaguar but hoped to lure the ex-car thief into going back to work. Sasser tried to help Rollin and still might be able to get the biker's charges reduced, so Dan planned to leverage the lawyer's help to get Hampton to literally ride again. The other ace in the hole was the fact that Hampton had been employed by Dan previously to swipe the Jaguar, but that scheme was nixed when Biaggio's daughter had driven off with it before Hampton could get his hands on it.

▲

Relieved to see Rollin's Harley outside the shop, Dan knew his friends were inside. Scotty opened the door, and they went directly to the retired men, relaxing in their usual seats.

"Good day, gentlemen," Dan said. He smelled the marijuana odor wafting off their flannel shirts and looked at Rollin.

Rollin put his hand on the table. "It was my bad. Cost me a hundred twenty bucks to get the bike back."

Hampton squirmed in his seat. "It cost me five grand to bail him out, but I got a feeling you need a favor. I ain't stealin' no cars. I'm retired, you forget?"

Dan sat beside Hampton. "Remember that Jaguar you were supposed to grab?"

"Biaggio?"

"Yes. He had his thugs slash Sasser's Cadillac's tires. I want to pay him back. I want the Jaguar gone."

"No way. No way," Hampton hotly protested.

Dan pointed to Rollin. "You want Sasser to do his best, don't you?" He eyed Hampton. "You want Sasser to get him a good deal, right?"

Hampton cringed. "Ain't got nowhere to take it."

Dan knew better. "Don't hand me that bull. I know the old chop shop disappeared. There must be a new one around, right?"

Hampton acknowledged Dan's suspicion with a nod. "For sure."

"What do you think you can get for it?"

"I'm guessing two, three grand."

It was Dan's turn to nod. "Now that's not a bad supplemental income, is it?"

Hampton sighed. "Well, I am down five big ones. Okay, so what's the deal?"

"Biaggio eats lunch every day at Cefalu with his boys. Tomorrow, around noon, I'll be there. That's your time to grab the car. It should be in the small lot at the back of his office. And wear a disguise. He may have cameras now."

"Thanks. If you see me in lockup, you'll know it didn't work out too good."

"Not gonna happen. You're a pro," Dan assured him. "Rollin can drop you off. Call me when it's done." Dan placed his card on the table. "Don't lose this."

The detectives left The Maple and headed to Dan's car. Scotty said, "You are crazy!"

Dan opened his door. "Get in. I'm not crazy." He gave Scotty a wry smile. "I must be out of my mind."

Chapter 34

Dan went home and had second thoughts about dropping in at Cefalu to harass Biaggio. I must be out of my mind resonated with the brash detective throughout the evening.

The smell of Connie's chicken potpie caught Dan's attention as soon as he got home. Seeing the nanny take it out of the oven, he said. "I'm gonna miss that."

She placed it on the counter. "Is that it? You'll miss my cooking?"

Dan smirked. "Well, I might miss you a tad."

"I'll miss you too." She pointed at him. "You know, I haven't ruled out coming back. It is something how time flies, and Thanksgiving is right around the corner."

"I hear you, but if you stay in Florida, we'll miss you. Who knows? Maybe we'll retire there someday."

"Just don't forget to take me to the airport on Friday. Should I put a note on the fridge?"

Dan smiled admiringly at her. "Are you sure you're not my mother's twin sister?"

Phyllis entered the room at that moment. "Are you two at it again?"

"No dear, we're having a friendly chat. Let's eat."

While the family dined, Phyllis said, "Mike called earlier and said he'll be here for thanksgiving. He's sending his itinerary. He'll be here Saturday."

"I'm sorry I'll miss him." Connie uttered.

The nanny went home after dinner was over and Dan relaxed in his recliner. He thought about what he was going to do tomorrow and stared at the TV without turning it on. Phyllis asked, "What's bothering you?"

"It's nothing, dear," he said as he clicked the remote and started to watch a Penn and Teller magic show, but his mind was in a different place, and he was distracted. There are people I'd like to make disappear. Damn Biaggio. And George Gunderson is a major pain too. I'm not afraid of Biaggio, and he sure doesn't like me. I'm going to freak him out tomorrow.

Phyllis said, "I know something is bothering you. Do you want to talk about it? You know it helps."

He knew he couldn't tell her about his intended meeting with Angelo Biaggio at Cefalu. "It's nothing. You know how these homicide cases occasionally get to me. Gordon Gunderson was only a year older than Mike."

"I remember the boy on the bike, Javier bothered you because he was Josh's age. We talked that out. I think it would help if you opened up."

"It's fine. I'm okay."

CHAPTER 35

Dan approached the headquarters back door and was suddenly stricken by the absence of the chain-smoking Landry. He just wouldn't stop. I feel for the guy.

Heading upstairs, his thoughts shifted to Angelo Biaggio. The daring detective knew going to the Italian restaurant and ruining another of the attorney's lunches would infuriate the dirt-ball lawyer. He was also sure Vincenzo and Pug would be nearby.

Approaching Scotty, who was standing at Bev's desk, he said, "Morning guys." He tapped his partner on the shoulder and hung up his coat. "We need to talk. Let's hit the head."

Scotty followed him into the bathroom. "You haven't said anything to Bev, have you?"

"You mean about Hampton and Biaggio? Hell no. I wish I didn't know about them either."

"Good. I need to call Hampton and remind him."

"How can you be sure the Jaguar will be there?"

"I can't. I can't even be sure Biaggio will be at Cefalu. It's a big gamble. I hope Sasser did what I told him and called in the tire slashing and theft of his sunglasses, so I can arrest Biaggio's thugs."

They exited the lavatory and went back to their workspace. Scotty said, "We ran out of Keurig pods. I'm going to get a coffee. Bev, come on. I'll buy you one."

Dan sat at his desk and phoned Hampton. Happy to hear his voice, the detective said, "Just wanted to see if you were up."

"Geez, Dan. Don't you trust me?"

"I do. You and Rollin going to be on time?"

"Yeah, he stayed here last night. We'll be there."

"Great."

"Call me when it's done."

Scotty and Bev returned and placed coffee cups on their desks. "I need to see Dixon," Dan said.

As soon as he got up, Bev waved her pen at him. "You two are getting awful chummy. What's going on?"

Dan eyed Scotty and saw him whispering to Bev as he walked toward the exit.

▲

Entering Dixon's office, Dan asked, "Did Hancock Sasser report his car being vandalized?"

Dixon nodded. "He did. I have an incident report. You wanna tell me exactly what happened?"

"Here it is," Dan said as he began telling Dixon the story. "I'm going to need a unit at Cefalu around noon. I'll be parked outside."

"I shouldn't ask this, but I think I already know the answer. Does Syms know?"

Dan shrugged. "Like you said, you already know the answer."

Dixon sat back. "It's gonna bite you someday."

▲

Dan's was parked across the street from Cefalu. The car's clock read 11:30 a.m. As he waited, he wondered, if by chance, Biaggio might not show. He kept watching customers enter the restaurant and glancing down the street in the direction of the lawyer's office. Fifteen minutes passed and there was no sign of Biaggio or his henchman.

Dan began to sweat as it crept closer to noon. He worried his plan could go awry. Where is Biaggio? I have to call Hampton. The moment of panic was broken twenty minutes later when he recognized his targets approaching Cefalu. He waited until they were inside and hoped the black and white would show up on time.

When noon came and the squad car wasn't there, the antsy detective stared at his watch. Where are they? Two minutes elapsed and he glanced at his watch again. Come on. Let's go guys. Finally, at six past noon, he saw in his rearview mirror a squad car approaching the restaurant. Dan got out of his Accord and stopped the patrolmen. The driver rolled down his window. "Hey, Dan. What's going on?"

"Park it. I'll explain."

Five minutes later, Dan and the two uniforms went inside Cefalu. Garlic wafted through the air as a hostess, armed with menus, looked at him and the policemen. Dan displayed his badge. Glancing to his left, he confirmed Biaggio, Vincenzo, and Pug were at the attorney's exclusive table in the far corner of the main dining room. "I'm here to see Mr. Biaggio. These policemen will stay here while I'm speaking with him." Addressing the uniforms, he said, "I'm going back there. Wait until I need you and then come to the table."

With soft music in the background, he carefully walked by white-collar diners and wondered how many lawyers were in the room. When he reached his destination, Biaggio tossed his cloth napkin on the red tablecloth. "What the hell are you doing here?"

Dan held out both hands. "Relax. We have to talk." Dan glanced at Vincenzo and Pug. "Nice to see you guys."

The two protectors quickly got off their chairs and faced Dan. "You can tell them to sit," he said to Biaggio. The less than pleased attorney pointed at his employees, and they took their seats.

With a half-filled wine glass and a plate of shrimp scampi in front of him, the stoic-faced lawyer said, "Talk and make it fast."

"Thanks. This won't take long."

The attorney took a piece of bread from a wicker basket that was next to a Chianti and said, "Damned right it won't."

"Angelo," Dan couldn't resist addressing him by his first name,

"I came here representing Hancock Sasser. Imagine that!"

Biaggio pointed a bread knife at the brazen detective. "Don't you call me Angelo. It's Mr. Biaggio to you. And that scumbag lawyer should have his license revoked."

Composed, Dan stared at the bossy attorney. "Angelo, Angelo, Angelo. Keep your thugs away from him."

Vincenzo again got up, and Pug followed suit. "Get out of here," Vincenzo yelled, catching the attention of other patrons.

Dan sneered at the goons, then looked back, nodded, and the two policemen neared the table. Pointing to Vincenzo and Pug, Dan sternly said, "Okay, boys, stay on your feet."

"What the hell is going on?" Biaggio demanded to know.

"Arrest these two and read them their rights," he ordered the uniforms. Biaggio started to rise. "Sit down, Angelo." Dan said.

"What the hell is this about? Where's your warrant?"

The detective placed his hands on the table and stared into Biaggio's eyes. "You're the lawyer. You know I don't need a warrant when there is just cause. These two clowns are on camera. They vandalized Sasser's car: slashed the tires on his Cadillac, broke into it, and stole a pair of sunglasses. I suppose you don't know anything about it. There's no mistaking these idiots from the video. They'll be downtown. I recall they've been there before. I guess you can see them in court tomorrow to bail them out."

Biaggio picked up his cloth table napkin and slammed it down. "You have some balls," the irate attorney yelled. "You haven't seen the last of me."

Dan waved his hand at Biaggio. "On the contrary, Angelo. I hear you'll be standing trial soon. Oh yeah, Sasser sends his regards."

Biaggio's outburst again caught the attention of everyone in the room and plenty of eyes were on the policemen and the cuffed thugs who were being escorted out of the restaurant.

Completing his mission, Dan got into his car and couldn't wait for Hampton to call him. He phoned his accomplice, who answered on the first ring. An elated Hampton said, "Dan! It went real smooth. No problem."

"Where are you?"

"On my way to the shop. Should be there in ten."

Dan let out a breath. "Good man. Let me know how much you get for the Jag. You did cover your face, didn't you?"

"Hell, yes. Got a Batman mask. But just one thing: there wasn't any Jaguar in the parking lot."

Dan put his hand to his forehead not believing the disguise Hampton had chosen. He was no less surprised by the Jaguar remark. "What did you say? No Jaguar?"

"Nope, but I got a hell of a Porsche though."

"A what?"

"Porsche. I sure want to run it."

Dan raised his voice. "Run it? You get that straight over to the chop shop. Don't you dare take that car for a joyride."

Dan heard Hampton huff. "No fun, Dan. You're a downer."

The detective calmed himself and broke a laugh. "A Porsche. You know it's his car?"

"Gotta be. He got a new tag, Angelo-one. Last one of these I had, I got it up to one twenty before being pulled over. I think that was the third time I went to the jungle."

"You get Biaggio's car to the shop, pronto."

"Will do. You laughing?"

"Bet your ass I am. Let me know how much you get. By the way, Hampton, you're the best. When I retire, I'll come hang out with you at the doughnut shop."

The resourceful detective drove back to headquarters and waited in his car for Hampton's call, but he worried the daring thief might well take the Porsche for a long drive after all. Fifteen minutes later, there still was no call. Dan went inside the building and up to his workspace.

"How's it going?" he asked his colleagues. Without waiting for an answer, he said, "I'm going to the boys' room."

"I was about to go too," Scotty said.

He and Dan walked down the hall. "Was Biaggio pissed?"

Dan opened the bathroom door, and they went inside. "What do you think? He nearly shit a brick when he saw me. I didn't waste time and told him to lay off Sasser."

Standing side-by-side at the urinals, Scotty asked, "What about his thugs?"

"Vincenzo and Pug were taken in. They should be downstairs. I had a couple of uniforms with me."

"The car?"

Zipping up and flushing, Dan explained, "Hampton took care of that. I'm sure Biaggio will be calling me. You won't believe it. He must have traded his Jaguar for a Porsche. Hampton got the new car and is taking it to the chop shop. You want to hear something funny? I told him to mask up before taking the car. He did; he wore a batman cover-up." They washed their hands and exited the lavatory. "Syms is going to have a hemorrhoid, you know."

"So will Biaggio."

"I'm worried about Hampton and the car. He promised he was heading straight to the chop shop, but he hasn't called me back yet."

Returning to their workplace, Bev took off her glasses, held them in her hand, and sneered at her colleagues. "What the hell are you two up to? I know women go to the bathroom together, but you two seem to be making it a habit." Scotty sat next to her as she put her glasses back on, and he fessed up he'd told her a story. She winced. "You lied to me about the girl."

Dan rolled his eyes at his partner. Scotty said, "I told her Haley had relapsed and needed your help."

Bev smirked and eyed Dan. "Do you mind telling me what you've done. I know it's not good."

Dan eased closer to the unsmiling, curious detective, and began to tell her the story when his cell rang, and he saw it was Hampton. The detective answered. "Where the hell are you?"

"Relax, I got three big ones for it."

Dan blew a sigh of relief. "What took you so long?"

"I kinda took the long route."

"You didn't take it up on ninety-one, did you?"

"Just a couple of exits, maybe three or four. You know it was fun."

"Hampton. Don't even think about coming out of retirement again. Next time you get nabbed, it could be the last."

"Hey, who asked me to do him a favor?"

"Okay, pal. You guys keep cool. And get off the weed."

"Not now. I hear it may be legal soon."

"Thanks. See you."

Dan turned back to Bev. She pointed at Scotty, "Save it, he told me. My turn to go to the bathroom.

Dan returned to his desk. "I have to call Sasser."

The friendly attorney's phone rang three times. "Dan" he said, "did you do it?"

"We arrested his goons, and Hampton stole the bastard's Porsche."

"I thought he had a Jag."

"So did we, but he has a Porsche now. I guess we can say he did have one."

"Damn, Dan. You're the man."

"I'm sure he'll call me, but you know as well as I do, I don't have any idea what happened to the car."

Sasser's laughter came right through the receiver. "Tit for tat, my kind of justice."

"One question: you can get Rollin a reduced charge, can't you?"

"Maybe. I'll talk to Judge Harper."

"Thanks, buddy."

Dan ran his hand across his forehead. He knew Biaggio would be bonding out his thugs as soon as he could. He also knew it wouldn't be long before he'd hear from the sleazy attorney.

Chapter 36

The brazen detective barely made it to his desk when Syms burst from his office and strode directly toward him. "Let's go. Hardison wants to see us right now. You've really done it this time." Dan feigned innocence, but he knew he was in trouble. "Come with me and shut up," Syms barked.

They marched upstairs to Chief Hardison, and Syms slammed the door shut. Hardison glared at Dan. "Sit, Detective," he commanded and gritted his teeth. "Do you have a story to tell me?"

Dan was wrong about Biaggio calling him. He'd called the chief. "What kind of story, sir?"

Hardison slammed his hand on his desk, then pointed at the detective. "Dan, if you want to walk out of here with your badge, you better start talking. Can you guess who called me last night? And I don't know how he got my number, but he's royally pissed."

"I have a pretty good hunch."

Hardison angrily said, "Hunch? Give me one good reason to let you keep your badge. Put it on my desk. When we're done, I'll decide who owns it."

Dan obeyed and placed his medallion on the desk. Syms looked into Hardison's eyes and held out his hands. "Hold it, hear him out. You know him. There's always a story."

Hardison sat and breathed hard again. "What? You're buying his shenanigans?"

Syms took his seat, and it was Dan's turn to take a deep breath.

"Here's the whole deal. My meeting with Attorney Angelo Biaggio was warranted. He had his goons vandalized Hancock Sasser's car."

"And you can prove that?" Hardison snapped.

"Yes. Sasser has cameras that clearly show Biaggio's thugs, Vincenzo and Pug, doing the damage. The incident was reported, so I had good reason to arrest them."

"My lord. Those are the same two you had hauled in last year." Hardison wiped his sweaty brow. "What about the Porsche? Someone stole it. Who?"

"I can explain that." Dan spilled the details.

Hardison slid his hand across his forehead. "You know, Biaggio is calling for your ass to be put in a sling and shot to the moon. He's demanding your suspension. I have to call him back."

Dan asked, "What will you tell him?"

Hardison thought for a second. "I'm going to tell him we're investigating your activities, and Dixon has a lookout for the Porsche."

"He'll be livid," Dan said. "Thank you, sir."

"He's already livid. He also contacted the night court judge and got his employees out of here before ten p.m. Go back to work."

Dan and Syms got up, and the detective pointed at his badge resting on Hardison's desk. "Is it okay if I take that?" Hardison handed it back to him.

Syms opened the door and walked downstairs with his detective. "I owe you," Dan said.

"Damn right you do. You owe me a big bottle of headache meds, and a couple of bonsais."

Dan had escaped without a bruise. "What happened?" Scotty asked. "I don't see any blood."

Dan smirked. "Nothing. In fact, I'm getting a raise."

"Right," Bev said.

Dan grabbed his jacket. "Biaggio called Hardison and went off on a tirade. He knows I had his car stolen. The chief is okay with it, and Syms came to my defense. Biaggio is demanding my suspension, but the old man isn't going along with it. I'm outta here."

"Where are you going?" Scotty asked.

"To see Dewey."

Dewey's Pawnshop was a place where Dan knew he could find a pair of sunglasses for Sasser.

⚓

Nearing the store, he saw the familiar pawnshop symbol, three balls suspended from a curved bar, hanging outside the door. The neon sign in the window flashed in yellow letters 'OPEN' and Dan entered the shop. He glanced to his left at the usual stockpile of electronics in one corner. He knew there was stolen merchandise among the inventories. Dewey's had been shut down twice due to tainted goods, but he always managed to reopen after paying fines and having stock confiscated.

Three customers were being helped by Dewey's employees. The shop owner, a cancer survivor, was behind the jewelry counter as Dan approached. Dewey was wearing a polo-style shirt, green like money, with the yellow pawnshop logo on it. The detective neared the counter, and Dewey raised his head. "You look good. Your hair is growing back," Dan said.

He shook Dan's hand. In his froggy voice, he said, "I feel good. How are you doing?"

"Great."

Dewey folded his arms. "What do you want this time? Another gun?" He took a step to his left toward the locked weapons case.

Dan had previously obtained a gun that he used as a plant in order to nab a suspect. "No, sunglasses. Ray-Bans. Got any?"

Dewey led Dan to a rack of assorted shades. "Here you go."

Dan spotted a tinted pair of Ray-Bans and pointed to them. "How much?"

Dewey took them off the rack. "Fifty-five. Try them on."

"They're not for me."

"You want a receipt?"

Dan laughed. "Are they returnable?"

"Hand over the money." Dewey gave a mocking smile.

Dan paid him. "Thanks. I have to run."

⋏

Dan drove to Sasser's office and was glad to spot the lawyer's Cadillac with new tires parked where it belonged.

Entering the reception area, he said, "Hi, Chantel."

"Hello, Detective. Did he know you were coming?"

"I think not, and I don't intend to stay long. I see his door is shut. Is he busy?"

Dan watched Chantel get up from her desk and knock on the door. Sasser had his phone to his ear and glanced at her. "What's up?"

"Detective Shields is here to see you."

"Send him in."

"I heard that," Dan said as he walked into the lawyer's office.

Sasser put his cell phone down and stood to shake Dan's hand. "My man," he said. "What brings you here?" Dan reached into his jacket pocket and placed the Ray-Bans on the desk. Sasser squinted. "Really? These look brand new."

"They are…sort of."

He picked them up and put on the glasses. "How do they look?"

"Great. Compliments of Angelo Biaggio."

Sasser laughed and stared at Dan. "Okay, Angelo. Thanks."

"Are you gonna take those off, or are you going to wear them all day? I have to go. I'll be talking to you."

Sasser removed the glasses. "Wait, how about a little barbecue?"

There was no way Dan was going to entertain that idea. "You trying to make me sick? Remember the last time?" He checked his pocket and removed his EpiPen.

"Oh, yeah. Too bad, I was treating."

Placing the medical device back inside his jacket, Dan said, "Next time, you can treat me to a dinner at Cefalu. See you around."

Chapter 37

Dan was glad to have Hardison off his back, and he was elated Syms had jumped in to go to bat for him. He knew his boss wasn't merely hinting at a bottle of Aleve and a couple of bonsais. The captain fully expected his detective to deliver the goods.

Dan started his day by making a quick stop to purchase the tablets, and then went to the home and garden center in pursuit of a couple of mini trees. Encountering the huge assortment of bonsais overwhelmed him. After browsing for several minutes, he saw a two he thought the captain would like. One was called a Dwarf Hawaiian. The other was a Dwarf Jade tree. He purchased them.

▲

With the bonsais in his hands and a bottle of pills in his pocket, Dan went straight to Syms without saying anything to Scotty or Bev. The captain smiled from ear to ear. "Well, well, what do we have here?"

Placing the garden center gifts, and the Aleve on the desk, he said, "Nice day, isn't it?"

Syms admired his presents. "It is now."

Dan inquired, "What made you step up for me yesterday?"

Syms grinned and put his hand to his chin. "Let's just say Landry's leaving was enough. I didn't want to lose another employee."

Dan turned to leave the office. "Thank you, sir."

As he neared Scotty, Bev, and his desk, he heard his desk phone, and noticed the caller ID. Dan sat, and for a second wondered if he should answer. Then he did. "Good morning, Mr. Gunderson."

"Maybe," George said. "What have you found out about Rosario and Amalia? Did you get him for drugs?"

If the hostile caller could have seen Dan's face, he would have known the detective wanted to shove his foot up the man's ass. "Listen, I appreciate your help. We did talk to them again, and we know about Rosario's past. I'm telling you he had nothing to do with Gordon's death. He was a good roommate."

"And the girl?"

Agitated, Dan raised his voice and harshly replied, "Okay, you want to know the truth about Amalia Kendrick?"

"Damn right, I do."

Dan knew what he was about to say would send the bigoted George Gunderson through the roof. Keeping his harsh tone, he said, "Okay, sir. You would be proud to have that young lady as your daughter-in-law. She's as good as it gets."

George's voice ran up a notch. "Who the hell are you to tell me she's good enough for my family?"

Dan retreated to his normal voice tone. "Sorry, I just thought you should know that there are terrific people like her and Rosario in this world."

"I think this conversation is over," George said.

"I agree, sir. Have a nice day."

Dan faced his colleagues. "George Gunderson was on the warpath again. I tried to bring him down a peg, but I don't see him changing his viewpoints."

"I bet he didn't like the kudos you gave Amalia and Rosario," Scotty said, based on what he had heard of Dan's side of the conversation, "especially suggesting she would be a nice addition to his family."

Dan laughed. "That didn't make him happy, but I understand his frequent calls. His son was killed."

"You sure ran past us with your hands full," Bev said. "Bonsais?"

"And Aleve," Dan replied. "I owed him for saving me with Hardison."

Then, there it was again, his desk phone rang. It was the officer at the main entrance. "What?" the detective asked. "Okay." He put the phone back on its receiver. "Ellie Wilcox is here. I'm going to get her."

Dan proceeded downstairs and came back with his unexpected guest. He motioned to Scotty to follow them into interview room one. Ellie had the familiar tote with her and placed it on the table. "This is crazy," she said. Dan saw the troubled look in her eyes. "I can't believe George called after the not-so-cordial meeting at the funeral and said he had to see me. I asked him why. He said it was important, so I agreed."

"Do you want some water or coffee?" Dan asked.

Ellie sighed. "No, thank you, I'm fine." She took off her coat and placed it over the back of her chair. Taking a deep breath, she sat, then uttered, "George knew about Gordon intending to write that damaging piece about him."

Dan asked, "How did he find out?"

"It was Keith. He told George, and they know I have these documents." She pulled two manila folders from her tote and opened them. "I already showed you tax returns. These are what he's afraid of."

A pile of papers was on the table. "Exactly what are these?" Dan asked.

"Letters, copies of emails that could send George to jail. It's all money transfers to foreign accounts. All unreported income."

Dan wondered why Ellie was showing Scotty and him the documents. "I don't understand," Dan said. "Why don't you take these and the tax returns to the IRS?"

"I might, but he's offering me a deal." She grimaced and swept her hand through her hair. "He was always secretive about his business deals. After we moved into that huge house and he opened his third branch, Natalie came into the picture. As I already told you, I knew he was having an affair with her. I went through his desk at home and found those Victoria's Secret receipts, as well as a lot of other things."

Dan leaned forward. "What exactly are you telling us?"

"I'm telling you he wants to give me a quarter of a million dollars to destroy these papers." She paused and said, "That's a lot of money to turn down. I met him at his office. He wanted me to come after hours when we could be alone, but I refused and went while employees were still there."

Dan said, "Are you going to take the money and destroy these?"

"I told him I would. He said he'd get a cashier's check."

Dan looked at her. "So why tell us this?"

"I don't have the check yet, and I don't trust him. He might do anything."

"When did he say he'd pay you?" Dan asked.

"Within the next ten days. He said he'd have to get the money from different accounts."

"Are you saying you think he could make you disappear, and the payoff is a lure to trap you?" Dan asked.

She took off her red glasses and rubbed her eyes. "Yes. He was really fast to offer me the bribe, and he got boiling hot when I said I'd have to think about it."

"But you agreed to take it," Dan said.

"I had to. He threatened me."

"Are you asking for protection?" Dan asked although he knew the police couldn't provide it without a formal complaint.

"I don't know. Not yet. At least you know." Ellie placed everything back into the folders, slid them into her tote, and put on her coat.

"I'll see you out," Dan said.

A few minutes later, he came to Scotty's desk, and they went to see Syms.

"You two look like you're being followed by a stalker," the captain said.

"Not quite," Dan said. "Ellie Wilcox was just here."

"You didn't tell me she was coming."

Dan said, "We didn't know either. It was a spur of the moment visit."

"Why was she here?"

Dan explained what had transpired between her and George Gunderson. "Wow, she could put him away," Syms said.

"Money talks," Dan said. He looked at the captain's trees that now had a paper turkey placed between them. "What the heck? Are you collecting turkeys now?"

"No. If you look inside the card, you'll see an invite to my brother's house for Thanksgiving. And what are you boys doing?"

Dan said, "Mike will be here, so it will be great."

"Very exciting." Syms eyed Scotty.

"We're headed up to Boston to Sallie's sister's house. Her husband's family will also be there."

"Enough niceties. Out," Syms said.

The detectives went back to their workspace, and Bev asked, "What was that all about?"

Scotty explained. Bev said, "That's pretty heavy stuff."

"Speaking of stuff, I should say stuffing. Are you all set for Thanksgiving?" he asked.

Bev smiled. "My in-laws are having it this year. Last year, it was my parents."

Dan said, "It's a little sad Connie won't be here. I have to take her to the airport tonight."

Chapter 38

It was bad enough George Gunderson was a thorn in Dan's side, but now Ellie Wilcox was throwing darts at her ex. There were also a few loose ends the detective needed to tie together. He addressed Scotty and Bev. "You know who bothers me?" He answered his rhetorical question. "Jason Ritter."

"How so?" Scotty asked.

"I don't know, but he's always seemed jittery, even from the start. He discovered Christine and Gordon and says he got there a few minutes before his show. We never asked what he was doing beforehand. We don't know if anything he said was true. And we never bothered to check his backpack."

Scotty looked at Dan. "Too late to do that now. Are you thinking he may have killed them?"

"He was there. That's all we know. And who knows what could have been inside his backpack both times we met with him? It's his edginess. His sleeping trouble may not be from what he says he'd seen; it may be our presence. If he's guilty, he's sweating bullets."

"Makes sense," Scotty said.

Dan shook his head. "I'm calling him. I also have a few questions for the security company. It's that code box. We know the cameras weren't working, but the box was. I'm guessing there's a record of what time it was accessed."

"Probably," Bev said.

He called the student who answered and agreed to meet the

detectives at the student center after his biology class. "We can meet him around ten-thirty," Dan said.

▲

Entering the building, Dan saw Jason seated near the center of the room. The detectives walked to him and took seats. "How are you?" Dan asked.

"I'm okay."

The student appeared calm, and Dan said, "You look better. You seemed nervous before."

"It was probably my insulin level. I carry some in my pack."

"You're diabetic?" Dan asked.

"Yes. When my sugar level drops too low, I get a little uneasy."

"Are you sleeping better?"

"Yes. I started seeing a counselor."

Dan concluded the student's edginess had been due to his diabetes. "Do you mind telling us where you were before you got to the radio station the night Gordon and the guard were killed?"

"I was sleeping. I got up and went to do my show as always. It was raining a little when I got there."

Dan said, "And then you buzzed Gordon, but he didn't respond, so you accessed the code box."

Jason sighed. "Then I opened the door, and you know the rest."

Dan took note of the student's much calmer demeanor and felt at ease about him. He said, "We appreciate you meeting with us again. Have a fine day."

Leaving the student center, Scotty said to Dan, "He seemed a lot more composed."

"He was. I'm satisfied he's not hiding anything. Let's head over to Bulkeley Security."

The detectives entered the building and Aaron Westland, who was talking with the two employees in the outer office, greeted them. "Any news?" he asked.

"We're still working it. We were at the student center. I'd like to ask you a couple of questions," Dan said.

"What would you like to know?"

"Can we go to your office?"

They proceeded into the manager's quarters and Dan said, "It's the code box outside the door of the radio station. Does that box record what time someone accesses it? We know Jason entered the code to get into the station because Gordon didn't respond to the buzzer. We also know cameras were out that night, but the box was working. Would Christine have entered the code?"

Westland said. "She would have used an override code that we had in place. Ramsey Dale assigned the students a code he frequently changed, but that system was antiquated and replaced a week after we upgraded the camera system. If you look at the box now, it resembles a small ATM. Every student who has access to the radio station has their own code, kind of like a PIN number. There is a master list and it's updated every time a new student is added or when one no longer needs access, and then they are removed. We can tell who entered the station, and when they entered."

Dan asked, "Did the old box record who entered by way of the station code?"

"It can only tell us that someone used the code, and the time they entered, but it can't identify the individual."

"Can you still retrieve the data from the Sunday evening, Monday morning when Gordon and Christine were killed?

"Yes." Westland went to the backroom where all the monitors were and came back with a printout. "Here it is."

Dan studied the single-page document. He noted four entries between 11:00 p.m. and 3:00 a.m. Recalling Jason said he got there at around ten before 3:00 a.m., Dan saw one near that time. "I am seeing an override entry, actually two. Christine was probably one, but who was the other person? The one at a little past two thirty was likely Christine, but the other entry at quarter past two may have been the killer."

"What about Watney?" Scotty suggested.

"I want to talk to him."

Westland said, "He'll be here later, around five p.m."

"Can you have him come down here now?" Dan asked. "Don't say we're here."

Westland called his employee and requested the guard's presence as soon as possible. "He's coming down, should be here within the hour."

The detectives waited with Westland. Soon, Watney's car pulled in, and the guard entered the outer office where Westland greeted him. "Follow me," he said.

Inside the manager's office, Dan said, "I want to ask you a few questions. Have a seat."

He did. "What's going on?" he asked.

"Tell us about the code box. You know the override, don't you?"

"Yes."

Dan looked into his eyes. "There were two people who used the override code the night Gordon and Christine were killed. We think Christine was one. That leads us to you. You were the only other guard on duty." Dan noticed Watney beginning to sweat.

"What are you saying?"

"I'm not saying anything. I'm asking. Did you go inside the radio station at all that evening or early morning?"

"No." He wiped his forehead and protested. "I picked up Doreen at a little after twelve and drove her back to her dorm. Then I came back here." Watney became quiet and wiped his brow with a handkerchief.

Dan remembered what Watney had previously told him. "Are you sure you were here playing video games after you dropped her off?"

"What?" Westland asked.

Dan held his hand up. "Bear with me," he said to Westland.

Watney's face became pale. "Yes. No." He closed his eyes. "I was here playing games before I picked up Doreen."

"Is that it?" Dan said. "You were here after you dropped her off?"

A bead of sweat appeared on the guard's forehead and he took a breath. "Okay. I was with Doreen in her room. We were." He silenced himself before he could say what they were doing, but he didn't have to admit they were having sex.

"After you and Doreen were done, you came back here?" Dan asked.

"Yes."

Dan looked at Scotty, and Westland stared at Watney. Dan said, "I suppose she'll verify your story. Was that the first time you two hooked up?"

"No."

Dan continued, "So, you lied to me when you told me you were here playing Minecraft the entire shift?"

"Watney!" Westland sternly said. "As soon as they're done with you, you can leave here, then come back to pick up your paycheck and turn in your uniform, your badge too. You're fired."

"We're done," Dan said. "We are going to speak with Doreen." He looked at Watney. "May we have her cell number?"

Watney recited it, got up, and stormed out of the building.

"Unbelievable," Scotty said.

They watched Watney leave, and Dan said to Westland. "I would have fired him too."

Dan didn't wait and as soon as they got into his car, he called Doreen. The young girl answered and after hearing what Dan had to say, she admitted Watney was with her. He turned to Scotty. "Doreen corroborated Watney's story. They were in her room."

▲

The names Melrose and Barbour had risen to the top of Dan's suspect list. "We have to bring them in for questioning. We have an idea where they are, and we have phone numbers, right?"

Scotty opened his notepad. "New Britain. They're supposedly renting a place near Central College and are planning to enroll next semester. Their numbers are right here. I'll start with Melrose."

Bev said. "What's your plan?"

Dan thought for a second. "I'd like to get them in here together." Dan sat up and thought again. "You know what? If they are guilty of either rape, murder, or both, they already have their stories rehearsed and know they'll have to answer questions."

"That's true," Scotty said.

Dan leaned on Bev's telephone skills. "How about you calling them? Tell them we know about the frat parties and in order to round out our investigation of Gordon Gunderson's death, we need to ask a few questions, and then they'll be free to go."

Scotty handed her the phone numbers. "I'll start with Melrose." Bev entered the number into her desk phone. When the call flipped to voicemail, she left a message with her number and added that it's important they talk as soon as possible. "Want me to try Barbour?"

"It's worth a shot," Dan said,

She repeated her effort and attempted to contact Barbour, but the result was the same as her call to Melrose.

"Damn," Dan said. "They better call you back."

"They might not want to," Scotty said. "We might have to go get them."

"Maybe," Dan said. "If we don't hear from them by mid-day Monday, we'll drag them in here."

"If we can find them," Scotty said.

"Let's get out of here and enjoy the weekend," Dan said. "Hard to believe Thanksgiving is this coming Thursday. I'm looking forward to picking up Mike tomorrow morning."

CHAPTER 39

It was Saturday morning, and Dan arrived at Bradley airport forty minutes before Mike's flight was due to land. He pulled up to the curb outside the baggage terminal. Signs clearly indicated parking was not allowed, and ahead he saw several cars with drivers in the process of picking up passengers. Transit buses from the nearby parking lots cruised the area as well.

Within minutes, an airport security employee approached him. Dan rolled down his window and was asked to move the car or circle around. He was clearly told he couldn't stay there. "Sir, I'm a police officer," he said and showed the man his badge as well as his placard. "I'm here to pick up the chief of police. He should be out soon."

"Okay, Detective."

Dan continued to wait and finally, his cell rang. "Dad, we just landed. I'm on my way out."

"Do you have bags? I'm outside the baggage area."

"I have a carry-on."

"Go down the escalator to the baggage carousels and come outside. I'm to the left of the first set of doors."

"I'll be right there."

Six minutes later, Dan watched his son step outside. He beeped the Accord's horn and got out, waving at Mike. Wearing an Arizona State sweatshirt and carrying his bag, Mike walked to his father's car, opened the back door, and tossed the luggage in. Dan said, "You look good. Hop in."

Mike got into the passenger seat and buckled up. "You look good too, Dad."

"How was the trip?" Dan started to drive away from the airport. "Fine."

"Mom can't wait to see you."

"Me too. And Josh and Kate."

Dan knew he had to tell Mike the rest of the story about Haley. "Listen, there's a lot more to Haley than I told you. You know she had done drugs. She swears she's been clean for a year or so. It's her baby, Joey's father." Dan continued telling Mike about Travis and the current situation. "I wanted to let you know."

"That's heavy, Dad. I still want to see her."

Dan smiled. "She doesn't know you're home, but her parents do." Switching gears, Dan said, "So, what's your hot girlfriend, Rachel like?"

"She's real nice. I'll show you her picture."

"Tell me the truth. How did you manage to squeeze a few extra days off to come home? We never had a Thanksgiving break, so to speak."

Mike said, "Okay. You're right. I'm skipping a few classes. Only Monday and Tuesday. There were none scheduled for Wednesday. Rachel has me covered."

"I kind of thought that. Don't tell your mother."

Dan's car rolled into the driveway, and the house's front door opened. Kate, Josh, and Phyllis were standing there waiting. Mike got his bag from the car, and his excited siblings rushed out to nearly tackle him before he managed to make it inside and give his mother a giant hug and kiss.

Mike unzipped his bag and handed Josh and Kate new hooded sweatshirts. "Can I take a shower?"

"Go," Phyllis said.

Mike showered and twenty-five minutes later, he came downstairs dressed in Levi's and a blue sweater and had a splash of cologne on. Phyllis smiled at him. "Hey, handsome. You smell good too."

Mike smiled. "It's good to be home." He looked at his siblings. "You guys miss me? I missed you."

Each wearing their new Arizona State sweatshirt responded in unison, "Yeah."

Phyllis said, "How about lunch? I went to the market and bought ham, cheese, potato salad, pickles, and cupcakes."

"Sounds good, dear," Dan said.

As soon as they finished their meal, Mike said, "I want to call Haley." He excused himself and went upstairs.

Dan was in the den when, an hour later, Mike came in. "How did it go?" Dan asked.

"Good. She sounds okay."

Mike's cell let him know he's just gotten a text. He looked at it and responded. "Rachel?" Dan asked.

"Yeah. Wanted to know how the trip was."

"You want to show me her picture?"

Mike went to his photos and showed Dan. "I think you understated the word nice. She's very pretty."

Mike put his phone back in his pocket. "Can I borrow your car later? I told Haley I'd pick her up, and we could go to Hanzel and Gretyl. We used to hang out there all the time."

"What time are you going?"

"About five-thirty."

"Take Mom's car. I never know when I might need mine."

Later that afternoon, it was time for Mike to pick up Haley and Phyllis gave him her car keys. "Thanks," he said.

As it approached ten p.m. Dan said to Phyllis. "I wonder where they are?"

"Do you want to call him?" she asked.

"I do, but Mike is a big boy. If he's not back by eleven. I'll call."

The worried father didn't have to phone his son. Fifteen minutes later, Mike walked into the den. "You guy's still up?" he mused.

"Not for long," Dan said. "You two must have had a lot to talk about."

Mike didn't bother to sit. "Yeah. She looks good. This has been a long day. I want to get some sleep."

Phyllis asked, "Where were you?"

"Oh, after we ate, we went back to her house. Must have been about seven or so. She wanted to put Joey down. Cute little boy."

"See you in the morning," Dan said.

Chapter 40

Dan, Scotty, and Bev had all survived the weekend without hearing the voice of Syms, but Hanson and Mal weren't as lucky.

Dan saw them leaving the captain's office and heading toward the squad room door. Hanson stopped. "You guys have a good weekend?" he asked. "The man got us out last night around eight."

"What happened?" Dan asked.

"Double shooting in the Blue Hills section," Mal said. "We're going to Woodland to talk with the survivor." He nodded at Dan. "You said I'd be seeing a lot of that hospital."

Hanson said, "He killed his partner, but got hit when they exchanged fire, and walked into Woodland an hour later. He was in surgery when we got there. The wound was not life-threatening, so we'll be talking to him, and he'll be put into custody as soon as he's released."

"Have fun," Dan said. He faced Scotty and Bev. "I bet you can't wait until you have a kid in college."

"Uh oh," Scotty said. "What's going on with Mike. He is home, isn't he?"

"He is and I'm a little concerned. For one thing, he has a hot girlfriend at college who is covering for him because he decided to skip a few classes in order to be home. I know that and so does he, but we haven't told Phyllis that tidbit."

"What's the problem?" Scotty asked as he and Bev listened.

"He admits he really likes his girlfriend, Rachel, but he also said

201

he still likes Haley, He said he never did stop liking her, and he spent more of his weekend with her than us. It wouldn't surprise me if they already had sex."

Bev chimed in. "Okay boys. Stop thinking with that thing between your legs. What's wrong with two old friends getting together. I'm sure they have a lot to talk about. You know, you make women out to be anxious to hop into bed with anyone who takes an interest in them."

Dan backed off. "You're right. I shouldn't assume things, but Haley has a little boy and she's not that stable right now. And Travis will never be out of her life."

Bev's phone lit up, and she said, "It's Melrose."

Dan and Scotty listened as she calmly spoke to him. Ending the conversation, she said, "Thank you. I look forward to meeting you both." Pivoting her chair, she smiled at the male detectives. "They're coming in this afternoon around one-thirty."

"I want to separate them. I'll take Melrose," Dan said.

Scotty nodded. "I guess Barbour is mine."

"I'll bring them up here and spring you boys on them," Bev said.

⚔

It was twenty past one when Bev was informed the young men had arrived, so she went down to greet and escort them to the squad room. "I want you to meet Detectives Dan Shields and Joe Scott. They'll be interviewing you."

Gregory Melrose was about Dan's height, had short brown hair, and wore silver-rimmed glasses. His dress slacks were complemented by an open corduroy jacket, revealing a knit pullover. Reed Barbour was taller, had thick black hair, a goatee. His leather jacket was also unzipped, underneath was a dark blue sweatshirt, and he kept it casual with jeans. Melrose inquired, "What's going on?"

Dan said, "Nothing. It's just routine. Mr. Melrose, please come with me into room one and have a seat. I'll be speaking with you."

Scotty eyed Barbour. "Come with me to the other room."

Dan closed the interview room door. Melrose sat and Dan took a seat opposite him. "Bev told you why you're here, correct?"

"Sort of. It has to do with Gordon Gunderson."

"You knew him, didn't you?"

"Not that well. He pledged and quit."

"And you are familiar with the Delphi article that he published?"

"Damn right. It got the frat kicked out, and it got us tossed out too."

"Was Gordon on drugs?"

"Not that I was aware of."

"What about you?"

Melrose uncomfortably shifted in his chair. "Hold it," he said. "I admit to having a marijuana habit, but I've never done drugs."

Dan didn't believe that response. He folded his arms. "Where were you on the night Gordon was killed?"

"Sunday?"

Unfolding his arms, Dan said, "Yes. Where were you at say two to three a.m.? That would be technically early Monday morning."

Blowing out a breath, he answered, "That's easy. We were at the the casino."

"Who are we?"

"Me and Reed. We were there from about seven p.m. to a little after two. We ate and played the machines."

"Which casino?"

"The Mohawk one."

"How did you guys do?"

"Actually, we did pretty well. I won two hundred, and Reed was up fifty when we left."

"Do you go there often?"

"Yes."

"Who do you know at the casino that could verify you two were there?"

Melrose raised his voice. "A lot of people." Then he said, "You can have the casino check our player's cards. We always put them into the machines. They'll verify we were there."

"And you left around two a.m. the morning Gordon was killed?"

"Yes."

Dan stared into his eyes. "Then you drove straight back to campus?"

Melrose squinted. "No. We stopped at a convenience mart. I filled up with gas, and we got a couple of coffees before getting back."

"Which store?"

"The same one we stop at all the time. The MaxiMart."

"Do you by chance have that casino card?"

"It's home. I keep it on a lanyard."

Dan, maintaining an even stream of questions, said, "We know you and Barbour organized wild parties, and you admit to having a weed problem. Who brought in the drugs?"

Melrose tensed up. "Drugs?"

Dan huffed and raised his voice one level as he fished for answers, not knowing for sure who supplied the narcotics. "Don't play games with me now. We know you and Mr. Barbour brought roofies to parties."

Melrose remained silent, and Dan sneered at him. "And what about the oxycodone?"

"Okay, we had pills."

Dan had an idea where they bought them. "Does the name Christine Kole ring a bell? She sold you oxy, didn't she?"

"Holy shit. I admit she did sell to us."

Dan knew the last part of this interview could get hostile. He tried to intimidate Melrose by standing face-to-face with him. "What about roofies? What about Trish Adams? Tell me about her."

Melrose's eyes bulged, and he began to fidget. "Who?"

Dan knew he'd struck a nerve and raised his voice again. "Who? You know damn well who. Isn't she the girl you and Reed Barbour raped?"

"Hell no. You can't prove that."

Dan couldn't believe that quick rash response. In his mind,

Melrose had just confessed to the act. The detective moved close to his prey. "What did you say? We can't prove it? How do you know we can't prove it? I think we can."

Melrose broke a sweat.

Dan backed off. "Tell me what happened that night at the big bash. As I heard it, you put roofies in her drink, dragged her upstairs, and enjoyed yourselves at her expense."

"No way. You're not charging us with that."

Dan glared into his glazed eyes and took a clear shot at him. "I didn't say I was, at least not now. She was afraid to report it then, but what if I told you she now remembers everything, and she's ready to press charges?"

"Bull," he said. "She didn't remember anything."

Dan wanted to kick the chair out from under Melrose as he leaned six inches from his face. "How the hell do you know she didn't remember anything? You remember everything, and we'll see you back here as soon as she presses charges."

Dan drew himself away and opened the door. "Stay right here." The angry lieutenant rapped once on the other door. Scotty opened it, and Dan said, "Step out for a second." Scotty did, and Dan told him what Melrose had said when asked about the rape. "Has Barbour mentioned anything about it?"

"I was getting to that. He claims they were both at the casino when Gordon was killed."

"That's one story they have down. Go in with Melrose. You don't have to say anything; just babysit until I come back. I'll go see Barbour and put the heat on him."

Scotty went into room one, while Dan entered room two. "Hi," he said. "I have a few questions for you. I already talked to Mr. Melrose." Barbour sat back and clasped his hands. "What can you tell me about Trish Adams?" Dan saw the scared look on the man's face.

"She came to a party with Gordon."

"Gordon got wiped at that party, didn't he?"

"Right."

"And his date, Trish Adams, was raped, wasn't she?" Barbour was silent, and Dan moved closer to him. Raising his voice, he repeated, "She was raped. Wasn't she?"

Hesitating, Barbour said, "That's what I heard."

Dan put his foot up on the chair and leaned in toward him. "You heard? Is that your answer? I have another answer because someone in that other room said there were roofies in her drink that knocked her out." Dan didn't tell Barbour that it was he and not Melrose who had said it. "Isn't it true that you and Melrose both raped her?" Barbour sat silently. "Look at me," Dan snapped. "Didn't you both rape her?" He raised his voice another notch. "You got her pregnant."

Barbour looked at Dan and jumped up. "Me? It couldn't have been me. I wore a rubber. He didn't. It had to be him."

Dan was close to a dotted-line confession, and he could taste it. He put his face close to the young man's. "You admit it. You and Melrose both raped her."

Barbour put his hands to his head and rested it on the table. "We had sex with her."

Dan eased back. "I just want to make it perfectly clear. You and Melrose both had nonconsensual sex with Trish Adams at that frat party."

He raised his head. "We were all high. So was she, and she encouraged us."

"You bastard," Dan said. "She was high and lured you into having sex?" He stared into Barbour's eyes. "She was out like a light after you slipped the pill into her drink. You carried her upstairs with Melrose and raped her. How many other girls have you two raped?"

Barbour remained silent.

"Stay here," Dan said. "I'll be right back."

Exiting the room, the savvy detective went next door and walked in on Scotty and Melrose. Dan motioned for his partner to join him in the hallway, and they had another short chat. "Look, Barbour admitted the rape. I need Melrose to confess. Time to switch up again."

Dan reentered room one where Melrose was sitting and calmly said, "Okay, now is the time to clear your mind and fess up. I just talked to your buddy. I know you dropped roofies into Trish Adams' drink and after she passed out, you both took her upstairs and raped her. He admitted you did. The only difference is he wore a rubber, and you didn't. What you don't know is she's pregnant with your kid. Look, we know frat parties can be wild, and this one was no exception, so you two had sex with her without her knowledge. That's called rape, my friend."

Melrose shook his head. "We didn't mean any harm. She was just waking up when we left the room."

Dan still pursued a confession. "So, in the name of fun, you...Gregory Melrose and Reed Barbour, rendered her unconscious, and you both raped her." The accused raised his head and sullenly looked at Dan. "Admit it," the anxious detective said.

Melrose closed his eyes and meekly uttered, "Yes."

"Stay here," he said to the student. Dan went back into the other room, and Scotty stepped out. "I just got a confession from Melrose. They both admitted to raping Trish Adams. I want to detain them. Go get cuffs and we'll charge them, read them their rights, and have them taken downstairs."

Scotty left and returned with cuffs. "A couple of uniforms are on their way up."

Dan and Scotty placed both men in the same room, verbally held them on rape charges and read them their rights. Syms rushed toward his detectives. "What's going on?"

"They admitted to raping Trish Adams. They're under arrest."

Two uniforms entered the room and took the detainees down to be booked.

Syms asked, "What about Gordon Gunderson?"

"They both have the same story about being at the casino at the time of the murder," Dan said. "We need to check it out."

Syms stared at him. "Tell me one thing: you didn't do anything illegal in getting a confession."

Dan proudly pounded his chest. "Nope. You can see the closed circuit and hear the interrogations. I never actually told either one we'd talked to Trish Adams or that she could identify them, but I did play them against each other."

"We have to write up the rape charge and get it downstairs." Scotty said.

After he filed the paperwork, Scotty came back to his desk. Dan said, "We need to verify their casino alibi. It's getting late now. Let's head there in the morning."

CHAPTER 41

It was a nice day for a field trip. Dan was on his way to the casino with Scotty riding shotgun, and said, "Melrose told us they have player's cards, so the casino should be able to track them to specific machines at exact times."

"True, but they can't tell us who used the cards. Anyone can slide them into slot machines."

"I assume they have cameras on the slots that can identify Melrose and Barbour. And they supposedly stopped at a MaxiMart on the way back. We're going there too."

"You think they're telling the truth?"

Dan hated to say it. "I do, but we can't take their word for it. Looks like it's a little over an hour to the casino." Halfway there, Dan received a call from Sasser. "What's up, Sass?"

"Bad news, I got bad news, Dan. Where you at? I hear traffic."

"On our way to the casino."

"You off?"

"No, we're quite on. We have to verify an alibi. What's the bad news? Are Biaggio's goons dogging you again?"

Assertively, Sasser answered, "Hell no. Those hounds aren't on me, but I have to drop the wrongful death suit."

"What?"

"It's Eduardo Ibanez. He died about a week ago." Sasser returned to his normal tone. "They went down to visit relatives and planned to be back after Thanksgiving. His wife, Ellina, has a large family in Santiago de Cuba. Eduardo had a heart attack, and she's not coming back."

Keeping his eyes on the road, Dan asked, "But you can still pursue the lawsuit, can't you?"

"That's the other bad news. I can't. Remember I said they never banked the money?"

"So?"

"They kept about ten for Javier's funeral and sent forty grand to her family. I didn't realize it, but Ellina never signed the paper. Eduardo is the one who signed the 'no harm' document. He can't be cross-examined to deny he knew what it meant. It's over."

"If you say so. At least Biaggio is out of your hair." Dan laughed. "I have to admit, I did enjoy getting in his face again at Cefalu, and having his thugs arrested."

Sasser sighed. "Thanks."

"Any word on Rollin?"

"I have to check when his hearing is. You gonna gamble?"

"Sass, just talking with you is a gamble."

"That's low, Dan. Good luck."

Continuing toward the casino, as they got closer, Scotty said. "That must be the MaxiMart."

"We'll stop there on the way back." Dan exited onto Mohawk Road and arriving at the casino, he opted to shun the valet parking option. He drove into the multi-level garage. "You'd think the whole world is here," he said as his car moved from one tier up to another, and finally pulled into a space on the fourth level.

They headed toward into the building. Several eager gamblers waited with them for an elevator that came seconds later. They all exited on the main floor and were immediately immersed in glitz and sounds of music as well as slot machine noise. Weaving their way down the circular corridor, the detectives came to a concierge station. Dan showed his badge and asked to speak with a manager. They waited and finally, a tall gentleman dressed in a business suit greeted them. Dan explained why they were there.

"We have more videos here than Warner Brothers," the manager named Trent Carlson said. "Come with me."

Dan and Scotty went with him and walked to a private area. The manager placed his finger on an identification pad that opened the door. The three men walked up one flight into a security room where a dizzying display of cameras watched over every nook and cranny of the place, except for restrooms. "What are the names of the men you are trying to find?"

Dan said, "Gregory Melrose, and Reed Barbour."

Carlson searched the database. "I have them. They're here frequently." Dan recited the specific date and time he was after. The manager tracked the data and verified their cards had been inserted into specific slot machines when Melrose and Barbour stated they were at the casino.

"Can you show us a video so we can identify them?"

"Let me pull it up."

With the video up on the computer screen, they studied the images. "It's them," Dan said.

Scotty agreed. "It is."

"They were here," Dan faced Carlson. "Thank you for your help, sir."

The detectives were escorted back to the main casino and Dan saw his partner eying the one-armed bandits. "How about a few tries?" Scotty suggested. "As long as we're here, we might win a few bucks."

"You mean lose a few bucks. Ten minutes."

"What if we're on a roll?"

The detectives sat side by side at machines and each inserted ten dollars. Dan had no luck, but Scotty had a couple of winning pulls before quickly losing his money. "Happy now?" Dan asked.

"Hey, you can't win if you don't play."

They walked away from the machines and headed toward an open elevator that took them up to level 4. Getting into his car, Dan uttered, "Next stop is MaxiMart,"

The convenience store /gas station was two miles from the casino and Dan found a space in front of the store. They went inside and luck was with them. Twenty minutes later they got back into the Accord. Scotty said, "That video shows them here. Melrose and Barbour are off the suspect list for the Gordon and Christine murders."

"At least we got them for sexual assault."

With Melrose and Barbour having been arrested for raping Trish Adams, Dan said, "We need to inform her that we have the two men who sexually assaulted her."

Scotty said, "That's one number we don't have."

Dan thought. "I can't call Amalia and ask for it, but I can call the RA, Kalani Moore." The quick-thinking detective did just that and obtained Trish's number. Using the desk phone, he said, "Here it goes. I want to keep it private, no speaker."

As soon as she answered, Dan identified himself. "Trish, I'm calling because we've been investigating Gordon Gunderson's death."

Dan could hear her start to cry. "I'm so sorry," she said. "And I cut off contact with him, but I still have a few things he gave me, including a sweatshirt he wore."

"Listen. Your good friend and roommate, Amalia told us what had happened at that Delphi party. We're sorry you were sexually assaulted." Dan heard a sigh. "We know you didn't press charges, but we've arrested Gregory Melrose, and Reed Barbour for rape."

Her voice was weak. "I thought it was them, but I couldn't be sure. I was so ashamed."

"You don't have to be. They're in jail and will pay for what they did." Dan paused. "And how are you?"

"I'm fine. The baby is due in a few weeks. Dan heard her weeping. "Do I have to do anything…like identify them?"

"No. They confessed. It's done. I wanted to let you know. Would you mind if I called Amalia and told her?"

"No, sir. Go ahead. I'll be talking to her later."

"Be well, Trish."

"Thank you."

Dan let out a deep breath and ran his hand across his forehead. "She said I can call Amalia." Recomposing himself, Dan contacted Trish's former roommate, and told her they had apprehended the rapists.

Chapter 42

It was dark when Dan headed home. He noticed driving at night was becoming bothersome because the glare from other automobiles' headlights seemed to splinter his vision, but he hated the thought of glasses.

His driveway was absent of Connie's Chevy Volt. When Dan opened the garage door, he didn't see Phyllis's SUV and wondered where she might be. Once inside the house, he saw his wife and asked, "Where's your car?"

"Mike has it. He's having dinner with Haley, and they're going to a movie."

"Really? He's spending a lot of time with her." Dan rifled through the mail on the counter. "What do you think?"

Phyllis sighed. "I think they're enjoying seeing each other. Leave it at that. Go up and change while I heat your dinner. The kids and I already ate."

Dan returned a few minutes later in jeans and a flannel shirt. Josh and Kate were in the kitchen looking for snacks. "How was school?" Dan asked them.

They each replied, "Good."

"Homework?" Dan asked.

Josh sat at the table with a glass of milk and cookies. "There's always homework. It's done."

Kate joined them with her snack. "I like homework."

While the kids enjoyed their snacks, Phyllis placed a plate of meatloaf and mashed potatoes in front of her husband.

"Meatloaf, my favorite."

"I thought Connie's potpie was your favorite," Phyllis said with a grin.

"She's gone now, so your meatloaf moved back up the list to number one."

"Thanks, I think."

After swallowing a mouthful, Dan said, "Lately, I'm having trouble with night driving. It's the glare."

"That's not uncommon for someone your age. You may need glasses."

Dan raised his fork. "Excuse me. What do you mean my age? You're only eight months younger than me."

"But I'm aging gracefully." She smiled at him. "You're due for an exam soon. Tell the ophthalmologist."

Dan continued eating his late dinner while Josh and Kate gobbled down their cookies and milk before scooting to the den to watch TV.

Finishing his meal, Dan was looking forward to a relaxing evening. Phyllis ordered the children upstairs to bed and Dan plopped himself down in his recliner. He clutched the remote as if it were a life vest and kept flipping sports channels until he found a North Carolina-Georgia Tech basketball game. Nearing halftime of the close game, the house phone rang. It was 9:50 p.m. Thinking it might be his boss, he reluctantly eyed the caller ID but didn't see Syms' name, so he picked up the receiver and heard Mike, as well as background commotion. "Dad, I need your help."

Startled, Dan asked, "Where are you? What's going on?"

"I'm at a club in Hartford with Haley."

It was difficult for Dan to make out his son's words because of the prevailing loud voices. "What's wrong, Mike?"

Frantically, he said, "I was in a fight."

Dan got out of his chair, "Are you okay?"

"My shirt is torn, hurt my hand, but I'm okay. The other guy isn't. The cops are here. I told them who I was, and a uniformed officer named Dexter said he knows you."

Dan could tell Mike was upset. "Calm down and let me talk to Dexter."

"Hey, Dan," the patrolman said.

"Dexter, what the hell happened?"

"Your kid beat the hell out of some dude. Broke the guy's jaw and made a bloody mess of his face. May also have busted a few ribs."

Phyllis entered the room. "What's wrong?"

"It's Mike. Tell you in a minute." Addressing Dexter, he asked, "What's the story?"

"The guy's being taken to Woodland Hospital."

"Can you stay there with Mike? Where are you?"

"The Applejack."

"I'll be right down. Who's the guy he beat?"

"The girl said his name is Travis McCarthy."

Dan yelled into the phone, "Holy shit! Hang tight. I'll be there as fast as I can."

With a concerned look on her face, Phyllis asked, "Tell me! What's going on?"

"Mike and Haley are at a club. Travis McCarthy was there. He and Mike got into a fight, and Travis was badly hurt. I have to go. I'll call you. Mike's okay."

Dan quickly rushed out to the garage, nearly forgetting a coat, so he ran back into the house, put one on and got into his Accord. Speeding to the club, he could only imagine what had occurred.

Two cruisers were outside the bar when Dan arrived. Police had emptied the place, and he went into Applejacks where he found Dexter with Mike, who was sitting in a chair next to a teary-eyed Haley. The remnant of a chair was against the wall. Relieved to see his son with only a bloodied, torn shirt and a slightly fat lip, Dan put his hands on Mike's shoulders. Then he saw the bandaged hand. "What the hell happened?"

Haley's wet eyes were red. "It wasn't his fault," she stated. "We came here to have a drink. Ten minutes after we sat down, Travis walked in and saw me with Mike. I think he was high, and he started ranting, accusing me of being a no-good mother and a whore."

Mike looked up. "Dad, that asshole put his hands on her, so I got in his face. He shoved me, and I hit him in the jaw, knocking him to the floor. They had to pull me off him." Mike pointed to the blood-spattered hardwood. "That's his tooth, not mine."

"Your hand?"

"It's not broken. The EMTs examined it. It's stiff and bruised, but I'll be fine."

Dan walked over to Dexter. "I'm glad you showed up."

"I'm glad he told me who he was. Otherwise, you'd be meeting him at the jail."

"I suppose you have to write it up?"

"You know I do. I may leave out a thing or two. Looks like a regular bar fight. Witnesses said Travis started it. Why don't you get them out of here?"

"Thanks, Dexter." Dan looked at Haley. "Have you called your parents?"

"Not yet."

"Do you have your license with you?"

She spoke, "I do."

"Mike, hand her the keys. Haley, you drive him home, then I'll take you back to your house."

"I'm okay," Mike said. "I can drive."

"No, give her the keys. Let's go."

Mike did as Dan ordered and walked with Haley who held Mike's unharmed hand. "I'll see you both back at the house." Dan drove behind them and called Phyllis. "Hi," he said. "Mike is fine. Haley is driving him back home. I'm behind them and will explain everything when I get there. Please have some coffee ready."

A half hour later, both cars pulled into the Shields' driveway, Dan parking beside Phyllis's SUV. The porch light was on, and Dan opened the door for Mike and Haley to enter the residence. The sight of Mike's torn, blood-stained shirt made Phyllis gasp. "Did you break your hand?"

"No." He hugged his mother.

She asked Haley, "Are you okay?"

"I am," she said, although her hands were shaking.

"Sit, have some coffee," Phyllis said.

"Mr. Shields, can you call my dad?"

Dan went to the den and called Haley's father. Returning to the kitchen, he sat, poured a cup of coffee, and looked at Haley. "I talked to your dad. I told him I'd take you home."

"Thank you, Mr. Shields." She began to cry.

Phyllis put her arm around the sobbing girl. "Haley, it's okay. How about me taking you home? I haven't seen your mother in a while." Phyllis handed Haley a few tissues.

"Thank you," she said as she dried her eyes.

When Phyllis got home more than an hour later, Mike had showered and was in the den with Dan. "What took you so long?" Dan asked.

"I was talking to Haley's mother. Maureen was very upset, and we chatted about Haley." Phyllis looked at Mike. "I invited them for Thanksgiving dinner, but she didn't want to impose on us. I asked if Haley could come, and she said she'd ask her."

Mike said, "I know she will. We talked about it." The young man got up and hugged his mother. "See you in the morning."

Dan said, "Time for us to hit the hay." They went upstairs and got ready for bed. "What else did you talk to Maureen about?"

"They've seen a big change in Haley in the few days since Mike has been around. They know she always liked him. I told her I can get help for Haley with one of our therapists."

Dan said, "Mike has to deal with his emotions. He has a girlfriend, Rachel, and I don't think she'd be happy to hear about this visit home. You know, Mike could have been arrested. He's lucky I have uniformed friends who also break a few rules."

"We have to let him do what he has to do," Phyllis said as she held Dan's hand under the covers. "Go to sleep."

Chapter 43

Dan had a heck of a story to tell his fellow detectives. He saw the clock on the front of the building that read 8:15 a.m. It also indicated the temperature was 39 degrees. Proceeding to the back lot, he parked in his normal place and then entered the building. The temptation to go downstairs was strong, but he skipped the jungle and headed straight to the squad room where Scotty, Bev, Mal, and Hanson were chatting. "Are you talking about me?" Dan inquired.

"Good guess," Scotty said.

"You have to hear this." Dan sat with a smug look on his face and spewed out how his son had beaten the crap out of Haley's ex-boyfriend, Travis McCarthy. Wiping away his huge grin, he said, "I'm going to see Dixon. I have to get the incident report from the fight. We got lucky because Dexter was there. Otherwise, Mike might have been arrested for assault. They took Travis to Woodland."

Dan entered Dixon's office. The captain asked, "How's it going?"

"I suppose you heard about my son's fight last night?"

"Dexter completed his report. I have it right here. Witnesses said Travis was the instigator."

"Can I get a copy of the report?"

Dixon shoved his across the desk. "Take this. I'll print another. Mike must be a heavy hitter because Dexter said Travis was pretty beat up."

"That idiot, Travis, said some nasty things to Haley, so Mike defended her."

"I'd say he more than defended her."

"Right," Dan said as he took the incident report. As much as he hated the guy, Dan had to find out how the scumbag was doing. The concerned detective knew there was a possibility that Travis could press charges and Mike could be arrested. "I have to get to the hospital. I want to check on him."

▲

Dan was back in familiar territory, Woodland Hospital. He walked to the front desk and asked if Travis McCarthy was registered. The receptionist told him Travis's room number was 241. Dan took the elevator up and entered the room. Travis was sitting in bed watching TV, and Dan asked, "How are you feeling?"

"What are you doing here? How does it look like I am? Christ, I have a broken rib, a missing tooth, and my face is busted up. That bastard should be in jail."

Dan, in a rare moment of silence, blew out a breath. "Listen, that tough guy you had the fight with is my son, Mike. He and Haley went to high school together."

"Holy Jesus. All I wanted was to talk to Haley about Joey. I want to see my son."

Dan said, "That's not what I heard. I heard you were high and saying nasty things."

"Damn it. She won't let me see Joey. I have a right. They have a restraining order on me."

Dan walked closer to the bed. "Look, I want to do you a favor if you do me one."

"What the fuck kind of shit are you pushing?"

"I'm not handing out crap. Here's the deal. I'll get the restraining order lifted, and I'll have Haley and her father work out something with you so you can see Joey. How's that sound?"

Travis said, "What's the rest of the deal?"

"You don't file charges against my son."

Travis blew out a breath from his bruised mouth. "Deal."

▲

Dan reported back to Dixon to tell him about his visit with Travis. "He has broken ribs, bruises, and a missing tooth. We made a deal. He won't file charges."

"What did you say to him?"

"It's simple. I'm going to make sure he can see his son."

"Sounds good. Have a good holiday."

"You too. Thanks."

Dan marched upstairs. Scotty, Bev, Hanson, and Mal were gone. The only one remaining was Syms, so Dan went to the captain's office and told him the story. "The squad room is deserted," Dan said.

"Good observation. You are a sharp-eyed detective. Mal is first up, then Hanson, then Scotty, and then it's a toss-up between you and Bev. I could put you at the head of the class if you wish."

"Hell no, I can use a few days without hearing your raspy voice."

"Then I'd advise you to get out of here before I change my mind."

Dan started to leave. "You know, you aren't such a bad guy. Don't eat too much turkey."

▲

Dan knew he needed Dave and Haley's approval in order to solidify the agreement he had made with Travis. The wheeling-dealing detective got home and called Dave Valente to explain what had happened and the tradeoff deal that had been agreed upon. "I'll go along with it, and I'm sure she will too," Dave said.

"I suggest Haley go to court and work out an equitable visitation plan with the judge."

"We'll do that. How bad was Travis hurt?"

221

"He'll be okay. It could have been a lot worse. Mike is fine. Thanks, Dave."

"Thanks, Dan. Haley will be having Thanksgiving dinner at your place. Then they'll come here for dessert."

Chapter 44

The turkey was out of the oven, sitting on a carving board and Dan turned to Mike to slice up the bird, but the injured son held up his bandaged hand. "Not today. It's all yours unless Josh can do it."

Josh's eyes lit up. "Can I?"

"Maybe next year," Dan said as he began slicing. White meat was placed on one dish while the legs and dark meat were served on another plate. Phyllis had already put out stuffing, cranberry sauce, green beans, mashed sweet potatoes, bread, and hot gravy.

Dan sat at the head of the table, Phyllis on the opposite end, Kate and Josh were to Dan's left, and Mike and Haley were seated to his right. Dan noticed how happy Mike was to have Haley sitting next to him. She, as well, looked pleased to be at the Shields' house.

"Who's playing this afternoon?" Mike asked his dad.

"I think it's the Lions and Bears, later the Cowboys and Redskins. Are you going to watch?"

"I might catch some at Haley's."

"My father is a Cowboys fan," she said.

Dan looked at Josh. "I guess it's you and me, buddy."

Phyllis said, "That's right. Leave the cleanup to me and Kate."

Haley said, "No, Mrs. Shields. I'll help."

"Thank you, Haley."

While Phyllis, Kate, and Haley remained in the kitchen, Dan, Mike, and Josh slipped away to watch football. It was ten minutes into the first quarter when Haley interrupted the males, and Mike

223

got up. "See you later," he said.

"Say hi to your parents," Dan said.

"I will, Mr. Shields."

Phyllis entered the den. "Dessert is waiting for you."

Dan said, "Let's go Josh."

After enjoying pumpkin pie, Phyllis said, "I think we should call Connie."

"Call her and put her on speaker," Dan said.

Connie was delighted to talk with Phyllis, Dan, and the kids. After ending the conversation, Dan said, "We should send her a puzzle." He then nudged Josh. "Let's watch the rest of the game."

▲

It seemed as if the rest of the day, Friday, and Saturday had passed in a flash, and Sunday morning arrived all too quickly.

The Shields family gathered at the breakfast table. Phyllis had made pancakes, bacon, and scrambled eggs. Mike reached for the maple syrup, and Dan said, "We have to be at Bradley by two. Who is picking you up?" Dan asked.

Mike poured the topping on his flapjacks and passed the syrup to Josh. "I can take a shuttle to school."

Dan saw Mike looking at a text. "Haley?" he asked.

"Um, no. It's nothing, but I am going over to her house to say good-bye."

Dan had a feeling he knew who had texted.

Shortly thereafter, Mike borrowed Phyllis's car and went to Haley's house. Dan said to Phyllis, "Remember that text Mike got earlier?"

"He said it was nothing."

"I think it was Rachel. I need to talk to him."

It was twelve-thirty when Mike returned from Haley's. One hour later, Phyllis had tears in her eyes when she hugged him. Mike gave his siblings big hugs too. "See you guys," he said to them.

Mike put his bag in Dan's Accord, and they headed for the

airport. "You won't be able to see Haley for quite a while," Dan said.

"I know. I can't be back for Christmas."

"We'll miss you." Dan hesitated. "Mike, you and Haley look very happy together."

"Dad, seeing her was great. You don't know how sweet she can be. Even though she has Joey, she is going back to school, and I do really like her, maybe more than ever. We talked about her coming out to Tempe during Christmas."

"What about Rachel? That was her who texted you this morning, wasn't it?"

"Yeah."

"So, she's your shuttle, isn't she?"

"Yes."

"Look, I'm not going to get on you about her. I was in college once, and there are a lot of good-looking young females." Dan paused. "And a lot of hormones floating around."

"Dad, Haley and I have a connection. I know you won't believe it, but we didn't sleep together, at least not since our senior prom."

"I wasn't going to ask, but thanks for the info. Mike, you understand that Haley doesn't need to be hurt again. That's why I was a little leery of you seeing her. I think your time away will tell you a lot."

"I won't hurt her, I promise."

"What about Rachel? I doubt you'll tell her about Haley."

Mike looked down at another text. "It's Rachel. She can't wait to see me."

"Great," Dan said. "What do you plan to tell her about your hand and swollen lip?"

"She knows. I told her I went to a club with a couple of friends and a fight broke out. That's not too far from the truth."

"That's true."

When they arrived at the airport, Dan got out of the car, as did Mike who placed his bag on the sidewalk, and they embraced each other. "Have a good flight. We love you."

"Love you too, Dad. Thanks for everything."

Dan got into his car and watched his son enter the terminal.

Returning home, Dan gave Phyllis a kiss. "He's a good kid, honey, and he likes Haley a lot. They really connected."

"I always did like her."

"I'm going to call Dave later."

It was 7:30 when Dan, sitting in his lounger, called Haley's father. "Hi," Dave said.

"How's everything going?" Dan asked. "I took Mike to the airport earlier. Did Haley tell you he won't be home for Christmas because he'll be preparing for the baseball season?"

"She did."

"Did she tell you she may go to Tempe for a few days?"

"We talked about it. I don't think that will happen. She won't want to leave Joey for the holiday. I'm seeing a better Haley and I hope she does go back to school in the spring."

"That's good to hear. We enjoyed her being here. Stay in touch," Dan said.

Phyllis heard the conversation. "What did you say to Mike?"

Dan took her hand. "I told him not to hurt Haley. Rachel knows about the fight, but not about Haley. I think you were right; Mike is a young man, and he has to figure it out. My sense is that he'll do the right thing, whatever that is."

CHAPTER 45

With the holiday and weekend behind them, the detectives exchanged Thanksgiving stories. Hanson said, "I take it we all had enough turkey. Me and Mal are going to Blues. Anyone care to join us?"

Dan said, "I do like their coffee a lot better than that Keurig pods." He stood and nudged his partner.

"Okay," Scotty said, "but I already ate."

Bev didn't move and Dan asked, "Are you staying here?"

She waved her hand at her comrades. "You guys should rent a booth there. Maybe install a hotline. You could probably get more work done there than here."

None of her male comrades responded to Bev's mild scolding.

▲

Hanson led his fellow detectives to a booth. A few seconds later their server had her pencil and pad in hand, took their orders and said, "I'll be back."

Hanson looked across the table at Dan, and Scotty. "I talked to Landry last night. He's still doing chemo, and he quit smoking. He says whatever hair he has is getting sparser, but it sounds like he's doing okay."

Ten minutes later with eggs, bacon, and hash browns in front of him, Hanson dug into his breakfast. Mal buttered his toast and sweetened his coffee, while Dan and Scotty had only coffee.

Mal's cell vibrated, and he answered the call. Dan saw the detective's brows furrow as he said, "Really?" After the three-minute conversation ended, Mal looked across at Dan. "You're not going to believe this. That was my old partner in Waterbury. They have Lorenze Poole in custody." Dan's mouth was frozen open as Mal continued. "They got him on a traffic stop last night around eleven p.m. The car reeked of marijuana. A search netted a few bags, a pipe, and a handgun. There was a knife and bloody blanket in the trunk. They ran him and also found an outstanding warrant. The car was registered to Spencer Gaddis."

"Anyone else in it?" Dan asked.

"He didn't say. The car is at the impound lot."

Dan had only one thought and put his half-empty cup down. "We have to go to Waterbury."

Scotty started to rise, but Dan had another idea and said to his partner, "Tell Syms." He pointed at Mal. "How about it? You and me. I think it would be better if we go. You know the territory."

Mal took a last bite of toast and chugged his coffee. "Let's do it."

They hurried to the headquarters lot and got into Dan's car. "You're my GPS," Dan said as Mal strapped himself in.

"You got it. Eighty-four toward Waterbury."

"This is a big break," Dan said. "Who's your ex-partner?"

"Alex Cortez, good guy. Twenty-four years on the force."

"I can't wait to grill Poole. I'm hoping Ahn Lee is alive, and he tells us where she is. But I have to tell you, I think he killed her." Dan sped toward their destination.

"I see you're eager to get him, but he ain't going anywhere," Mal said.

Dan eased off the pedal. "We need to see the Audi." He hit the car phone button and called Scotty. "Did you tell Syms?"

"I'm with him now."

"Put him on speaker."

"Dan," Syms said, "be careful. I know you."

"Don't worry. Mal is bigger than me."

"You know what I mean."

"Okay. If I get a chance to see Poole, I'll go easy. Talk to you later."

"I heard about your interview style," Mal said. "And easy isn't it."

They passed the last Southington exit. "I need to call Cortez back," Mal said. "He can take us down to lockup."

"See if he can get Poole into an interview room."

Twenty-two minutes later, Dan parked his car in a visitor spot outside the police station. Mal led the way through a sliding glass door. The officer at the front window asked, "Mal, are you back?"

"Only for a while. This is Lieutenant Dan Shields. Cortez knows we're coming."

"I'll let him know."

"That's not necessary. I still remember the way." Mal led Dan down a hallway to their right. They went inside the detective quarters, and a uniformed patrolman who knew Mal said, "Hey. Just can't leave here so fast, can you?"

"Relax. We're here to see Cortez and a suspect named Poole."

Mal introduced Dan to Cortez. "What are his charges?" Dan asked.

Cortez read from the booking sheet. "Traffic violation, doing fifty-five in a thirty zone, possession of marijuana, having a concealed and unregistered weapon, false representation, resisting arrest, and the outstanding warrant for a probation violation."

Dan said, "He's a bad guy. I'm sure he shot and killed two people in Hartford. We also believe he kidnapped a female named Ahn Lee. She's missing and may be dead."

Cortez shook his head. "That might explain what was found in the trunk. We have a bloodied blanket as well as a six-inch knife. I'll get him up here. Room two," Cortez said.

"We'll be in there," Mal said.

Upon entering the interview room, Dan said "I have a feeling he's going to clam up."

The door opened. Cortez, a policeman, and the cuffed detainee, dressed in a green jumpsuit supplied by the police department, entered the room. The officer sat Poole down, anchored the detainee's cuffs to the metal holder on the table, and stood in a corner of the room. Cortez said, "I'll be back in my office."

The jet-black haired criminal, with a scarred face, looked away from Dan. "Nice to meet you," the detective said as he stated his and Mal's names. There was no response from the tight-lipped detainee. "Okay," Dan said. "Where is Ahn Lee?"

"Who?"

Dan certainly didn't like that response and ran his hand across his forehead. "Do you really want to play that game?"

"Who did you say?"

"You heard me."

"Don't know where she's at."

Dan got close to him and raised his voice, "What did you do with her? We know you carried her out of the house in the bloody blanket that was found in the trunk of the Audi."

"No way."

Dan had a hunch this conversation with Lorenze Poole was going to end soon with the suspect not admitting anything, but the detective persisted. Stepping back, he said, "Let's move off her. Why did you kill Spencer Gaddis and Chester Hadlyme? For your information, Hadlyme was the innocent Batman at Stackpole."

Poole squinted. "Wasn't me."

Dan put his foot up on a chair. Glaring into the man's brown eyes, he barked, "Okay, you piece of shit. Don't talk. We have enough to send you back for a long time." Knowing this statement to the repeat offender wasn't true, at least not yet he demanded to know. "Where is Ahn Lee? Where did you ditch her?"

Poole shifted his body and with fire in his eyes, he smugly stared back at Dan, and shouted, "Know what? This is bull. I want my lawyer."

That signaled the end, and Dan couldn't ask any further questions. He stared coldly at the criminal he knew had killed at least two people, and the disappointed detective backed away. "I guess you can get Cortez now," Dan said to Mal

A couple of minutes later, Mal reentered with Cortez. The officer who had remained in the room, got Poole up and escorted the detainee back to a cell. Mal said, "He lawyered up."

Cortez said, "I saw. I was watching."

Dan asked, "When is his arraignment?"

"Tomorrow morning. He'll be in court at nine."

"Do you have the gun from the Audi as well as the blanket and knife?"

"Yes."

Dan said, "I suspect it's the same gun he used to kill two people. I'd like to run it over to ballistics. Then we can take the blanket and knife for print and DNA analysis."

"Let me retrieve them. I'll sign the stuff out from property." Cortez returned with the items and handed them to Mal.

Leaving with the evidence in their possession, Dan asked, "Where's the impound lot?"

"About two miles from here."

They got into Dan's car. "Take a left out of the driveway."

He followed Mal's guidance and came to the lot where the Audi was located. Mal pointed to the left. "Park over there."

They walked fifty feet toward a small building, and Dan eyed the slew of vehicles behind a gated fence. Mal went inside and came out knowing the location of the Audi. "Follow me."

Approaching the car, Dan took out his phone. "I want to get a few pictures. Open the door."

Mal took a few steps and pulled on the driver side handle. Upon entering the vehicle, the detectives searched the Audi's interior, including the glove box. "How about flipping the trunk lock?" Dan asked.

Mal clicked the trunk open and walked to the rear of the car. "Blood for sure."

"There's the ski cap he wore when he shot the first batman."

Dan snapped pictures of the red spots. "Damn it. She was in here.

That bastard dumped her somewhere."

"We should ask the boat crew to search the Naugatuck River," Mal suggested.

"Maybe, but she could have been dropped anywhere from Hartford to here. Let's go. I want to get that gun to ballistics and the other stuff to Kara."

Dan knew he had to have the bullets taken from the bodies of Gaddis and Chester Hadlyme from evidence back at headquarters. With the gun now in their possession, he needed a match to those slugs. Dan figured he would then have enough to add murder charges to Lorenze Poole's existing ones. After getting into his Accord, Dan called Scotty. "We're leaving Waterbury now. We talked to Poole, but he clammed up and asked for a lawyer. We have his gun, the blanket, and a knife. I want to get to Farmington, and it's on our way back. I need you to meet us at the ballistics unit with the bullets we have in evidence."

"You got it," Scotty replied.

"Tell Syms."

▲

Dan and Mal got to the ballistics facility, and there was no sign of Scotty's car. "Looks like we beat him," Dan said. "I can't wait to get the gun tested."

Scotty pulled in a minute later and walked to his partner's car as Dan and Mal got out. Scotty eyed the gun. "Ruger."

"Yup," Dan said, and they headed inside the single-story brick building. Eager to have their evidence scrutinized, Dan opened the door and led his fellow detectives into the room where Avery Welles was seated at his desk. "Hey," Dan said. "Time to get to work."

The ballistics expert asked, "What have you got? Hi Scotty."

Dan introduced Mal. "He's new to our department, came from Waterbury where we obtained the Ruger in this bag. We need it tested." He pointed to the bagged bullets Scotty had in his hand. "We're hoping for a match."

Avery stood. "Follow me."

They proceeded into a soundproof room where the Avery slipped on a pair of latex gloves and took the empty chambered weapon out of the bag. "I have some thirty-eights." He inserted a bullet, and placed coverings over his ears. "Stand back."

The detectives stepped back and stood against the wall while Avery fired the slug through a hole into a box that contained a Jell-O-like material. He then removed the spent bullet, and they all went back to the outer office. The ballistics expert placed the bullet into a rotating scope-like piece of equipment with two slots. The device reminded Dan of a key duplicator. Scotty handed Avery a shell that had been removed from one of the Batman victims, and the technician rotated the scoped machine while looking into a magnifier. "They match," he said.

Scotty handed him the second bullet. The results were the same. "Ditto," Avery said.

"Great," Dan said. "We got him for murder, two counts."

"I'll document these findings, and you can take the report with you," Avery said as he placed the Ruger into the evidence bag, and handed it back to Dan. He also put the bullets into the baggie Scotty had given him and handed it back.

Fifteen minutes later, the signed document was in Dan's hands, and they left the testing facility. Walking to their vehicles, Dan said to Scotty, "Mal and I still have to drop off the blanket and knife with Kara. We'll see you in the morning."

"Let me have the Ruger, I'll have it placed into evidence along with the shells."

Dan and Mal headed the short distance to the forensics lab to see Kara. Dan carried the blanket and Mal took the knife into the CSI office. "Hi Kara," Dan said. "Have you met Mal Jones?"

"I have now. Nice to meet you. I heard you were on board. Where's Scotty?"

"He's on his way back to home base. Mal and I went to Waterbury where they have Lorenze Poole in custody. We have his gun and just had it tested. It's the weapon that killed the two

233

Batmans. We think this is the blanket Ahn Lee was wrapped in, and we suspect the knife is the one he used to kill her, although we can't prove that without her body. He lawyered up and remained mum about Ahn."

Kara took the bagged items. Dan asked, "Did you get prints from the apartment above hers?"

"Several, including Gaddis, Poole, and Ahn Lee."

Dan realized there was one more thing to do. He had to write up murder charges. The detectives said farewell to Kara and made their way back to Hartford.

As soon as he and Mal got back to headquarters, they marched in to see Syms. The captain sneered at Dan, "Why the hell haven't you called me?"

"Simmer down," Dan said. "We have him for murder." He proceeded to tell his boss the details. "Poole is being arraigned tomorrow in Waterbury on the other charges. I'm going to write him up for two counts of murder. We can't charge him with three. At this point, Ahn Lee is simply missing."

Mal said, "Let me call Cortez. He should be able to hold the arraignment for up to seventy-two hours. We can add the murder charges and then proceed."

"Maybe we can get him back there, and I can take another crack at him."

"Not without his lawyer being there," Mal said.

"Yeah, but I still want to give it a try even with the lawyer in the room. I can present them with the evidence, and maybe he'll cave."

CHAPTER 46

Dan and Mal headed back to Waterbury the next morning and met with Cortez, who said, "I've added the two counts of murder to his charges and got the arraignment pushed to tomorrow."

"Nice," Dan said. "We still need to find Ahn Lee. Mal suggested searching the river but unless we get a lead, that could be a wasted effort."

Cortez said, "We may be in luck. Poole met with his attorney last night. His name is Francis Durant, and he walked out of here after Poole fired him."

"What? So, he has no lawyer?" Dan asked.

"Not at the moment."

Dan looked at Mal and said, "I want him."

"We'll be in interview room one," Mal said to Cortez.

"I'll get him up in a few minutes. I'll be watching from my cube."

Dan paced the floor as he and Mal waited. "What a break. I don't believe it," the lead detective said.

Once again, the detainee was escorted in by a uniformed officer who anchored down the suspect and remained in the room. Dan glared at the killer. "Now's the time, Lorenze. Right here and now. Tell us the truth. You can't run away from it. You know where you're headed. How about talking to us?" The seemingly tired, but defiant suspect sneered at the detective. "Talk to me," Dan reiterated. "Do you want to clear your head of everything?"

Their captive looked down at the floor. Dan and Mal eyed each other and didn't say a word. Inwardly, Dan thought, He's gonna do it. He's gonna talk.

Finally, Poole lifted his head. "I didn't want to hurt her."

Dan said, "How about starting from the beginning...all the way back to Cheshire?"

Poole stared at the wall in back of Dan. "Gaddis knew these women. He knew I owned a few, but he wanted Ahn for himself because he got her pregnant. I had a better place for her in Atlantic City, but Gaddis said there's no way I was taking her." He looked into Dan's eyes. "That bastard. I'm the one who brought her here. He pointed a gun at me and told me to disappear, so I decided to take the crazy asshole out."

"What happened at Stackpole?"

"I heard he was going there dressed as Batman to get free drinks. I went there and saw him coming out of the bathroom, so I drilled him."

Dan sat back. "When did you realize you got the wrong guy?"

"A couple of hours later when he showed up at Ahn's"

"And then you took him for a ride and finished the job."

"I did. He was high, and I shot him when he got into the back seat of the car. Ahn was scared shitless."

"Then you torched your car after dumping him behind the diner?"

"I had to. All that blood, and I figured there might have been cameras there."

"You were right," Dan said. "What happened to her?"

The killer gritted his teeth, and in a remorseful tone said, "She was defiant and wouldn't go to Atlantic City." He paused. "Ahn said she was going to the police. I had no choice."

"Where is she?" Dan asked.

"The river."

"Where did you dump her?"

"Not sure. By a boat launch in Cheshire."

Dan had one inconsequential question. "Just curious, why did you bother to lock the back door?"

"I don't know. I guess I just did it. I went back inside for the suitcase, grabbed the appointment book and her keys off the table, and locked the door. The criminal then lowered his head onto the table and mumbled under his breath.

Dan was sure he heard him praying.

Cortez entered the room with a piece of paper in his hand and placed it on the table. Poole looked up. Cortez handed him a pen. "Sign this," he said.

The guilty killer didn't have to read it. He signed the confession, and the uniformed officer escorted Poole back to his cell.

"I thought it would be worth a shot, but I never expected him to confess as easily as he did," Dan said.

"Neither did I," Mal said. "Goes to show, you never know."

Cortez shook their hands. "Great job, guys."

⚜

Dan had called Syms to tell him the news and when he and Mal returned to headquarters, they went directly to the captain's office to replay the interrogation and Poole's confession. Exiting Syms' office, Dan saw Scotty and Bev talking with a well-dressed visitor and approached the man. "Sass, what are you doing here?"

The slick lawyer was wearing a Stetson and an expensive looking, long, gray outercoat. "Just passing through. Haven't been here in a while."

"No, and you haven't met Mal."

"My pleasure," The lawyer said. "I see Syms is here. Gotta see him."

Sasser started walking down the hallway toward the captain, and Dan followed him. When they entered his office, Syms said, "Nice hat. You look good."

Dan again asked, "Why the visit?"

Sasser took his hat and coat off. He and Dan sat next to each other. "I was at the courthouse and figured I'd drop by to see my friends." He eyed the back table. "You still growing trees?"

"You still slinging crap?" Syms asked.

"You know, your lieutenant did me good."

"I know, and he's a lucky guy because Biaggio isn't liked around here, and Hardison backed Dan."

"Okay," Dan said. "Tell us a story."

"About the courthouse…I was there with Rollin. I spoke with Judge Harper and got his charge reduced. Rollin got off with a thousand-dollar fine, no probation or anything. Harper is a good man."

Dan knew the old Sasser had a way of convincing judges to get cases dismissed or charges reduced to minimums. "You didn't pay him off, did you?"

Sasser huffily responded, "Hell no. That old Sasser is long gone. I'm straight. Rely on my good looks and charming personality."

"Come on, Sass. Tell me the truth." Dan had his doubts about there not being a payout.

"I didn't, Dan. Judge Harper is okay. No lie. Hey, I gotta go. I'm due for a haircut. Gotta look sharp."

"How about that guy?" Dan stated after the lawyer left.

"A real gem," Syms said.

Dan grinned at his boss, "Yes, he is. Just like me."

"Get out."

Dan went back to his workplace where Bev, Scotty, and Hanson were gathered around Mal who had told them about Poole.

▲

Leaving the police station, heading home with a sense of accomplishment in nailing Poole, Dan knew there was another case to solve. He thought about Gordon Gunderson and Christine Kole and set his sight on finding their killer or killers.

CHAPTER 47

With Gordon Gunderson, Christine Kole and a yet to be identified suspect on his mind, Dan approached his desk and saw Scotty sitting with Bev at her computer. "What are you two looking at?"

Bev said, "You better take your coat off and pull up a chair."

"What have you got?"

"Facebook," Bev said. "I've been here over an hour browsing it." She drew Dan and Scotty's attention to Gordon Gunderson's page. "Look. Rosario, Amalia, Keith are here and so is Cody. Hang with me." She switched to Christine Kole's page. "Take a look at her friends."

The male detectives observed as Bev scrolled the page and she pointed to Melrose and Barbour. Then she moved the cursor to Cody Wilcox."

"Whoa," Scotty said. "They knew each other. Cody and Christine knew each other."

"I'll be damned," Dan said.

"Hold onto your seatbelts." Bev said as she brought up Cody's page, and they browsed his profile. She drew attention to a few pictures as well as some posts, and Dan shook his head, and said, "There's a photo of Cody and Christine together."

"This is unbelievable. Are you serious? This is crazy. He's supposed to be in Iraq," Scotty said.

"Doesn't seem that way," Bev said. "From his posts, it appears Cody was discharged with post-traumatic stress disorder several months ago."

"What the hell is going on? Ellie Wilcox said he was in Iraq, as did Keith. They lied to us. Why?" Dan asked.

Bev was on a roll. She found Ellie's Facebook page where Dan saw a photo of Cody and a different one of Gordon. "Can you print the pictures?" Dan asked.

"Take some with your phone."

Dan did as Bev suggested. With these revelations swirling around in his head, he tried to make sense of it. He wondered. What does this all mean? "We need to bring Ellie Wilcox back here, and we need to find him. I'm guessing Keith didn't know Cody wasn't in Iraq. Ellie better have some answers for us."

Scotty said, "George Gunderson might be able to tell us a few things as well."

Jolted with this stunning information, Dan recalled a comment Hampton had made. "Scotty, remember Hampton told us he'd seen Ellie at the doughnut shop with her son?"

"I do."

Dan rubbed his chin. "Hampton said they were hugging, and I told him it wasn't her son, that it was Gordon. It may well have been Cody." Dan took out his cell. "I'm calling Hampton." The phone rang once, twice, three times, four. "Answer it, Hampton." After the sixth ring, it went to voicemail, but Dan couldn't leave a message because the box was full. "Damn him."

"What about Rollin?" Scotty asked.

"I'll try him." Dan repeated the effort, but his attempt to contact Rollin met the same result. Determined to pin down the identity of the person Ellie Wilcox had met, Dan said, "Grab your coat. We're going to the doughnut shop. They'd better be there."

"What about Ellie Wilcox?" Scotty asked.

"We'll deal with her later. Let's go."

The detectives headed to the familiar hangout. "I think we're going to get to the bottom of Gordon Gunderson's death soon, and Ellie Wilcox is holding keys that we need to get our hands on. I can't figure it," Dan said.

"Why lie about Cody?" Scotty replied. "Could he have killed Gordon and Christine?"

"He could have. What else did she lie about? And I'm bothered by her supposedly being in fear of George Gunderson and alleging if she disappeared, he might be responsible."

▲

Dan was relieved to see Rollin's Harley when they got to The Maple. That was a sure sign he and Hampton were inside. Dan opened the door and the detectives walked toward the two retired men. "Hampton!" Dan shouted. "Why didn't you answer your phone?"

Hampton nervously shifted his body. "You look like you stepped in a pile of dog doo."

"I haven't got time for small talk." Dan looked at Rollin. "And you didn't answer yours either. Tell me something, That woman we met here, remember her?" He was staring at Hampton. "Both of you mentioned you'd seen her here before, but you said she was with her son, and I said it wasn't her son."

"Geez, Dan. So what?" Hampton uttered.

"Do you remember what that kid was wearing?"

"Khakis."

Rollin scratched his head. "They wasn't khakis. They was more like fatigues."

Dan looked at Scotty, pulled out his phone, and showed photos of Cody and Gordon to both Hampton and Rollin. "Do you recognize anyone?"

"Yeah," Hampton said. "The first one."

"Cody," Dan said.

"Who's Cody?" Hampton asked.

"The woman we met with. You were right, that's her son. Thanks." Dan looked at Rollin. "You got lucky. Sasser did you a favor."

Rollin smirked and waved. "Good dude."

241

"Enjoy your retirement, gentlemen." Dan said.

▲

With these new twists, Dan and Scotty rushed to see the captain. "What's going on?" Syms asked. "You two look spooked."

"Not quite," Dan said. "But we do have a puzzle that's beginning to come together. Bev showed us what she'd found on Facebook." Dan brought Syms up to date. "As of now, Cody and Ellie Wilcox are suspects. I have a phone call or two to make."

Dan sat at his desk and called Ellie, but her phone instantly rolled to voicemail. "Good morning, this is Detective Shields. Please call me when you get a chance. We have some news about George that you'll want to hear. Thanks." He said to Scotty, "What are the odds she'll call me back?"

"Good question, especially if she wants us to believe George made her disappear."

"Exactly." Dan snapped his fingers. "I'm calling George Gunderson." He quickly entered the house number.

Natalie answered, "Hello?"

"Natalie," Dan said, "we have news about what happened to Gordon and the guard, Christine. It's urgent that we speak with you and George as soon as possible, like now."

Natalie sighed. "What is it?"

"We need to see you both right now."

She huffed. "George is in New Haven with Keith. He's staying at Keith's tonight and flying out of LaGuardia tomorrow to Phoenix."

"Oh no," Dan said. "This is very important. Can you call and ask him to come back to Simsbury?"

"I don't know. I'll try."

"Please call me back."

The detectives waited for her return call. Dan kept his eyes on his watch. Ten minutes had passed. Come on, what's taking you so long? Another minute elapsed, and his phone lit up.

"Detective," George said. "What is it that's so important?"

"Mr. Gunderson, trust me. It's about Gordon. We need to see you and Natalie immediately."

"I'm in New Haven."

"We know that. How long will it take you to get home?"

"With luck, an hour or so."

"We'll be at your house." Dan was about to end the call when something crossed his mind. "One more thing, can you bring Keith?"

"What?"

"Please, you'll understand later."

"Damn it, okay. We'll see you in a while."

Chapter 48

Traffic slowed their journey to Simsbury. Dan said, "It could take a while. This is stop-and-go."

"If George comes this way, he'll be late too."

"He may have another route from New Haven. All we know right now is Ellie lied about a few things, and Cody is not in Iraq. We can't arrest them. We have no proof yet. I hope George can give us some meat to chew on."

Traffic got worse, slowing to a crawl, narrowing to one lane due to what seemed like never-ending road construction, or as Dan called it: road destruction. To make matters worse, it seemed he was stopping at all the lights. "Not a green one yet and we're still fifteen minutes away. Do us a favor, call the house."

Scotty did and Dan heard him say, "That's great. We should be there in about fifteen minutes." Scotty hung up. "He's there with Keith."

Thirteen minutes later, the detectives arrived at the house. Natalie opened the door. George was standing behind her with his ear to his cell phone, acknowledging their presence with a hand wave. He pointed to the parlor, and the detectives followed Natalie to the room where they had previously chatted. Keith greeted them, along with the friendly dog. A couple of minutes later, George, dressed in an expensive-looking dark suit, white shirt, and patterned tie, put his phone in his pocket and took a seat beside Natalie. "What have you got?" he asked.

Dan said, "First, we want to know everything you can tell us about Ellie and Cody."

George held his wife's hand. "That could take a while."

Dan asked, "Are you aware that she met Gordon at a doughnut shop not long before he died? She also met Cody there."

"What?" George threw his head back. "I thought he was in Iraq."

"Me too," Keith said.

Dan said, "We found out he was discharged with PTSD about six months ago."

George grimaced. "What are you telling us?"

"Tell us more about Ellie." Dan looked over at Natalie, who sat with her legs crossed. He then looked into George's eyes. "You clearly stated Cody was the reason for your divorce."

"He was."

Dan eyed Natalie again and then re-engaged George. "Forgive me for what I'm about to say. Ellie called Natalie a slut and said she was the reason for your divorce."

George clutched his wife's hand and angrily protested, "She said what?"

"I won't repeat myself. She told us the minute you hired Natalie; you began having an affair."

Natalie angrily uttered, "Me? They were separated for five months and in divorce proceedings."

"For Christ's sake, we had every right to date," George assertively stated.

Dan's inclination was that Ellie lied about Gordon and his desire to expose his father. He had to dig deeper. "Gordon wrote that article about the fraternity. Were you aware of what else he was going to write about?"

"Not really," George said. "I'm sure it would have been political, global warming, or something other cause."

Dan said, "Would it surprise you if Gordon was planning to publish information about you and your business dealings?"

"What's that supposed to mean?" George asked.

"Ellie claims to have evidence of backroom deals and falsified tax returns that she was going to provide Gordon so he could expose you."

George got up, paced the floor, and raised his voice. "That's preposterous. Everything I have I earned. She's just mad because she's the one who insisted on a prenup. Bad enough I pay her alimony. Look, maybe she thinks because I became successful after our divorce, she got shortchanged." George sat again next to Natalie and shook his head. "I don't believe this pile of crap."

"I have to ask you something else. Ellie said she met with you to tell you she had all this documentation. She planned to make sure your political future was laid to rest. Also, Ellie stated you offered her a lot of money to go away."

Seething, George harshly replied, "She what? She said I'm attempting to bribe her to keep her mouth shut?"

Dan focused his eyes on George's. "It sounded that way to us. You said you met Ellie at a PWP meeting. What else can you tell us about her?"

"Ellie went to nursing school but decided to nix that career and became a travel agent. She moved here from Maine where she was working for a travel agency and took a job here at Savitt Travel in Avon. I know she had Cody before she got married. We dated and things happened. She probably never mentioned that she quit her job after we got married, but she went back to Savitt after our divorce. What are you telling us? You think she had Gordon killed?"

Dan leaned forward. "We're not sure at this point. We have reason to believe Cody may be involved. There's a strange tie to him and the security guard who was killed. We've cleared the Delphi members, except for an unrelated charge."

George rolled his eyes. "That no-good piece of shit."

"We haven't found him, and we can't get in touch with Ellie. She also suggested that if she disappeared, it would have been because you reneged on the money deal and made her go away."

"Really? If I ever do see her again, I'll make sure of it."

Dan held his palms out. "We'll take care of her. If we're right, she'll pay the price."

"I'll be in Phoenix for a couple of days," George said.

Dan asked, "Do you have Gordon's laptop?"

"Yes," Keith said. "It's upstairs. I took it when I cleaned out his dorm room."

"May we borrow it?"

Keith got up. "I'll get it." A few minutes later, he returned with a black computer case with the laptop inside, and handed it to Dan.

"Thanks. We'll be sure to return it. By the way. Why did you leave the bike there?"

"I had no use for it."

As soon as the detectives got into the Accord, Dan said, "I want to have Bev browse the computer. She's a lot better than we are."

⋏

In what seemed like record time, Dan got back to headquarters. Anxious to see what Bev could dig up, he placed the computer case on her desk. "This is Gordon Gunderson's laptop. How about browsing it?"

"Okay, but you better take a breather and have a seat. She looked at Scotty. "You too." While you boys were out, I learned Ellie's husband, Cody's father, was shot to death. It appeared he shot himself with his own gun. It happened in Bangor, Maine."

Scotty said, "I bet if we look up the incident, we'll find something in the newspaper."

"I like the way you think. I did exactly that," Bev said. She reached for the printout beside her computer. "Read this."

Dan and Scotty studied it. "I don't think George Gunderson knows about this," Dan said. "The incident was called suspicious because they found Cody's prints on the weapon. It says when Ellie and Cody got home, Cody picked up the gun before she phoned it in. They closed the case and deemed it suicide."

Scotty kept reading. "Cody was eleven."

Bev went onto his Facebook page a second time. "Cody has been to the veterans' hospital for psychiatric treatment for his PTSD. You might find him there, but it looks to me like he may be staying with another veteran named Kenny Tower, who is also PTSD."

Dan put his hand to his forehead. "That's the connection. Christine Kole's grandfather said she worked part-time at the hospital. They knew each other from there. I bet she sold him pills. If Cody was the killer, he had to know the cameras wouldn't be working. For some reason, she told him. She probably gave him the override code too."

"Why would she do that?" Scotty asked.

"Who knows, maybe they were high and maybe they were having sex, but she told him."

Bev unzipped the black case, removed the laptop, and began browsing file names. "Here's the Delphi piece. It looks like Gordon was working on a couple of articles. One looks like global warming; another appears to be about race relations."

"Do you see anything with George's name? Any indication of a story about him?" Dan asked while peering over her shoulder.

"There doesn't appear to be anything about him." Bev kept scrolling through the list of documents. "This is it. 'Murder in Bangor.' She clicked on the document and began reading.

"Print it," Dan said. "I think we have our smoking gun."

Bev hit the print key and seconds later, the article was in Dan's hands. He said to Scotty, "Let's go see Syms."

Raising his head upon seeing his dynamic duo Syms asked, "You have something?"

"We do." Dan placed the paper in front of his boss, who read it and reached for his Aleve. Stunned, Syms said, "Gordon knew the story. He knew Ellie had shot and killed her husband. She had Cody pick up the gun so his prints would be on it, and she was slick enough to have worn gloves when she shot him."

"And I think she conspired with Cody to kill Gordon," Dan said. "We have both motive and means. Now we must find them. Ellie is not answering our calls, but we think we know where Cody is."

"Good work. If you need warrants, let me know."

"Thank Bev...she dug up all of this."

Dan and Scotty returned to Bev. "I've got a phone number and address for Tower."

Scotty glanced at the address. "Not far from the doughnut shop, Goodyear Street."

Dan whipped out his cell and started to punch in the phone number. Remembering Bev's soft demeanor, he asked, "Bev, will you call Tower?"

"What do you want me to say?"

Dan thought while scratching his chin. "We can't alarm him or Cody, and we can't say we're detectives. We need another angle. The veterans' hospital, but you can't say you work there or are representing them."

"Got it," Bev said. She used her desk phone and called. A male answered. "Is this Kenneth Tower?" she asked.

"Yes, who is this?"

"My name is Beverly Dancinger. I understand that Cody Wilcox is also at this address."

"Yeah," the man replied. "You wanna talk to him?"

"I need to talk with both of you. I'm calling to follow up on your last visits to the veterans' hospital."

The speaker was on, so Dan heard Tower shout out, "Hey, Cody, some woman from the VA wants to come check on us."

Bev heard Cody talking, and Tower said to Bev, "Not today, he has some stuff to do."

"I understand. I have a report to file and need to see you as soon as possible."

Tower again asked Cody before answering Bev. "We'll be around tomorrow morning."

"Is ten a good time?"

"Fine."

Bev verified the address. "Great. My associate and I will visit you then."

Dan smiled at her. "I don't know how we got along without you."

She grinned. "Me neither."

"George Gunderson said Ellie worked for a travel agency, Savitt Travel. They may know where she is." Dan looked up the number and called the business. After a brief conversation with the owner, he said, "She left the company three weeks ago. Apparently, Ellie has a sister in Bangor who owns a bookstore and planned to go there to help run business because her sister is handicapped. I have a hunch we might find Ellie Wilcox in Bangor."

Bev turned to her computer and Googled bookstores in Bangor. "There's two independents: Bangor Books and Stationery, and Sharon's Book Nook." She wrote down the phone numbers. "Want me to call them?"

Dan thought for a second. "Not yet. Save the numbers. If she's there, I don't want to let her know we've found her. Let's wait to see what Cody can tell us tomorrow."

Chapter 49

Bev had set up the visit to Kenny Tower's house and minutes before she and Dan were to head out to the residence, she saw Dan lean over to Scotty and say something she couldn't hear. "I'll be right back, then we can leave," The cagey detective said.

Pivoting toward Scotty, she asked, "What is he up to?"

"Your guess is as good as mine."

Bev put her hand on her hip holster. "I got a perfect score, remember? And you're less than three feet away. What is he going to do?"

"Okay. He's done it before."

After the explanation from Scotty, Bev said, "I should have thought of that. I won't tell him I know his little secret."

Bev stared at Dan when he returned to their workspace. "Are you done with your business?" she asked.

"Let's go, lady."

▲

Goodyear Street was indeed not far from The Maple. Dan pulled up to a brown ranch-style house with yellow shutters and an American flag that was mounted over the front door. There was a short driveway with a carport and a green Jeep parked in it.

Dan and Bev walked to the front door, and she rang the bell. A man in a wheelchair opened it. His hair was long and unruly, as was his black beard. Most noticeable was his prosthetic leg. Bev said, "Hello. Are you Kenny?"

"Yes."

"I'm Beverly Dancinger. This is my associate, Dan Shields."

The rail-thin man said, "Cody is in his room." Tower's stutter was prominent.

"Can you get him?" she asked.

He wheeled his chair across the hardwood floor, past a gray, well-worn couch. With the TV blaring, he yelled, "Hey, they're here."

Dan scoped out the place and saw, strewn around the room, an array of photos of soldiers and scenes from war-torn places. The fireplace appeared to have been recently used, and the mantle had more military photos on it. Cigarette butts were in ashtrays on both sides of the couch; however, it was the aroma of marijuana that filled the room. He glanced at the loud TV and saw what appeared to be an old war film. "Can you turn that down?" Dan asked.

Picking up a remote, Tower clicked the off button.

Dan and Bev removed their coats and plopped themselves deep into the couch. As they waited for Cody to enter the room, Dan noticed a small plastic bag with two pills inside next to one of the ashtrays. The kitchen was in view, and Dan spotted what appeared to be drug paraphernalia, including a syringe, on the counter. The visual inspection was interrupted when his suspect entered the room.

Cody, long-haired, sporting a modest-length beard, was wearing a tan tee and fatigue pants. Dan took the average-heighted man to be every bit of 220 pounds. Bev briefly rose. "Hello, Cody." After introducing herself and Dan, she again sat. Cody perched himself in a chair alongside the wheelchair.

Dan said, "Thank you both for your service. We know you've had traumatic experiences and have spent time at the veterans' hospital."

"Yeah," Cody said. "I'm going back next week."

Bev opened her purse and took out a notepad and pen. Addressing Tower, she asked, "If you don't mind, would you tell us what happened to you?"

Tower pointed to a photo. "That's my unit. The guys in the truck were my buds. We hit a mine, got blown up, and four are dead. I guess I'm the lucky one." Kenny's eyes widened, and he banged his hand on the chair.

Bev said, "Sorry you had to endure that devastating event."

Kenny wheeled himself into the kitchen. "Anyone want a beer?"

"No, thank you," Bev and Dan each responded.

The veteran returned with two cans and handed one to his roommate. Bev addressed Cody. "We know you suffer from PTSD."

Dan watched Cody's eyes drift from left to right and suspected he was high.

"Hell yeah, can't sleep through the night." He chugged some beer. "Damn explosions go off in my head. I got pills."

"What kind of pills?" Bev asked.

"Regular pills. Pain meds."

"Oxycodone?" Bev asked.

"Got those too," Cody said.

"Too?" Bev queried. "What else are you on?"

Cody chugged again and stood. "See my frickin' arm? Sometimes crystal meth is the only way to make it through the day. You gonna report us? None of this is our fault."

Dan chimed in. "No. We'll get off that."

Cody sat again, and Bev asked, "Have the counselors ever asked you about your childhood? I think it would be helpful if you told us about those times. Any events stuck in your mind that you think about or would rather forget?"

Tower said, "Hated school, got pushed into the army, and look what happened."

Cody began to fidget. Bev crossed her legs and looked into his eyes. "I think it would be helpful if you talk about what it was like before you went to Iraq."

Cody's head bobbed, and he blurted out, "I had a bastard father."

Dan's ears perked up. It sounded to him as though Bev was about to crack open an egg. She asked, "How so?"

Cody's glassy eyes seemed to be frozen as he went back in time. "He drank a lot, and I saw him beat my mother a few times, but she wouldn't leave him."

"So, you wished she had left him?" Bev asked.

"Yes." Cody ran his hands through his hair. "Asshole. We fixed his ass."

Dan sensed Cody was getting close to talking about the shooting as Bev continued. "I'm not sure what you mean. How did you fix him?" she asked.

Cody leaned forward with his hands on his knees. Dan could see the hatred in his eyes, and Cody grew silent.

Bev broke the silence after a few seconds. "It sounds like something bad happened. An accident or something?"

Dan was in awe of Bev. Cody swung his hand up. "It was an accident, but it was no accident." He quieted again.

Bev leaned forward and offered her hand. "You seem very disturbed. It sounds very painful. Get it all out."

Cody stood and then sat again. He put his head down and rested it on his knees as Bev again extended her hand. He reached for it. "My mother, my mother." He stared into Bev's eyes but suddenly became silent.

"What's wrong, Cody?" Bev asked.

"I can't talk about it. I was only eleven."

Bev said, "It's okay, Cody. You need to get it out of your system."

Dan listened as Bev pried that door open.

Cody looked up to the ceiling. "Mom, I know you had to do it." He closed his eyes.

"Cody," Bev said, "what is it? Keep talking."

He opened his eyes, looked at Bev, and blurted out, "She killed him. Shot him dead." Cody seemed to be in a self-induced trance and rambled on. "She shot him with his own gun."

He began to shake, and Bev tried to calm him. "It's okay, Cody. Take a few deep breaths." He did as she asked and breathed hard.

Dan sat back, finding himself in the unusual position of keeping his mouth shut, and let Bev continue. "Cody, listen. We spoke with your mother. She told us about your stepbrother, Gordon."

Cody's eyes opened wide. "Gordon? What about him?"

"Tell us about him," Bev said.

Cody began to nervously pace the room, growing silent again.

Dan broke his silence and assertively said, "Because he's dead. You killed him, didn't you?"

The young man stared at the male detective.

"Cody," Bev said, "we know you met your mother at the doughnut shop on Mapleton. We know Gordon knew what you just told us. He wrote about the shooting and was planning to publish it."

Cody shook his head and shouted, "Motherfucker!"

"What's going on?" Tower asked.

Dan replied, "It's about Cody killing his stepbrother."

Cody flung the beer can across the room, the remaining liquid spewing out. "I had to kill him to save my mother."

"When did you decide to kill Gordon?" Dan asked.

"After I met my mother at the doughnut shop. We talked about it, and she convinced me it was the only way to quiet Gordon." He began to pace the room. "I need a hit."

Bev cut in. "Cody, calm down. Please sit again. Everything will be okay. I'm sure you are relieved to get all this off your chest. Take a few more deep breaths." He appeared to do this as she asked, "Where is your mother?

"I'm not sure."

"Did you know she was planning to go back to Maine?"

"We talked about it. My Aunt Sharon has a bookstore in Bangor."

Bingo, Dan thought. Cody just told us where his mother might be. He switched gears and took over. "We know you knew Christine Kole and obtained pills from her, pills like the ones in the bag on the end table."

Cody covered his eyes. "She was nice. Came to the hospital and served meals. Sometimes, she'd come back, and we'd talk."

"Talk?" Dan asked. "You mean get high and talk? She sold you the oxy pills, and you knew she was a guard at the college. She told you the cameras would be out that night, and she told you about the code box override, didn't she?"

"Yeah, and I knew Sunday night would be a good chance to get Gordon while he was alone. I knew he hated the sight of needles and sure enough, he passed out before I shot him up." Cody lifted his head and again placed his hands on his knees.

"You forgot one thing," Dan said. "You forgot Gordon was left-handed and wouldn't have shot himself up in that arm. You also didn't expect Christine to be on duty that night, did you?"

"No. She came in as I was about to go down the stairs. I panicked and pushed her. She fell and I snatched her bag off her shoulder before I left." Cody looked at Dan. "Wait a minute. Who the hell are you anyway? You sound like cops."

"Okay, Cody," Bev replied. "You're right, we are detectives."

Dan eyed Bev and whispered, "I'm wearing a recorder and have the confession on tape. We can take him in."

Bev softly said, "I know. Scotty told me you might do that."

"It could get dangerous," Dan whispered. "The mention of arrest could set him off, and there may be weapons here. I need to call for assistance."

Cody's face displayed fear. "I can't go to jail. I can't go to prison."

Bev looked into his eyes. "Cody, listen to me. No one has mentioned jail or an arrest. We're just talking. I see you're hurting. Stay calm."

Dan asked, "Can I use the bathroom?" Tower pulled back his chair and pointed down the hall.

Once out of sight, Dan called headquarters and requested help to arrest Cody. To be safe, he asked for two units to assist them.

Returning to the couch, Dan intently watched Cody. The wary detective kept his hand close to his jacket where his gun was concealed.

Bev looked at Tower. "Do you have family here?"

"Just my mom. She's almost ninety, has Alzheimer's, and is in a home. I never see her. She doesn't know who I am anyway."

Dan looked at his watch. Five minutes had passed. Why does it always take so long? He wondered if he'd given the correct address.

Cody walked toward the hallway. "Where are you going?" Dan asked.

"Piss."

Dan followed him and waited outside the door until he was done. Then without putting his hands on the man, he followed Cody to the living room and told him to sit. Glancing at his watch again, Dan thought, Ten minutes. Where are they?

He looked out the window next to the front door and saw two black and whites. Four uniforms were approaching, and Dan let them inside. Cody made a sudden dash for the back door and was quickly wrestled to the floor by two policemen. They pulled him upright, and Dan said, "Cuff him." He then looked at Cody. "You're under arrest for murder."

Bev read the detainee his rights.

Dan asked Tower, "Can you get him a coat?"

Tower retrieved a jacket, and Dan placed it over their suspect's shoulders. Following the uniforms outside, Dan said, "Thanks, guys. We'll meet you back home."

"Mr. Tower, we wish you the best," Bev said. She joined Dan outside where Cody was placed into the backseat of a cruiser.

Dan called Scotty. "We're on our way in. Cody Wilcox is in custody. He admitted killing Gordon and Christine. They've got him in a cruiser, and he will be booked. I'll tell you the whole story when we get there."

Chapter 50

The arrest of Cody Wilcox closed part of the Gordon Gunderson/Christine Kole case. Dan, Bev, and an informed Scotty went to Syms' office where the sly detective revealed his recorder. "We have his confession right here," he said as he placed the tiny device on the captain's desk.

Syms listened to the recording. "Good work. He fessed up."

Dan said, "We think Ellie Wilcox is in Bangor with her sister who owns a bookstore."

"We don't know for sure," Bev said. "Ellie doesn't know me, so if I call the bookstore and ask for her, that should tell us."

"If she is there, we need to contact the Bangor police department and have them pick her up. They need to reopen the John Wilcox file," Dan said.

Syms rose. "We have to get this story in front of Hardison." Dan went with the captain while Scotty and Bev returned to their workspace with the understanding that Bev would make the call to Sharon's Book Nook.

While Dan was in the process of giving Hardison the progress report, Bev entered the office. "She's there. She actually answered, and I asked if they had Grisham's new book."

Hardison said, "I'll find out who the Bangor police chief is and discuss what we've uncovered. We need to get that recording to them, or at least a transcript, and let them handle it."

It had been a week, and Dan hadn't heard what was going on in Bangor. He saw Hardison walking down the hallway toward Syms. "Chief," Dan said.

Hardison stopped. "Follow me. Scotty and Bev, you all need to hear this." They entered the captain's office and took seats. "Here's the story. The Bangor police read the transcript I sent, and they reopened the John Wilcox file. The assigned detective found Ellie Wilcox at the bookstore and brought her in for questioning three days ago. She denies everything and claims Cody's PTSD makes him hallucinate and make up stories. She stated Cody is unable to deal with reality."

Dan was curious. "Did they say why they never went after her? The story in the paper was sketchy but certainly sounded like there was more to it."

"There was a lot the paper left out. According to the police chief, who was then a narcotics officer, the former chief closed the door on the case. It seems John Wilcox was known to be abusive. But here's the real kicker: Ellie was having an affair with the chief's son."

"Wow," Dan said. "Sounds like they might not be able to get her on that murder unless she confesses, and that's not likely."

"Maybe," Hardison said. "If they do a full-blown investigation, the ex-police chief, as well as his son, might be indicted. It's a mess, and she may well have gotten away with murder."

"What a nightmare," Dan said.

Hardison replied, "The good news is that they intend to follow the story and let the pieces fall where they may. It could end up in a long battle with a lengthy court case. We might have to let them extradite Cody, but that's putting this horse before that cart. They haven't arrested her; they questioned her."

"We can still get her and charge her with conspiracy to commit murder in Gordon Gunderson's case," Dan said.

"I talked to the DA about that," Hardison said, "He advised we can go forward and have Cody tried for murder one, two counts. He thinks it will be hard to prove Ellie Wilcox conspired to kill Gordon, if what she claims is true…that he hallucinates, and with PTSD… that's plausible."

Dan said, "We know Ellie is at the bookstore, and we have to get her back here. We need to tell her that Cody keeps asking for her. She is his mother, and she might want to see him."

"I think 'keeps asking' is too weak. It should be more like, he's ill and has talked about taking his own life. That should get her. I can call the bookstore again. They don't know it was me who previously called," Bev said.

The untrusting Dan said, "What if she isn't there? What if the Bangor police questioning made her run to Canada or somewhere else?"

"In that case," Bev said, "all I can do is leave the message and make it sound really desperate. I'm sure her sister will get the message to Ellie."

"Brilliant," Hardison said. "Do it."

Dan nodded and said to Bev, "You do have a way about you. Make the call."

The detectives marched to their desks. Bev called the bookstore and Sharon answered stating her name. This time, Bev identified herself and left the message. She then turned to Dan. "Sharon said she'd give Ellie the message. Evidently, she hasn't seen her sister in a couple of days, but she has spoken with her."

"That could mean Ellie did get out of town. She may be running away from it all," Dan said.

"I'm not sure any mother would run away from her son," Bev said. "We have to wait. I have a hunch she'll at least call."

⋏

Two days later, Ellie Wilcox showed up at the Hartford Police Station. She spent an hour visiting with her son, and then was escorted into interview room one where Dan and Scotty greeted her.

Not smiling and visibly tired, she sat across from the detectives.

"I never expected to be seeing you here like this," Dan said. "You had us all fooled."

She frowned. "Not good enough as it turns out. Don't be hard on Cody."

Dan scratched his head. "But he killed two people at the radio station."

"Cody really got messed up in Iraq."

"We know, and we're sorry about that." Dan veered from his hardline questioning and began mimicking Bev. "It's pretty apparent you had a rough first marriage, and Cody saw a lot of things he didn't like. It can't be easy watching your mother being beaten." Dan witnessed her tough exterior begin to crack.

Ellie reached into her purse for a tissue. "It was bad, very bad. I felt trapped, couldn't leave because I didn't know what he'd do to Cody."

She began crying, and Dan faced her. "I'll be right back." He returned with a cup of water, handing it to her.

"Thank you," she said. "I couldn't take it any longer. John drank and got mean. Cody begged me to leave, but as I told you, I couldn't. There was only one way out, so I shot and killed him with his own gun."

Dan filed that admission. There it was, she confessed to killing her husband. He continued. "Is it true you were having an affair with the police chief's son?"

"I didn't think it was an affair, even though he was married, and I was married. It was just sex. But John knew and beat me for the last time, so I shot him." She drank the water and wiped her eyes. "Cody was there."

"And he told Gordon all about it, didn't he?"

"Yes, and he told Cody, he was going to write about it. I knew I had to do something. I called Gordon and told him I had a lot of evidence that could bring his father down. I knew Gordon disliked many of George's ways. I met him at the doughnut shop to show him a few of the same papers, I showed you, hoping to exchange my information for having him not tell about what happened in Bangor."

Dan watched as she began to shake. "But Gordon wouldn't go for it, would he?"

She wiped her eyes again. "No. Then I met Cody at the doughnut shop, and we discussed what to do about Gordon. Cody didn't like the fact that Gordon intended to expose us."

"Whose idea was it to kill him?"

"I suppose it was both of us."

Ellie's meeting with Cody at the Maple had been confirmed by Hampton and Rollin, and Dan assumed the retirees didn't see the other meeting, Gordon with Ellie.

"But there was the text you sent Gordon that Sunday evening," Dan said.

Ellie sighed. "I wanted to give it another try, and apparently Gordon was willing to listen because we were going to meet again that Tuesday." She began trembling and her eyes were teary. "But Cody seized the opportunity that Sunday night to go to the radio station and kill him."

Dan was curious about all those files, the documents she'd shown them. "What about those papers? You had a lot of dirt on George Gunderson that we know wasn't true. Where did you get those phony documents?"

She sighed. "Funny thing about the internet. You can find stuff out there that can be doctored to suit your needs. It really wasn't that difficult to come up with manufactured paperwork, including tax returns. Will I be able to see Cody again?"

"I think that can be arranged. One more question. Did he talk about Christine Kole?"

"No, he never talked about her, except to say he was sorry."

Dan knew he had just heard Ellie admit guilt. Incredible, he thought. He'd gotten confessions to two murders, John Wilcox, and Gordon Gunderson.

Dan rubbed his hands together and stared into her saddened eyes. "You're being arrested for conspiring to murder Gordon

Gunderson."

Ellie bowed her head. "I wish none of this ever happened."

Dan read the confessed murdered her rights. "We will be in touch with the Bangor police, and they will be charging you with the killing of your husband, John Wilcox. Please remain seated. An officer will be here to escort you downstairs." Minutes later, she was cuffed and brought to the booking room.

Dan went to his workplace and asked Bev to join Scotty and him with Syms. "We arrested Ellie Wilcox for conspiracy in Gordon Gunderson's murder, but she also admits to shooting her husband. We need to get the interview video to the Bangor police so she can stand trial for murder there after her conspiracy case is adjudicated here."

"Agreed," Syms said. "Come on, we have to bring it to the chief."

They entered Hardison's office and filled in the chief. "We've got her for conspiracy in the Gordon Gunderson case," Dan said. "She also confessed to killing her husband. The Bangor police have to be informed, and they'll have to move forward with charging her for murder."

"I'll get on it," Hardison said.

Syms and Dan went back to the squad room and rejoined Scotty and Bev. "Let's make a few phone calls. George and Natalie have to be told, as do Christine Kole's grandparents, Ramsey Dale, Aaron Westland, Rosario, and Amalia." Dan reached for the desk phone. "I'll contact the Gundersons and the Koles. Bev, you can call the students."

"I'll take Ramsey and Westland," Scotty said.

An hour later, the calls had been made, and Dan clasped his hands together. "We have closure, if you can call it that."

"You are correct," Bev said. "There really is no such thing as closure. It's a word we throw around, but families of deceased loved ones never have closure. Their dead loved one is never walking through the door again."

Dan's cell rang, the voice on the other end was his wife's. "Oh no," he said. "Thanks." He quickly got up and grabbed his jacket.

"What's wrong? Where are you going?" Scotty asked.

Dan smirked. "To the eye doctor. Phyllis just reminded me of my appointment."

Epilogue- ten months later

Randy Landry had succumbed to cancer a month ago. His death left the detectives with heavy hearts. Syms placed a picture of the deceased detective on the squad room wall.

Cody Wilcox had been scheduled for trial, but ten days after his hearing, he was found hanging in his cell, having committed suicide.

Ellie Wilcox was awaiting trial for conspiracy to commit murder in the death of Gordon Gunderson. She was not charged in the killing of Christine Kole. The murder charge in the death of her husband, John Wilcox had been filed. She would likely stand trial at a later date in Bangor.

Lorenze Poole was sentenced to life on three counts of murder. He was serving time at Northern Correctional Institution in Somers.

Angelo Biaggio and Rozalie were not imprisoned. They indeed had gotten suspended sentences, paid fines, and were on probation. The insurance fraud charge was dismissed.

Reed Barbour and Gregory Melrose were each given the minimum sentence of five years for rape and were sent to the Cheshire Correctional Institution.

Hampton and Rollin were still getting government funds and hanging out at The Maple.

As expected, Connie moved to The Villages.

George Gunderson began his campaign for a run at the Governor's office.

Mike finished his school year, and his baseball season was over.

Having ended his relationship with Rachel, he and Haley took up where they had left off. She completed her first semester back in college and had gone to court, obtaining sole custody of Joey, while granting Travis supervised visits.

▲

George and Natalie Gunderson were about to receive unexpected news. It was a Sunday afternoon. Dan had arranged a visit to their home with Rosario, Amalia, and two other guests.

He picked up the visitors at the student center, drove to Simsbury, and pulled into the Gundersons' driveway. The sun was bright on this warm, late summer afternoon. Dan had sun protectors on over his rimless prescription glasses. He also had Gordon's laptop to return.

Natalie Gunderson opened the door with her husband beside her to see Dan, Rosario, and Amalia, as well as two other people. George said, "Detective, thank you." He turned to Rosario and Amalia. "I owe you two an apology. Welcome to our home."

Dan handed the computer to George and said, "Thanks for letting me borrow this." He introduced Trish Adams to the couple. Trish had a paternity test done to determine the identity of her daughter's father. The fact was, she had gotten pregnant before she'd been raped, and the DNA results proved someone other than Melrose or Barbour had fathered her child.

"Hello, Mr. and Mrs. Gunderson," Trish said as George and Natalie stared at the baby girl in Trish's arms. The new mother said, "Meet your granddaughter. Her name is Gina."

THE END

About the author

Mark L. Dressler was born and raised in Hartford, Connecticut. A retired former corporate manager and successful businessman, he began writing in 2014.

His popular Dan Shields mysteries Dead and Gone and Dead Right are set in his hometown, while revered female detective, Lex Stall, takes on Manhattan in Dying for Fame.

Mark's riveting novels have earned him recognition by the Hartford Courant, who named him a most notable author.

His TV appearances on CT Style with Teresa Dufour at News 8 WTNH in New Haven and on Real People with Stan Simpson at Fox 61 in Hartford have solidified his stature as one of Connecticut's favorite authors.

Additionally, Mark has been honored by Boston Children's Hospital for his charitable donations from partial proceeds of his books.

The author is a member of Mystery Writers of America as well as the Connecticut Authors and Publishers Association.

Mark's books are available on Amazon in Kindle and paperback. You may also purchase his books from any bookseller.

Follow Mark on Facebook at:

www.facebook.com/MarkLDressler

Email him at mark.dressler17@gmail.com

THE MARK L. DRESSLER MYSTERY COLLECTION

THE DAN SHIELDS SERIES
(The detective who breaks all the rules)

DEAD AND GONE (2017)

Dan Shields is drawn into the gang world when a drug bust goes wrong. Police, as well as gang members, are killed, and the money is nowhere to be found. Dan soon confronts the thug who shot and nearly killed the detective six years earlier. The savvy sleuth follows a twisted path leading to an unexpected discovery that stuns the entire police force.

DEAD RIGHT (2019)

Dan Shields and powerful attorney Angelo Biaggio engage in a game of life and death. It was the lawyer's car that had struck and killed a twelve-year-old boy on a city street. Without stopping, the vehicle sped away from the scene. As the detective homes in on the driver, the lives of Dan, and his family are placed in grave danger.

⋏

THE LEX STALL SERIES
(Manhattan's tenacious female detective)

DYING FOR FAME (2020)

Lex Stall draws aim on an edgy suspect who had discovered Fredrike Cambourd's bullet-riddled body in the artist's Manhattan basement studio. The person of interest has an alibi, but it soon crumbles, and she is determined to get to the truth. What Lex discovers is more than she could have imagined.

Note: Dan Shields makes a cameo appearance in this story.

A peek into the next Mark L. Dressler thriller that features Lex Stall, Manhattan's Tenacious Female Detective.

WRITE TO THE END

The ransom letter demanded $100,000 for the return of Svetlana.

Noted mystery author, Essex Westbrook resided at Manhattan's Grand Truman Hotel. His 26th floor suite was the size of eight guest rooms.

It was well past midnight and the curtains in his office were partly drawn, allowing neon lights to filter into the workspace. An empty coffee cup sat on his desk while his fingers tapped the computer's keys as if they were Steinway ivories.

At 3:10 a.m. the pajama clad, sixty-three-year-old novelist input the last words of his next thriller, Night Killer. Careful not to wake his wife, Westbrook tucked himself into their king-sized bed and dozed off. Six hours later, he wakened, but wasn't surprised not to hear her. She routinely took early morning walks, bringing back coffee from a local café.

Donning his bathrobe, he yawned as he entered the main living space to retrieve the daily newspaper. Instead, he saw an envelope that had been slid under the front door and wondered what was inside. He opened it and read the dastardly letter.

Made in the USA
Middletown, DE
18 February 2022